The Hometown Legend

Also by Maisey Yates

Secrets from a Happy Marriage
Confessions from the Quilting Circle
The Lost and Found Girl

Four Corners Ranch

Unbridled Cowboy
Merry Christmas Cowboy
Cowboy Wild
The Rough Rider
The Holiday Heartbreaker
The Troublemaker
The Rival

Gold Valley

Smooth-Talking Cowboy
Untamed Cowboy
Good Time Cowboy
A Tall, Dark Cowboy Christmas
Unbroken Cowboy
Cowboy to the Core
Lone Wolf Cowboy
Cowboy Christmas Redemption
The Bad Boy of Redemption Ranch
The Hero of Hope Springs
The Last Christmas Cowboy
The Heartbreaker of Echo Pass
Rodeo Christmas at Evergreen Ranch
The True Cowboy of Sunset Ridge

For more books by Maisey Yates,
visit maiseyyates.com.

MAISEY YATES

The Hometown Legend

CANARY STREET PRESS

If you purchased this book without a cover you should be aware that this book is stolen property. It was reported as "unsold and destroyed" to the publisher, and neither the author nor the publisher has received any payment for this "stripped book."

CANARY
STREET
PRESS™

Recycling programs for this product may not exist in your area.

ISBN-13: 978-1-335-00628-8

The Hometown Legend

Copyright © 2024 by Maisey Yates

All rights reserved. No part of this book may be used or reproduced in any manner whatsoever without written permission.

Without limiting the author's and publisher's exclusive rights, any unauthorized use of this publication to train generative artificial intelligence (AI) technologies is expressly prohibited.

This is a work of fiction. Names, characters, places and incidents are either the product of the author's imagination or are used fictitiously. Any resemblance to actual persons, living or dead, businesses, companies, events or locales is entirely coincidental.

For questions and comments about the quality of this book, please contact us at CustomerService@Harlequin.com.

TM is a trademark of Harlequin Enterprises ULC.

Canary Street Press
22 Adelaide St. West, 41st Floor
Toronto, Ontario M5H 4E3, Canada
CanaryStPress.com

Printed in U.S.A.

To Flo, the best editor any writer could ask for.
I will never be able to express how much you mean to me,
both as a partner on my stories and as a person.
You're simply the greatest.

CHAPTER ONE

RORY SULLIVAN WAS BORING—HISTORICALLY.

So when she looked up from where she was seated beneath a tall pine tree, in her most sacred spot on Four Corners Ranch, to see a man who might have been conjured straight from the pages of one of her favorite novels—or from the pages of her diary—she blinked twice.

Especially because in her notebook she had just written: *Get a kiss (kiss from a stranger?).*

And then he was there.

A man.

A stranger.

She was working on her list.

The Summer of Rory.

The list that she badly needed to get her life in order. Because everything was changing at Sullivan's Point. Everything was changing with her sisters, and their lives, and she was happy for them. Thrilled. But it had underscored some deep and hard truths about herself that she had been trying to ignore.

She wasn't living. Not really. She was cocooned in the safe existence of her family home, protecting herself from potentially difficult social situations. Protecting herself from life.

And she had been going over the list of things that she had failed at for all of these years.

Entry one.

Climb the damn mountain.

Get a makeover.

A more shallow entry, but one that resonated none-theless.

And then she'd written entry three:

Get a kiss.

That was right where she was at when *he* appeared.

Broad-shouldered, standing a good distance in the thicket of trees. He had on a black cowboy hat, a tight black T-shirt. He had a beard and long shaggy hair, ink running down both of his arms in complex patterns.

She would have said she didn't find any of those things appealing, but in that moment, he stole her breath.

Golden sunlight filtered through the trees and made everything feel like it was under some kind of magic spell. Like *she* was.

She had never looked at a man and had a reaction quite like this before. Visceral. Deep. Raw.

Rory was untouched. That was part of the problem. She was leaving Pyrite Falls in just under a month to go start her new job in Boston, and she had never even been on a date.

The stark truth was that she couldn't go to Boston a virgin. If she went to Boston a virgin she was going to be a virgin until she died. Because how was she going to explain to a guy in the dissolute city that she had never seen a penis?

She had never even kissed a man. You weren't allowed to be a virgin and a legend unless you were a nun. And even then, you had to do some pretty intense stuff to reach legendary status, and considering she wasn't selling all worldly possessions and devoting her life to the poor, maybe she was going to have to see a penis.

She wasn't writing that out on her list. She was going to start small.

Oh. No. She didn't want to start small with penises.

Her whole face went hot and she looked from her notebook, back to the stranger again.

He was still there. He wasn't a hallucination.

She'd never felt anything like this before. This intense. This gripping.

She had had a deep and near-fatal crush on her best friend's older brother when she was in school—which had resulted in the most intense humiliation she had experienced up until that point—but that was all.

There had been greater humiliation in her life following that. But there had never been a more intense attraction to a man.

Until now.

It almost made her giddy.

Because who was this girl, the one sitting there staring at this stranger, suddenly overwhelmed by the desire to cross the space and kiss him?

She stood up.

Was she actually going to do it?

He didn't say anything, but she knew that he saw her.

He was staring at her the way she was staring at him.

Did he think she was beautiful?

She was dressed in a long floral dress that touched her ankles; it didn't show a hint of skin. She knew that men liked skin.

Normally, she wouldn't do this. Normally, she would say something, or…apologize for being there, when he was clearly there, and hadn't meant to run across her.

She wouldn't stand there, staring, taking in every detail of him that she could see from that distance.

And for a moment, she let herself get lost.

She didn't know him.

He didn't know her.

They were alone together in the woods, and she was...

She wanted to be brave. Was she that brave?

She took a step toward him, and he just stood there, his expression fixed.

She tried to take in a shuddering breath.

He shifted, and her eyes went to his hands. They were large hands. Masculine and rough.

What would it be like to be held by a man like that?

What would it be like to feel desired by him?

Her mouth went dry.

A few months ago she had decided that she was going to change everything. That was when she had accepted the job offer in Boston. After months of trying to find something, anything that would make the most of the skills she had as a property manager. After Quinn had gotten engaged to Levi, and she had realized that her little sister was doing things that Rory herself was never going to. Not at the rate she was living. Or not living.

Shrouded in fantasy, driven by need, she took another step toward him.

Then two things happened.

Her phone buzzed in her pocket, a reminder she had a meeting with her sister. And she saw herself. Really saw herself and what she'd been contemplating.

She was about to walk up to this man—this stranger

who could be a serial killer for all she knew—and kiss him.

She'd heard it said before that the character in a book or movie didn't know what genre they were in. Truth be told, neither did she. If she were in a romance novel, it would be reasonable to go and kiss him.

But what if she was in a horror movie?

Or what if he just doesn't want you?

So Rory did what she did best. She turned, and she ran.

And she didn't look back.

WHEN SHE FINALLY got from her spot in the woods to the farm store, she got out of her car and looked into the back of her sister's truck, which was parked out front. There were baskets full of vegetables in the back, and she knew that Fia must just be stocking up for the day.

She grabbed a basket of zucchini. She pushed open the door to the store and sighed. Her heart was still thundering like a spooked horse.

Nothing happened. You didn't do anything.

He probably thinks you're a weirdo, but so does everybody. You're Rory Sullivan, the Pimento Tooth- pick. Scrawny, gangly, obsessed with whatever book you're reading and writer of cringe poetry. So he thinks you're weird? Big deal.

It felt like a big deal. Because he'd been beautiful.

The single most compelling thing she'd ever seen in her life.

Why had she been such a coward? Maybe kissing him would've been stupid, but she could have at least talked to him. Instead, the minute he moved she had scampered off like a frightened deer.

She wanted to do something. She started stacking the zucchinis in their rightful place, which was doing *something*, but not quite how she meant it.

"Hi, Rory," came the sound of her sister's voice.

Rory jumped, still skittish. "Oh. Hi."

"Yeah, hi."

She stopped for a moment. "Fia?"

"Yes?"

"Do you ever date?"

She was quite certain her sister didn't. The great implosion between her and Landry King was the stuff of Four Corners legend, and she seemed to do her best to stay clear of men. Or if not clear of them entirely, then at least she kept it on the down-low. Because after all that, she hadn't really wanted everybody in on her business anymore. Which Rory could understand. In theory.

"Why?" Fia asked, her eyes narrow.

"I just feel like I need to shake things up."

"You're moving to Boston."

"I know that. But I… I'm tired of living life through books. And pictures of beautiful places online. It's not the same."

"No, it isn't. But it's safer."

"I just… In a romance novel, if you saw a gorgeous man standing in the middle of the woods, you would kiss him," Rory said.

"*Would* you?" She sounded skeptical.

"You don't read romance novels, how would you even know?"

"I don't read romance novels because I don't get caught up in all that kind of stuff. I have my own dreams. It's better not to depend on someone else."

"In general I agree, but…" She thought of him again.

She didn't want to live like this anymore. She didn't want to live with regrets. She wished she would've just done the bold thing. Except, that was very impractical, because if you went up kissing dangerous-looking men like that, they were probably going to assume you wanted sex.

That thought sent a sensation up between her legs.

She kind of *did* want sex. That was the thing. If only she hadn't had sex because she had some kind of intense commitment to her virtue. But no. It was because she was a coward.

She needed to add sex to her list.

"I hope you're not busy tonight," Fia said. "With mystery men or otherwise."

"Oh. Sorry. I have two online dates, and I thought I would try to make it to both of them in a series of increasingly slapstick events." At least that had happened in a book she'd read recently.

Fia gave her the side-eye. "So you aren't busy?"

"No, I'm not busy," she said. The idea of her having *one* date was hilarious, let alone two.

"Well, we have a very last-minute rental request, and since the house up on the ridge got vacated last month, and we haven't had any other inquiries, I want to accommodate."

"Okay. Is it clean?" she asked.

"I had it cleaned when Sandra moved out, but it could probably use a once-over." Their tenant had been clean and quiet, but dust did tend to accumulate.

Rory tried not to ponder all the dust she'd likely accumulated by sitting around doing so little with her life.

"Yeah. Sure. I can do that."

"Great. Sorry to throw that on you."

"Oh, no. I'm practicing. For my new job," she said, testing the waters softly with that subject.

"Yeah. Well, then I'm giving you more work experience. Which I would try to avoid doing so that you wouldn't leave me, but you already secured a new position."

"I need to leave," said Rory.

Fia looked at her for a long moment. "I know you do. As much as I need to stay."

"This place is in your blood. I get that."

"Yes, it is. And more than that, I feel like... I was made to feel like this place couldn't be mine. Like I wasn't going to be able to make it work. And I have. I'll never leave it. No matter what."

"And I love that for you. This is the best part of my being here. But I'm just going to die a spinster with ten cats if I don't do something."

"You don't have a cat," Fia pointed out.

"Not yet. But there's still time."

"There's nothing wrong with being a spinster."

Rory cringed. "I didn't mean that. I didn't mean *you*. Besides, you have..."

Fia scowled. "*Don't* say Landry."

"I didn't." She had been thinking it, though. The thing about Fia was that she had a legend. The legend of her and Landry King. And why they hated each other so much. What had passed between them all those years ago?

Rory didn't have a legend. There was nothing about her that was interesting.

She knew Fia hated to be the subject of all those rumors, but Rory knew for certain that it was worse to be uninteresting.

"You know the person moving into the house," Fia said, making a clear and obvious decision to change the subject now that Landry King's name had been introduced.

"I do?"

"Yeah. Your friend Lydia's brother. Gideon."

Her heart tripped over itself and then she managed to hit the zucchini stack with her elbow and send at least five of the long green veggies rolling to the floor.

"What?"

Gideon. Here. Gideon who had been a distant inspiration in her mind because really thinking of him was too big and too bright.

Gideon, who apparently still made her stomach go tight and took her breath away.

Gideon.

Gideon was staying at Sullivan's Point? She'd known he was coming back to town sometime in the next week, but she'd assumed he'd be getting his own place, or staying with his mother and sister.

She thought of the man in the woods again. No. That couldn't have been…

Gideon didn't look like that. He did not look like an invitation to sin and vice.

The last time she'd seen him he had been clean-shaven with his hair high and tight, as he had gone off into the military.

He had always been muscular, but not like that man. That man looked like he lifted tires in his spare time.

Or maybe whole buildings.

"He needs a place to stay and he called asking about one of our rentals. I told him it was free." Rory bent down quickly and started picking the zucchini up. "Was that the wrong thing to say?" Fia pressed.

"No..." She leaned out long and grabbed a rolling zucchini, standing and trying to position them on the display. "No. I just assumed that he would be moving back home."

"It's a long story. I guess he's buying back the family ranch that they lost after his dad died. But it isn't ready yet, and I think that wasn't part of the plan. The owners have some kind of contingency they added to the sale. Anyway. He can't move in over there for a while, so he needs a place to stay in the interim. I didn't get the sense that he especially wanted to stay with his family."

"Oh. He's rebuying the family ranch?"

Lydia hadn't mentioned that. She wondered if Lydia knew. The loss of her father combined with the loss of the ranch shortly after had been so traumatic for her— for her and her mother. And now Gideon was being... Gideon.

Being heroic again. Getting the land back.

It was very Gideon. Also very fitting with his mystique.

She did her best not to think too deeply about that, or him.

But he had a mystique, whether Rory wanted to ponder it or not. A soldier, now on his way to being a cowboy via restoration of his family's legacy.

There was going to be a plaque in town for Gideon Payne someday.

And while Rory herself didn't want to aspire to a plaque—considering she had never gone to war, that would only ever be some kind of sad memorial she wasn't especially in a hurry to get—she did want *something*.

When people talked about her, she didn't want the words in their mouths to be negative. When they talked about her, she didn't want them to say she was sad or silly. Rory Sullivan, that quiet girl. Rory Sullivan, the quitter. Rory Sullivan, a nerd.

Or worse yet, for them to not even notice she was gone at all.

The truth was that was more than likely the path she was on at the current moment. *Rory Sullivan, who? Oh, did she leave? Didn't notice.*

Yeah. That was Rory.

And it was never Gideon.

Gideon Payne was a war hero. Gideon Payne was the best athlete Mapleton High had ever seen.

"I guess he probably doesn't need a welcome basket and a guide to the area," she said.

"Everybody likes a welcome basket, Rory. Even if it's a welcome-back basket."

"Well. I'll get on that. And I'll get the place clean. Do you know when he's expected?"

"When's the parade scheduled for?" Fia asked.

She laughed. "I thought that was this weekend."

"Oh. Well, then he's coming ahead of the parade. Because I think he said today sometime. But it might be late. I don't know. I suppose you could text Lydia and ask. Otherwise, I have his contact information somewhere."

"It's okay. I'll just make it my focus for the day."

She was happy, actually, to have an excuse to work on something as solitary as cleaning.

It would give her time to think about how exactly she was going to accomplish her goals.

And to forget about the mystery man and her moment of temporary insanity.

But maybe being somewhat adjacent to Gideon would be helpful.

After all, being in proximity to a local legend might give her some ideas on how to achieve legend status herself.

People told stories about him down at the diner. There was a hamburger named after him—The Legend.

He had been the football star at the local high school. He had set records in track and field in the state of Oregon—which was unheard of in a school the size of theirs. He had been the golden boy.

The one everyone admired.

There were whispered stories about his looks and his sexual prowess—which Lydia had always gagged and retched about because, after all, he was Lydia's older brother. Rory had secretly been scandalized, heartbroken and intrigued. Though she could never ever tell Lydia. He was Lydia's older brother, after all, and everyone liked Gideon most of all. Rory having a crush on him would have been a huge betrayal.

It was the one secret she'd ever kept from her friend, but consequently she also didn't often ask Lydia about Gideon because she felt like it seemed…obvious.

Anyway, there was a point where everyone had known. After…The Diary Incident. When the mean girls who'd tormented Rory had upped their game and subjected her to the most wounding, deeply humiliating experience of her life.

And Gideon had saved her.

He was a hero. *Her* hero.

But heroes didn't stay around. They had to go off and join the military. He'd left town under a cloud of confetti, riding on a white convertible and waving.

Her heart had broken.

Because the one person who'd made her truly brave was leaving.

She'd kept up on his accomplishments through the years via Lydia's mom's Christmas letter she sent out, but otherwise…

She hadn't kept up. She hadn't felt worthy of it, or of him, really. After all, he'd never mocked her when her love poetry had been made public. Instead he'd walked into the school with his hand on her shoulder and when one of the bullies had approached them, he'd told them to go straight to hell.

Don't let the bastards get you down, Rory. You're meant for bigger things than this place.

No one else had ever said anything like that to her. No one else had ever looked at her and seen more. But then she'd gone away to school and she…she'd run. She'd felt like she'd let him down in that way, even though he was off fighting in a war and she was sure he didn't actually keep tabs on what his little sister's best friend was up to.

So she'd tried not to think about him.

Until three years ago when he'd gotten injured in Afghanistan.

Rory, Gideon was hurt in an attack today. They're flying him to Germany.

She could still remember her friend's desperate, tearful phone call.

And the way she'd sat, hollow and barely able to breathe, waiting for more news.

How could Gideon be injured? He was too strong for that. Too full of life.

He most especially couldn't die.

She hadn't breathed again until Lydia had called to say he was stable enough to move to a military hospital in the States.

He had broken ribs, a broken pelvis. Shrapnel wounds. Burns. A concussion but, all in all, it had been minor compared to what you expected when you heard someone was injured in a bomb blast.

Lydia and her mom had gone to stay in Atlanta for a while after that. When Lydia came back, Gideon had been released and was home with his wife. Rory had gone back to following only vague updates.

She knew he'd been honorably discharged after his injury and given an award for his bravery. She knew that he'd split from his wife.

Even now that made her chest feel strange and sore.

The truth was Gideon Payne was *iconic*, and not just as Rory's first and fiercest crush. Not just her hero. He was iconic to this town and everyone in it.

Rory had never been iconic of much of anything. Perhaps the emblem of a small troupe of trembling chickens, or the patron saint of lowly burrowing animals, or…beige.

All of which had gotten worse after her father had left the family.

What had begun as a nervous disposition and vague awkwardness had turned into some pretty full-blown anxiety.

The only place she could have adventures was in books.

At least then she could be the fearless ship's captain.

Or the beautiful interesting girl who got the attention of her best friend's older brother.

Hypothetically.

Because when you couldn't count on the one thing you had always felt like you could, what else was out there waiting to betray you? She had never quite been certain of the answer to that question, and it had made things—like rope climbs and team-building hikes—seem terrifying.

Likely, it was a contributing factor to why she had only lasted a couple of months away from home.

She was clinging to what was familiar.

Because so little was.

But she was determined to see things from a different perspective. If you wanted a different reputation, you didn't wait to be at the mercy of the world. You had to decide. You had to take control. Yes, as a child, she'd had no control over whether or not her father stayed.

But she was a grown woman now, and she had control over whether or not she took charge of her life.

He'd built her up back then and she'd let those guys at college knock her back down.

But Gideon… Well, he'd been knocked down, too. And he was still coming back triumphant. That was what she needed. Some of that triumph.

And she knew that Gideon would come with triumph.

Because unlike Rory, he was a local legend.

He had left with the parade, and he would return with one, too.

CHAPTER TWO

GIDEON PAYNE CAME back to Pyrite Falls in silence, under cover of darkness.

Far from the way he'd left, with the roar of the crowd and the sun shining brightly.

He wanted it that way.

He'd spent the day driving around familiar mountain roads, and after talking to Fia Sullivan about coming to stay at Sullivan's Point, he'd gone for a walk in the woods.

And there she'd been.

He had never seen a more beautiful woman. Not in his memory.

Granted, he hadn't gotten laid in two years, but the truth was he hadn't even wanted to.

Seeing that creature in the woods, her red hair long and curling. The sun had been shining behind her, making that demure dress transparent, showing the shape of her legs, her hips… She'd been perfect.

She was probably a Sullivan.

The Sullivans were all redheads; he remembered that much from when he had lived here all those years ago.

But he didn't want to put a name to her. Not in that moment. He just wanted to enjoy that one thing finally felt normal.

His cock worked. Praise the Lord.

In the grand scheme of things, that felt like a mighty miracle.

The need to reach out and touch her had been… She must've seen it in his eyes.

That must've been why she ran away.

He had frightened her.

That wasn't terribly surprising. He couldn't be civil at the best of times, and when lust had grabbed him by the throat for the first time in years, he imagined he'd looked feral.

The people of Pyrite Falls would be surprised to see him now.

His sister had texted him about a parade of some kind, one marking his return. He didn't want one. Maybe when the good citizens got a look at him, they wouldn't want to throw one.

But he had nowhere else to go. No other ideas for how to climb back out of the pit he was in.

Rock bottom was an interesting place. And he had no real interest in staying there.

He was better. Better than he'd been, anyway. He'd been on the outcropping just above rock bottom for the last year or so.

He'd spared his family the worst of it.

At least, he'd tried.

He hadn't managed to spare Cass the worst of it, but that was marriage, he supposed.

For better or worse, going down in flames together.

After the marriage had ended, however, his continued undoing was something he'd had to fight through on his own.

He was getting pretty damned tired of fighting, though. Truth be told, that was partly why he was back here. This was the last place things had been easy. This was the last place where they'd made sense. And he'd known who he was when he lived in Pyrite Falls, and he had no fucking clue who he was now.

He had a feeling he was never quite going to be able to get back to the man he'd been. Hell, he knew that.

He had the scars to prove it. Both physically and mentally.

But, maybe this would be easier. Something had to be.

Anything was easier than sitting in the hollowed-out shell of his military career, and the dissolution of his eight-year marriage.

Well, maybe not anything; some deployments had certainly been worse. But most things were easier than that. At least here he would have a purpose again. That had been the problem. That had been the slow slide all the way down. Having nothing, no idea what to do next, no idea who he was anymore.

Cassidy had said he didn't know how to smile anymore.

And she was right. That was the problem.

She'd been right about him. Everything she'd shouted at him in a desperate rage to wake him up, to reach the man she'd married, had been true.

He couldn't even be angry at his wife for ending things. Because he wasn't the man she'd married.

He was unable to be the husband that she wanted him to be. *Needed* him to be.

All of those things were true.

She'd said it was like he'd died in Afghanistan.

He couldn't argue that.

But maybe being back here would make him feel more like himself. Maybe.

But there was a reason he'd come back initially under the cover of darkness.

There was a reason that seemed preferable.

There was a reason it seemed a little bit easier.

He'd get the lay of the land before anyone was expecting him. Including his mom and Lydia.

He hadn't told them about his intent to buy the ranch because he'd been afraid of it falling through. He'd been irritated when the sale had been held up, because he'd just been waiting for that to bite his ass and not be the heroic move he'd been hoping it would be.

Now, though…

He was sort of grateful for the reprieve.

He'd told them he'd had a hiccup with the place he was buying, and even though he'd managed to get it ironed out quickly, it had made the exact date of his getting to town fuzzy. He'd left it that way deliberately.

He could've stayed in Georgia for another month.

But he was so done with that place. So done with having to be confronted by any of the places where he'd once been Staff Sergeant Gideon Payne.

Because that man was gone.

But maybe Gideon Payne, rancher, could follow in his father's footsteps and find a life.

Damn.

Regret hollowed out his gut.

His dad was gone.

He'd come home for the funeral, but there was something so stark about it now that he was home.

He hadn't been back in four years. Not since his mom had sold the ranch. That distance had allowed him a healthy amount of denial.

And hell, he'd been in another world.

The military was all-consuming. His life away had been all-consuming. Until it wasn't.

Until he'd been injured and left with nothing but his own echoing thoughts. His own weakness. His own failure.

What a nightmare.

In the end, coming back home felt like the only answer. Though right at the last minute was when he'd started feeling pressured by the whole thing. The stay at Sullivan's was a godsend in that way.

He didn't know any of the Sullivans all that well, apart from Rory, who was his sister's friend. He didn't know her now. He knew her as a teenager who chattered his ear off and sang tunelessly to the car radio on the way to school.

If he could find affection for his past self, for his memories, he'd have looked back on that time with warmth.

As it was, all he could do was look back and envy that idiot kid he'd been. The guy who'd felt bulletproof.

Well, he was not, it turned out, blast-proof.

He thought of the angel he'd seen earlier today.

And he pushed that to the side.

He'd forgotten how many complications a man could find in a small town.

He'd chosen to come back home. He'd found himself in a weird-ass place these past few months. He didn't have the stomach to stay in Georgia, not when it was littered with the debris of his life, blown all to hell by a bomb from Afghanistan.

When he'd gone on deployment he'd always felt thankful that while he might be moving into the line of fire, his wife wasn't. His home wasn't.

He'd been wrong.

That bomb blast might have happened overseas,

but it had sure as hell blown up that life on Dogwood Street, in Atlanta, Georgia, where he'd once had that perfect life.

He hadn't been able to stand being near any of that. He'd considered going off somewhere new. Somewhere no one knew him. There was a hefty amount of appeal in that.

Also a lack of accountability that scared the shit out of him.

So he'd finally considered coming back home. He knew why he'd decided on this. It was just…doing it was harder than he'd anticipated.

He'd never imagined his life ending up like this.

After the blast, right at first… Right at first, it had been okay. Cass had been that brave military wife. The one who stood by her husband through his injuries. The one who sat in the hospital with him. She'd thought this was the testing of them, the making of them.

He'd believed that, too.

They'd both been wrong.

She'd found her breaking point.

He'd found his.

It was fair.

This wasn't the life he'd promised her. If he could have left himself, he would have.

Hell, he'd tried.

He pulled his truck onto the dirt road that he knew would lead up to the rental house, based on his instructions.

He drove until it seemed like he had to have gone way too far. But he seemed to recall that Fia had said specifically that. That it would feel like he'd gone too far, but he had to keep going.

There was maybe a metaphor in there somewhere. But he felt a little too weary to try and grasp it in his hands.

So he just drove on. He turned off the road onto a narrower dirt road that went straight up the side of the mountain.

He was thankful he had a four-wheel drive. And everything that he owned was in a duffel bag in the back of the truck.

It just wasn't much was what it came down to. His life, and everything he cared about anymore, fit into a bag.

He could never imagine such a thing a couple of years ago. He'd lived in a beautiful house filled with things. Furniture and decorations and clothes.

The day Cassidy told him to leave the house and not come back, he'd put all the things he wanted into one bag. It had been pretty easy. There was something in that, too. But, he wasn't in the mood to think on that, either.

It had made this move easy, and that he could be grateful for. He had all the time in the world to rebuild. If he even really wanted to.

There was nothing wrong with living simple.

It appealed to that part of him that still felt like a military man, even though he wasn't. Even though he never would be again.

He would always be marked by the military. That was for sure.

So he supposed it was fair enough to think of himself that way.

He kept on going.

He was surprised when he saw lights shining through the trees, and when he pulled into the driveway, he saw what was a very neat, bigger-than-expected cabin.

It was all lit up and welcome, and the porch light was on.

He sat in his truck for a long moment, examining that feeling. Of the light being left on for him.

He could remember coming home late in the latter days of his marriage. And that light being off.

Because she wasn't waiting up. Not anymore.

He couldn't blame her.

It wasn't her fault. She couldn't have kept on being there for someone who wasn't there for her. That was the truth of it. He wasn't owed endless service just because he'd been wounded serving the country. She was his wife. She had needed things, too.

But damn, he'd missed that sense someone might be waiting for him. More than he cared to admit.

He cleared his throat and got out of the truck, moving around the back and grabbing his duffel bag. He walked up to the steps and looked at the way his shadow cut through the light. He didn't need to pause and ponder that metaphor. It was self-evident. It was him, all the way around at this point. He was the shadow. If he could've just been better, then…

He'd ruined Cassidy's life. Sometimes that was like acid in his soul.

She married him… In that white dress, looking so beautiful and so full of hope. She was an Army brat. She knew the deal. She was in it for the long haul. She was the kind of woman who could withstand the deployments, the moves, all that stuff. She was perfect. And he had somehow managed to ruin all her dreams.

Because neither of them had really had an idea of what the long haul could mean.

Tragedy happened to other people.

Other men were broken apart by war.

Other men were hobbled by brain injuries, PTSD and addiction.

He'd now learned too well that the line separating him from *other men* had been a trip wire. And once it had been activated, everything had been blown to hell. Now there were no lines left.

He was the shadow.

And hell, he couldn't blame her for keeping the porch light off so she didn't have to see it anymore.

He shook his head and walked up to the front door. He had a code to open up the padlock that contained the key, centered right there next to the door.

That worked easily and quickly, and it was a weird thing to marvel at such a small detail being easy.

But he wasn't used to easy. Not at this point.

He walked inside and looked around. It was clean. Freshly so, and it beat the hell out of the mildew in the apartment and old motel rooms he'd been staying in.

Cassidy hadn't wanted spousal support from him. But there had been some gaps in pay while he'd been moving around, and while he'd waited to get his disability from the military. And after he put all that money down on the ranch.

He'd been living lean. That was over now. He had the money.

Still, he hadn't stayed anywhere this nice in some time.

It was the cleanliness that got him.

He moved deeper into the room, and there was a table. And on that table was a giant basket. Inside the basket was a bottle of wine, which he immediately took out and moved off to the side.

It wasn't difficult for him to be around alcohol, but he wouldn't be opening the bottle.

There was food in there, which he did appreciate. Candies and nuts, some bread and muffins. The basket overflowed, really.

It was amazing, and his stomach was growling. He went over to the fridge and opened it. There was a glass bottle with milk, some butter, a pie. He opened up the freezer and saw a tub of vanilla ice cream, and he gave thanks to a God he rarely acknowledged anymore.

He took the pie out of the fridge and cut himself a generous slice. That was one of the perks of living by himself—there was no one here to judge him. He heated the pie up in the microwave, then put a generous scoop of ice cream right on top. He didn't care much about exploring the rest of the place, not when there was a blackberry pie for him to dig into.

It felt like home.

This place.

Homemade pie, a big scoop of vanilla ice cream and a clean kitchen.

He sat there in the silence, eating.

It wasn't a parade. But he didn't want a parade.

He thought of that woman again. Surrounded by sunlight. It made something warm bloom inside him that he hadn't felt in a long time.

As welcome homes went, this was just about perfect. He hadn't even turned the lights on. He looked around the dim room, the only sound his fork on the plate and the steady ticking of the clock on the wall.

"Welcome back, Gideon. Welcome back."

CHAPTER THREE

THE THING ABOUT Rory was that she'd always been a quitter. Something she was thinking about as she sat in the farm store, working a shift while Fia harvested more from the garden.

The farm store she'd be leaving next month.

Quitter behavior. Some might argue.

She'd first realized she was a quitter when clinging to the bottom of a rope in PE, looking up and doing mental calculations on how difficult it would be to get to the top. She was never going to make it. She'd realized that she could struggle and strain and get halfway, and then fail, in spite of getting mostly there...or she could just stop before she started.

She opted for that.

She'd failed PE, which she hated. She'd had straight A's otherwise.

The grades were very important. Because she wasn't athletic, she wasn't popular. Her braces, glasses and knobby knees had precluded her from being part of the elite set. And her grades were all she had.

For all the good they'd done her.

Unlike most of the Four Corners kids, she'd gone to high school an hour from the ranch. Another aspect of her...quitter-ness. She just hadn't been able to deal with her family during that period of time and the opportunity to put a little distance between herself and the turmoil at home had been a blessing.

She'd met her best friend, Lydia Payne, at a parade in town that her mom had taken her to when she'd been eight years old. Lydia had decided to collect Rory and make her into a pet of sorts, and Rory had soaked up the attention. In her own household, she was often lost.

Less confrontational than Fia. Not a rancher like Quinn. A little less—a *lot* less—brave than Alaina.

When she'd gotten into middle school, she'd begged to be able to go to school in Mapleton, along with Lydia. Her parents had agreed, since it didn't mean any extra work for them, given transportation would be handled by Lydia's older brother.

That had given Rory her own space. Her own time. A little room to breathe.

That was when she'd started fantasizing about a life away from Pyrite Falls and Four Corners. Maybe if she had even more space around her, she'd feel that much more free.

The problem was she'd still been a quitter.

Her quitting continued to the team-building hike they'd had to take one year in school, and she'd gotten midway up the rocks, looked down, scared ten years off her life and refused to go any farther.

She'd achieved her dreams. She'd gotten into college far from Pyrite Falls, Oregon, and away from her family. Away from everyone who knew her.

For three months.

She'd spent a semester in absolute misery and had turned with her tail between her legs after experiencing the most humiliating night of her life. She'd thought one of the guys wanted to make out with her; instead, she'd ended up abandoned in a closet for an hour and when she emerged, she'd had beer dumped on her while they'd laughed about small-town virgins with tits that weren't any bigger than mosquito bites.

She'd confided in her friend Lydia about the humiliation, and Lydia had been pragmatic: *It could be worse. You were at a frat party. You could have been a statistic.*

But then, in addition to being a quitter, Rory Sullivan could never be a statistic.

Because she was too invisible to be counted as a statistic.

She was certainly invisible in her hometown.

It was one reason she needed to get out. She'd always felt like she wasn't going to be the hometown girl who blossomed when she went away. She'd had years to figure out how to blossom in Pyrite Falls, after all, and it hadn't happened. She'd been picked on at school, and even the one time…even the one time she'd thought she'd triumphed, it hadn't been enough.

Everyone thought they knew what to expect with her, and as a result she lived down to those expectations.

Not anymore.

She had a plan. She had a job lined up, which felt like a small miracle, since she had often felt like maybe she had torpedoed her chances of success of any kind when she left school.

But she'd been working at the ranch ever since then, and had also been part of establishing the new Sullivan family farm store. She had gotten so much experience coordinating that, and additionally she had experience managing rental properties. Even though it wasn't a lot of experience, it was still experience. It had started with houses on the ranch, and had expanded to a cou-

ple of places in the outlying area since people realized
she had been doing such a good job with them at Sullivan's Point.

That had opened up an opportunity for her outside of
Four Corners. It hadn't been her intention when she had
started doing it, but it was certainly her intention now.

She felt like those doors were open again, ones she'd
thought she'd closed forever with her youthful coward-
ice, and now she saw a new chance.

She wanted to take that chance.

To be worthy of the boost she'd been given all those
years ago, that she hadn't been able to do enough with
then.

She'd been blindly applying for jobs in cities for
the last couple of months, and finally she'd gotten one.
There was a building manager at an apartment complex
in the north end of Boston, a beautiful historic building, and the long-time manager was retiring, leaving
the vacancy.

And that meant…finally, she had a chance to start
over. Finally, Rory had the chance to reinvent herself.

She was older now. She was ready now.

She wasn't a scared eighteen-year-old away from
home for the first time. She'd had a lot of time to sit in
her failures.

To sit in the quitting.

She wasn't going to do it anymore.

Of course, she had some regrets about leaving. Because yes, she thought as she parked her car in front of
the store, it meant leaving the store. Arguably quitting.
Though this was quitting to begin.

Her best friend, Lydia, still wasn't happy about it.
And her sisters weren't especially thrilled, either.

Though at least they were understanding. Because they knew. They knew what it had been like for her growing up. They knew what it was like for her now.

And they were all…paired off.

Well, not Fia. But that didn't surprise Rory. Fia didn't want that kind of thing, and Rory wasn't sure she did, either. Or rather, she had other things to worry about first.

Such as getting a date. Getting kissed.

Not being such a loser.

Well. She was on the right path.

She had four weeks left in Pyrite Falls. And she had a plan.

Her Summer of Rory.

It was such a funny thing, but she'd been thinking a lot about reputations and legends. Rory Sullivan had, for the longest time, been known as a quitter. A weird girl, best ignored—which was easy enough because it wasn't like she was going to push her way into a social group. Somebody you didn't want to invite to your birthday party. Somebody that you poured beer on after abandoning her in a closet.

Rory was a wet blanket because her reputation preceded her, and she allowed it to define who she was. She was done with that. She was redefining herself.

Perhaps not by kissing strange hot men in the woods, but there were other ways to have a rebirth. She was certain.

Thank God for Lydia, because without her, Rory wouldn't have had anyone. But Lydia liked that Rory's humor was quiet and a little bit sly. She liked sitting in a corner, too, even though Rory was confident that Lydia didn't have to do that if she didn't want to.

Rory had always been a bookworm. Content to experience adventure in the pages of those books, because she was too anxious to do it any other way, and it was far too easy for her to let herself back out of things when she was uncomfortable. But if she was going to make this move to Boston, if she was going to start over, if she was going to reinvent herself, then that meant she had to get a firm foundation underneath her.

It was funny that all of this was happening when Gideon Payne was coming back home.

His name elicited a reaction from everyone. He was a legend in town.

But the reaction he elicited in her was different.

Personal. Somewhat embarrassing. Definitely deep.

She stared down at her journal, an ironic thing to be looking at while thinking of Gideon. But writing things down had always been formative for her. And yes, that had backfired on her that time in middle school. But she wasn't a teenager anymore.

Thank God.

This list was a part of her plan. A big part of it.

But she wasn't going to share it with anybody. And anyway, this was all part of her whole process. She didn't need to feel silly, because she was happy enough with what she was doing. She didn't need to feel silly, because she stood by the decision she was making to change her life. And maybe all of this would blow up in her face, but this was about being active, rather than passive.

Well. Quitting was active. In its way.

She had actively shoved herself into the category of the *beige secondhand sweater*.

If she were an article of clothing, that would be her.

She wanted to be a pair of stilettos. A miniskirt.

A bit exciting, a little racy.

How could she go to her new life in Boston when she hadn't even conquered the life she had here?

She started to feel warm and peeled her sweater off.

And nearly groaned when she realized that she had a beige T-shirt on underneath.

She was still wrestling with the sweater when Fia walked in, carrying a basket overflowing with fruits and vegetables. Bright pink and golden raspberries, sun-warmed apricots, carrots with cheerful green tops. She loved that. She would miss it.

"Can you go check on our new tenant today?" Fia asked, setting her heavy basket down.

Gideon.

Rory's heart gave a very unnecessary thump.

"Yeah," said Rory, setting her notebook down.

"Good. You might bring him some more food. I know that you put coffee and milk and the like up there for the morning, but he's probably going to need lunch."

The reaction she felt to actually going there when he might be home was something like…panic. And she couldn't explain why.

"Do we provide room and board now?" she asked, her heart pounding in her ears.

"No. But he is… He's Gideon Payne. He has a Purple Heart. He took Mapleton High School to state in football. Nobody else has ever done that."

"You didn't even go there," Rory pointed out.

"No. Maybe I didn't. But you have to admit, it's impressive. This is a tiny little area, and it's never really been on the map for much. But when it has been…it's been him. Well, and Sawyer Garrett putting a mail-order bride article out there on the internet, and getting picked up by worldwide news outlets. There was that. But otherwise, it's Gideon. He's a war hero and he's…"

"I get it. Are you sure you don't want to go deliver the stuff? You seem like you have a little bit of a crush on him." If that sounded pointed, it wasn't on purpose.

If it was deflection, she didn't mean it to be.

She was just about to see the man she'd had a totally teen-years-defining crush on for the first time in forever and it was just fine.

She wished, she really did, that the timing of this were different. That she'd run into him again after she'd become interesting.

Or at least even half of what he'd told her she could be that day he'd rescued her at school.

Lord knew she wasn't now.

Not that she harbored secret fantasies about anything happening, it was just that…of course she wanted to be a little more amazing when coming face-to-face with the man who had defined masculine beauty to her when she'd been fifteen. Who wouldn't?

"I don't," said Fia. "I'm merely giving admiration where admiration is due. Because I am good like that."

"Let me tell you, Gideon Payne is just a regular guy. I think it's great that his reputation precedes him, and as a war hero, he deserves some credit. But… Don't forget that I am still very good friends with his sister. And I used to see him around the house quite a bit. He is a *regular guy*."

Her heart fluttered as she said it, like it was calling her a liar. She wasn't lying. He was a man. An amazing one, sure. But he wasn't…the demigod her mind had built him into all those years ago, so she and everyone else could calm down.

"Okay. If you say so," Fia said.

Rory remembered him all clean-cut, and the last time she'd seen him had been right before he went into the military, so not only had he been clean-cut with that square razor-sharp jaw, but he'd had the high and tight haircut that made his looks even more severe.

He was basically Captain America.

And good for him. *Good for him.*

She went to the store, putting together a little care package to bring up this afternoon since Fia was bound and determined to overextend the hospitality.

She thought about what kind of thing she might do in a much larger apartment complex, where there were a hundred and twenty units.

It was massive.

But she would also have more resources. She'd already done many video calls with the other manager, learning that there were other resources available to her should there ever be emergencies. She wouldn't be on the hook personally for repairs. Her job was simply to facilitate all these things and make the tenants feel like life in the apartment complex ran smoothly.

They were premium apartments. And Rory would be getting one as part of her job.

She tried to imagine that life. A life nestled in this beautiful city she'd never been to.

Bricks and noise and streetlights, all things that they didn't have in Pyrite Falls.

It was such a huge step, but one that she felt was necessary.

It was the kind of step a heroine in a rom-com might take. A small-town girl making it to the big city and finding new friends. Drinking martinis. Having a shopping montage. Meeting a man who thought she was different and interesting instead of a faded wallflower. She wanted that.

"Okay," she said. "I'll drive up to greet him."

It was strange because she wasn't feeling nervous about it or anything; she did know him, after all. And also part of her job was talking to a lot of people she didn't know.

It was her function on the ranch, and off. She made a lot of phone calls to people she'd never met, she had a lot of meetings with people she'd never met, and she was willingly jumping feet first into a job that would require more of the same.

Meeting people just didn't fill her with a sense of anticipation or anxiety. Funny, because so many things did.

But for some reason, as she drew closer to the cabin, she felt a strange tightening of anticipation.

Maybe because he was kind of a legend. Maybe because she hadn't seen him in so long.

The last time she'd seen them, he'd been headed off for basic training. He had been back since, but she hadn't…visited with him.

She had collected a list of facts about Gideon over the years. Things she'd kept written secretly inside her own heart, and definitely not in a diary anywhere. If you didn't learn from your mistakes, what was the point?

But she knew he'd been deployed to Afghanistan, that he'd gotten married. She knew he'd been to classified locations that Lydia wasn't even allowed to know details about. He'd been injured in the line of duty. He'd gotten divorced.

Rory wondered if he would be different.

For some reason, that thought didn't hit until right

when she pulled up to the cabin. Because he was a legend. And legends felt fixed. Statues, plaques, immovable objects that stood as a testament to a moment.

He'd been injured. But in her mind she'd imagined him walking on crutches and waving bravely to a crowd of people. A man in a parade, like always.

How bad had it actually been?

She realized her own images of the whole thing had been cinematic. A man with an artful cut on his cheek bravely lying in a hospital bed with his family by his side before returning back home.

She got out of the car and took the basket with her, walked up to the front door and knocked. His truck was there, so she imagined that he was, too. She didn't exactly know what he was doing with his time until the ranch was ready for him. Visiting his family, likely, but it was fairly early in the day.

The door opened, and she stood there, face to chest— until she tilted her chin up—with a stranger.

Because this was not Gideon Payne. Not as she remembered him.

This was the stranger from the woods.

Oh, no.

Oh, no.

Immediately, she felt like she was on fire. Like she might die from being this close to him. Or die if she didn't get closer.

She could hardly see him for all the raw magnetism she felt just by standing in front of him, but when she took a breath, she took stock of all the differences.

He wasn't the smiling boy with a loud laugh and an easy manner. Gone was that clean-cut look, that aggressively homegrown handsomeness.

He was big. Much bigger than he'd been back then. His chest was deep, heavily muscled. He was lean, but he was the kind of muscular that looked like he could effortlessly flip a tire. Or lift a car.

His hair was long, dark and shaggy, and he had a heavy beard.

She had to look, hard, for any feature that made him recognizable as the man he'd been. This wasn't Captain America.

Those blue eyes, though.

They were familiar. But different somehow, too. There was no humor there. No warmth. No recognition as he looked at her.

Not from earlier. Not from back then.

He wasn't scarred. At least, not that she could see.

He had tattoos. She'd noticed the tattoos from afar, but hadn't been able to tell what they were. Up close she could see. Smoke, and fire, it looked like. A dragon. And on the other arm, water. Waves and a large sea serpent. She felt silly staring like that, so she didn't manage to take a visual tour of the other arm before she looked up to meet his gaze.

Her mouth felt dry. Her heart was pounding hard. She hadn't realized it, because she'd been all distracted trying to take in the differences in him. Trying to find something familiar.

"Gideon?"

"Yes."

"I... Rory. Rory Sullivan," she said. Still, she didn't see any recognition. It wasn't like they'd been friends but he had driven her to school every day. She hadn't expected him to forget her completely. Was she really that beige? They'd...they'd talked on those car rides.

She'd treasured them. He'd saved her. It had mattered to her. And today she'd thought... Did he not think about her at all? Had he not actually noticed her yesterday? "I'm Lydia's friend."

"Oh," he said.

"My sister wanted me to come by and make sure that you were getting settled in okay. And to bring a bit more food. Since we figured it might take you a couple of days to get settled and assembled. I manage the houses that we rent out on the property. In addition to some around town." She didn't know why she added that last part. It wasn't relevant to him.

He probably didn't care.

She cleared her throat and pressed on. "Anyway. I just wanted to bring you this."

"Thanks. Did you make the pie?"

"Oh. Yes. I did. We have blackberries in our garden, and..."

"You remembered ice cream."

"What's pie without ice cream?" she asked, smiling. Or trying to. "You found the coffee and everything, too, right?"

"If I hadn't, I would never have answered the door. I wouldn't have been upright."

He was talking, but it was all clipped and short. Like he didn't want her to accidentally get the idea he wanted to carry on a conversation.

"Anyway. Here you go." She handed him the other basket.

He took it, and didn't ask what was in it. "Just a second."

He turned and went into the house and reappeared

a moment later with a bottle of wine. "You can have this back."

"Oh. Is that not… It's not a kind that you like or…"

"Don't drink. Thanks."

"Oh. Yeah. No problem. I'm not the biggest… I don't love wine myself. But a lot of people do. So I like to put it in the welcome baskets and… I guess I should ask."

"Don't worry about it."

Except she was worried about it.

Because she worried about a lot of things, and that seemed like a pretty reasonable thing to worry about. She imagined that you probably shouldn't make assumptions about people's alcohol consumption.

She'd always seen it as a nice thing, but…

"Don't overthink it," he said. "I just didn't want it to be wasted in my cabinet, otherwise I would never have said anything."

"Okay. I won't overthink it. Well. That's a lie. I will overthink it. Because I overthink everything."

He shifted, and something about the way the light hit his face then gave her a small glimpse of the boy she used to know. "That's a difficult way to live, Rory."

"Is there another way?" she asked.

"Yeah. Personally, I try not to think of much of anything. I find that helpful."

"Helpful to what?"

"Sleeping at night. Being able to get through the damn day without having a nervous breakdown. Quite a few things."

"Oh."

"Yeah. So… Thanks. I'll see you around." She didn't know what she'd expected. But it wasn't this. It wasn't that she thought he would be excited to see her or anything. They didn't know each other. It wasn't that she thought he would ask her in. It was just that she remembered him being so...gregarious and friendly. She hadn't expected it so much as it had just seemed like a given.

He'd always been that way... It was like the party was drawn to him. He was a human flame, and everybody else were moths.

But he seemed to relish that role. He always had.

Every time she'd ever gone to Lydia's house there had been a group of people there hanging out with her older brother.

He was the perfect one. Women loved him. Men loved him. Everyone loved him.

High school kids, adults, everybody.

And he seems to thrive in that spotlight.

But not this man.

She held the bottle of wine close to her chest and walked back down to the truck.

She hadn't even gotten to ask him about the parade.

Was there really going to be a parade, or had someone been joking about that? It seemed like a reasonable thing to expect for Hometown Hero Gideon Payne.

But she wasn't sure that this Gideon would want a parade.

She wasn't sure of much of anything, which was normal for her. But she had to admit that she felt like the certainty of Gideon might have set her on the right track.

But that wasn't happening.

Her phone pinged, and she had a text from Lydia.

You have time to meet for lunch?

Yes.

Maybe she would ask Lydia a little bit more about her brother.

She drove down to town and pulled into the Becky's parking lot.

She hadn't verified for sure that it was where Lydia wanted to meet, but there wasn't anywhere else that wasn't too far afield.

The little diner was made from rough-hewn wood and had a bright blue door.

It was so named for an old miner called Becky who had come out here to find gold but had done better serving up hash browns.

Even though Becky himself had been deceased for going on seventy years, the name remained.

It was right next to Smokey's, the only bar in town.

A place that Rory herself didn't frequent. To say the least.

It just wasn't her thing.

When she walked into the diner, she saw Lydia sitting there. She smiled and gave her a wave.

Rory crossed the space and sat down at the table. "It's good to see you. We've been so busy since the store opened."

"And you've been busy shoring up your plans to abandon me."

"I'm not abandoning you, Lydia." Her stomach twisted with guilt. "Or at least I'm not trying to. I'm just trying to…"

Lydia reached out and patted her arm. "You're allowed to go have a life. I'm sorry. I'm not trying to make you feel guilty."

"It's okay if you do. It's fair."

"It isn't." Lydia frowned and her friend's sadness cut her deep.

"You could come with me. I could use a roommate."

"You don't need a roommate. Anyway, I can't leave now that my brother is back. That would be a terrible welcome-home gift."

"Right." She cleared her throat. "I saw him this morning."

Lydia's eyes narrowed. "He's here?"

"Yeah, he's… He's staying at Sullivan's Point."

Lydia looked miffed. "He didn't… He didn't tell me that. He didn't tell me or Mom that."

Well, now she'd gone and upset Lydia even more, and she hadn't meant to do that.

"I'm sorry. I assumed that you knew."

"I didn't. But communication with Gideon has been… It's been a challenge the last couple of years."

"Oh." She felt a strange, hollowed-out feeling. She wouldn't have understood what Lydia might mean if she hadn't seen him today. If she hadn't tried to talk to him.

If she hadn't come away from it not certain if he even knew her or not.

Lydia sighed and rubbed her forehead. "It's embarrassing to admit this, Rory. But… I haven't talked about it because I didn't know how to admit that my big brother isn't himself anymore."

She saw the pain on Lydia's face and she felt so *guilty*. Why hadn't she dug deeper into how he was doing? Why hadn't she realized her friend was upset about this? That she was hurting?

"When he got out of the hospital we thought the worst of it was over. He was healing. But it wasn't that simple. Things I attributed to being cooped up in the hospital—his temperament changes—they didn't go away."

"Temperament changes?" She thought of how he'd been today. Terse. Unsmiling.

"I guess. He's different. He stopped reaching out. He doesn't talk to us unless we make contact, and he makes it hard for us to get a hold of him. He didn't even tell us when he and Cassidy split up. *She* told us. And after that…sometimes we didn't know where he was for weeks. I… I couldn't admit that to anyone, Rory. That my perfect brother wasn't perfect."

"Lydia…"

"I know. I'm a terrible person. But it's not about embarrassment. It's about the way everyone here sees him. He's a legend here, you know that. It would be like telling them he…like telling them he was dead."

"No, I don't judge you. I'm just sorry I didn't know."

Lydia shook her head. "Don't blame yourself. I didn't want to think about it unless I had to. I avoided it unless I had to. We just…kept it between us, me and Mom. We did not expect him to move back. But we're glad. It's been a lot of…worry. But I just keep hoping that since he's coming back, he's ready to be himself again. Though his hiding that he's already here is a little…eh."

She thought of him, in the woods when time had stood still for a moment, and at his house. He definitely wasn't what she'd expected. She would have had a hard time imagining the Gideon she knew not contacting his mom and sister.

But the man she'd seen in the woods had been dangerous. The man she'd seen at the house had been altogether feral.

She could imagine that man not communicating with…anyone.

"Well, he is here. And I'm sorry that I didn't realize that that might be shocking information."

"It isn't your fault. My brother is thirty-one years old. He can certainly manage himself if he wants to. He's been to war. He's just… I don't know. I'm hoping that it all gets better now that he's here. And maybe he needed a few days to accept the fact that he's back and people will be reporting on his movements. Just like old times."

"The local girls practically put out APBs on him. Tracking his every move." She tried to lighten the conversation because Lydia was upset and Rory hated that.

Lydia looked at her for a little too long. They had a pact not to ever mention The Diary Incident, and Rory stared back as if daring her to break the pact.

Lydia looked away. "Yeah. Basically."

"You're worried about him."

"Of course I am," said Lydia.

They ordered; Lydia got a steak, while Rory opted for a hamburger. It didn't benefit you to get crazy at a small-town diner. Best to stick with the basics. That was something else that Rory would enjoy about Boston. The food possibilities. In that brief moment she had lived in the city when she'd gone to college, she had discovered so much food. It had been her absolute favorite thing. She and her sisters were foodies by nature. They baked, they made preserves, they grew their own food. It was part of who they were.

But she had limited exposure to broad varieties of food, food from other countries, fusion foods, modern cuisine…

Here they had one diner. And you could order a hamburger.

But she put her focus back on Lydia.

"I can keep an eye on him. Make sure that he's okay. I mean, he's going to be at the ranch until even after I leave. I can always…treat him a little bit special."

If it would make Lydia feel better, she was all for it.

It has nothing to do with you fixating on him? she asked herself.

No.

She wasn't fixating. She was…getting ready for a whole different life, she wasn't going to backslide all the way to a crush on Gideon Payne.

But the truth was she cared about him. She always had. He had been there for her when she needed him. If she had the chance to be there for him now, why wouldn't she be?

"How long has it been since you've seen him?"

"Since he left the hospital. After that, everything with him and Cass fell apart and…and then he kind of ghosted everyone."

"Do you know what happened?"

Rory didn't personally put a ton of stock in marriage. And she could admit that that was part of why she hadn't applied some deep meaning to the fact that he had gotten divorced. People got divorced. All the time. It didn't mean anyone was evil.

It was funny she felt that way. Because her sisters were in marriages that would most definitely last. She had no doubt about it. They were uniquely suited to each other. And all around Four Corners that was the case. Her sister Alaina's best friend, Elsie, was married, and Rory couldn't imagine Elsie and Hunter with anyone but each other. Ditto for the other couples on Four Corners Ranch.

But happy endings were only really guaranteed in books. And Rory wasn't foolish enough to believe they were commonplace outside of them.

"I'm sorry," Rory said. "I think I'm a little bit cynical about marriage because of my parents. But your parents were married until…"

"Yeah. Until my dad died. And they would've been married so much longer if he hadn't gotten sick. They were forever kind of people. And I know it never occurred to Gideon that he wouldn't be. I mean, that's why you get married. He could've slept around. He could have had any woman he wanted. He pretty much did when he lived here. And I think did for a while when he was in the military. Not that I want to think about that, but you know…"

"Yes. They made it impossible for you not to think about it."

"Yes. Anyway. It's that exactly. But yeah, I think it devastated him. The end with Cassidy. And… I just don't even know what all his problems are. Because he closed us out completely. And now he's coming back. Almost like nothing happened."

"Maybe to him it didn't." She thought about her dad. The way he called them periodically as if he hadn't abandoned them. As if they didn't have very good reasons for being angry with him. He liked to act like nothing had happened. Like he hadn't cheated on their mother. He hadn't left them when they were vulnerable teenage girls.

Hadn't nearly broken poor Quinn. Hadn't tormented their mother with his infidelity to the point where she'd become so impossible to live with that Fia had run away for a while.

He liked to call them up like it hadn't been six months since his last call. Like it hadn't been a few years since they'd seen him in person.

It was something men seemed to be able to compartmentalize. Maybe that fundamentally was why she just didn't have very high regard for marriage. She didn't trust men.

So she remained alone.

If she could've chosen her sexuality at the beginning of time, she'd have totally picked liking women. It would be way more sensible. Rather than being huddled in fraternity party closets and then getting beer spilled on her the only time she had ever really attempted something physical with a guy.

But something like that… Well. It was enough.

"It isn't like that. Not with him. I don't know what he's thinking. But he's almost like a different person. The Gideon that I know told us everything. He was always excited, interested and interesting. Not this person I can hardly get two words out of, and now he's in town without even letting us know."

"He is different," Rory said, looking down.

"What does he look like?"

She looked back up at her friend. "Bearded?"

"You're not sure if he's bearded?"

"No. I'm sure that he's bearded. I was just trying to decide if that was the defining characteristic."

"Oh. Well. Bearded is a change."

"Long hair. He's… He's huge. I mean, weight-lifting huge."

"He's always been fit."

"Yeah, but not like this."

Lydia grimaced. "Oh. Great, so my brother is now a long-haired, bearded guy with a gym body. There women are going to be *feral*."

Rory laughed. She couldn't help it, because at least in the middle of her very serious distress, there was this amusing distress.

And she did not tell Lydia that she had been fully immobilized with lust at the sight of her brother's new look. Keeping that to herself was true friendship. "Well, you've weathered it before. You can certainly weather it again."

"I'm going to envy you moving to Boston. My family needs me."

"Yeah."

"Rory…will you please check on him? I feel like he doesn't want to see me."

"That can't be it."

"It can be, actually. He's here and he didn't tell us."

"I promise. I'll check on him."

She thought of that day she'd seen Gideon in the woods. When she'd been writing in her notebook.

Get a kiss (kiss from a stranger?).

That made her feel all trembly.

But he wasn't a stranger, it turned out. He was Gideon.

So she wasn't going to think about him and kissing in that context.

No, tonight she was going to bring him dinner, for her friend. That was all.

CHAPTER FOUR

GIDEON WAS STILL reeling from coming face-to-face with the angel that had stopped him in his tracks in the woods. Still knocked on his ass from having to face the reality of the fact that his little sister's best friend had been the one to knock the libido back into him on a sunny day when he had *not fucking asked for it*, thank you very much.

And that was when his sister called. Mad.

"Why didn't you tell me that you're here?"

He sighed. "I needed a couple of days."

This reminded him of the darker days, when he'd been secretive because he had to be. He'd been full of shame. He'd been hiding things on purpose. But since he'd made amends with all of that, as best he could, he didn't believe in taking on shame he hadn't earned.

So, he was going to be up-front about his reasoning with Lydia, even though he could hear the hurt in her voice.

"And you couldn't tell us that you were here?"

"No. Because being back home is kind of a loaded thing for me. I know you might not get that, but it is. I'm not the same person that I was when I left."

"I know, Gideon," she said softly. "You haven't been the same person for a while. I just wish you would let me…know you."

"I'm sorry. I'm still figuring this out. I needed time. Because you know, everyone here is going to expect me to be...me. And I'm not. I needed time to be here and get my bearings before I jumped into the middle of this."

Before he jumped into being back here as performance art, which it was bound to become.

He hadn't been unaware of that when he'd decided to come back here.

But it had been an uneasy bargain.

It was the kind of choice you made when all your choices were dead ends and this one might, maybe, actually be something.

That moment in the woods...when he'd seen her, and she'd seen him. That had been the most pure, clear moment he'd had for a long damned time.

But it hadn't been clear. Not really. Because she wasn't an angel, she was Rory. And no matter how much his body might like it, he wasn't going to get anywhere near her.

He'd ruined Cassidy's life, but at least he hadn't known he was a ticking time bomb—bad analogy but still—when he'd married her. He knew it now. Rory was off-limits.

"We're your family. *We're* not a town that has blown you up into this weird, out-of-proportion hero."

He had to hand it to Lydia for getting to the heart of the matter.

The problem was there was more to this matter than just the heart of it.

His mom and Lydia hadn't spent any time with him since the accident—by design, he hadn't wanted to expose them to his worst, thanks. But he was different and he didn't know if they were prepared for that or not.

You could have prepared them.

Rory had looked at him like he was a stranger.

Well. In the woods, she'd looked at him like...

No.

Back in the day she'd been a sweet kid. Chatty. Endlessly, but he'd liked it.

She'd had a crush on him, which he'd thought was cute. There had been some drama at her school about it and he'd felt like he needed to stand up for her because...she was a kid. A crush was harmless. She'd been sweet and she certainly hadn't deserved to be treated like that.

When she'd shown up at the house, he'd been unfriendly to her and he felt bad about it, but it was like he couldn't make his face work the way it used to. Couldn't find it in him to smile. Not even for the girl who'd made him pie.

What a dick.

"Is there *really* going to be a parade?" he asked.

An egotistical thing to ask in most cases. But this was Pyrite Falls, and he was Gideon Payne. It wasn't ego, it was just...the way it was.

"I think they were planning a small thing with a welcome-home banner. But not really a parade. But we're a Purple Heart City because of you and..."

So. A parade.

"I know. But I don't have to *do* anything, do I?"

Lydia was hesitant. "You probably need to go."

"Right. Well, I'm not all that comfortable with things like that."

"Gideon..."

"That's what I'm trying to tell you. I wanted some time to be back here on my terms because there are expectations of me. And I knew that there would be. Hell, I could've gone and moved to the middle of nowhere if I didn't want any expectations on me."

As soon as he said it, it made him feel near panic. Like he was falling into an abyss.

He didn't have his military career. He didn't have his marriage. He didn't have all these things that he had defined himself by for years. If he cut ties with his hometown on top of it, with his family, he might as well...

He might as well have just died overseas.

He let himself have those thoughts now. Because he recognized that when he didn't, they became worse. Survivor's guilt was a real thing. Unfortunately, he hadn't finished his counseling. He'd had a fair amount of it in the hospital, and then once he'd got home, he'd been consumed by trying to get back to where he was before.

He'd convinced himself he didn't need therapy, he just needed to get back to normal.

So that's what he'd done.

He'd gone home. He'd tried to be the husband he had promised to be. Tried to ignore the pain. Tried to ignore his mood swings. And when he couldn't, he'd just medicated it. Every day demanding another pill, and another and another. Until what had started as a quest for *normal* got lost in the haze. Until what the pills had done was worse than the pain, worse than the mood swings.

What he'd learned was that those pills hadn't made his pain go away. They'd deferred it.

When the world had collapsed, he'd felt it all.

The devil always came to collect.

Always.

After more than a year of denying every dark thought

and ending up in hell anyway, he'd come to the conclusion that you might as well think the dark thought. It was inside you whether you gave it a voice or not. Best not to surprise yourself. Especially not when your defenses were down. Best to know, fully know, the kind of capacity for darkness that lived inside you.

"I'm sorry. But...how could we have known this would be hard for you, Gideon? You haven't told us anything."

"I didn't have anything to tell. I needed to make a plan. When Cassidy left, I didn't know what to do."

Left. That was funny. And kind of a lie.

She'd kicked him out. But she left him emotionally, so he found that an easier way to put it. He was the one who'd physically left, but at her request.

"I'm sorry," Lydia said, her voice acidic. "But I don't have any sympathy for Cassidy. She abandoned you when you needed her the most."

"I left her when she needed *me* most," he said. "I didn't call you, Lydia. I didn't call Mom, because I was in no state to be...around people. Cass was living with me. She had to deal with the fact that I wasn't the same person all day every day. She had to deal with my injuries, with my career ending, with uncertainty about where our money was going to come from, and I couldn't be there to reassure her. It was all because of me, and I couldn't... I couldn't make it okay."

"That is an awfully kind interpretation," Lydia said.

"I'm not trying to be *kind*. But I loved her for a long time. You don't just stop loving somebody. I still see the woman I married when I think of her. Not the end of everything."

"Good. You see it. I'm glad you see it because I can't especially. I can't."

"And this is why I needed some time. Because now you know I'm here, so here you are with your opinions. The town will be there with their welcome banners. And I just needed…"

Silence and pie.

"I'm not your enemy."

"I know you're not. I love you, kid. I'm here to be with you and Mom. Even though it's hard. But be patient with me, okay?" He needed to be here. Without connections, all he had was that abyss. He couldn't face it.

"Okay."

"I'm officially here from tomorrow. Promise. I will go into town, and I will stand underneath the banner. Swear it."

"Okay."

"We'll talk in the morning."

"All right."

He hung up with her, and got online, started looking at some different hiking supplies and other outdoor equipment.

He wasn't here to try and compete with the ranchers. In the sense that he wasn't going to get cattle, or sheep, or try to grow produce. He would probably have some animals for his own use, but what he'd decided he was going to do was put some tiny homes on the property, and offer ranch days. Complete with trail rides and other activities. The McClouds had a therapy portion of their ranch, but it wasn't recreational. There was nothing in the immediate area like this, and he had a feeling he could make a profit at it. His dad had tried to compete with Four Corners for years. As far as Gideon was concerned, that was a losing proposition. They were too big to fail. And he had no interest in getting up in their business.

He had a plan. And he had some time to float him until he could get that plan into action.

Leading hikes and horse rides sounded like an ideal thing for him. He did great outdoors. He had infinite survival skills from his time in the military. And keeping his endurance up was good for him. Yeah, he had his injuries, but a trick hip wasn't going to stop him from hiking up a mountain. It might keep him from being able to do everything that needed doing out in the desert, but not simple tourist hikes. And anyway, the real issue wasn't in his body. It was his brain.

Hell of a thing.

He'd never been focused on mental kinds of things. He was physical.

Not that the blast had impacted his IQ, but he'd never fully appreciated all the things your brain was in charge of. Which sounded dumb. It *was* dumb. He had taken it for granted, until those shock waves had rattled his brain around in his head like ten car accidents, and years in the NFL getting tackled, giving him concussion after concussion all in one moment.

It had taken time for the medical teams he'd seen to realize that his issues were more severe than they'd first thought. That his injuries were more extensive. More internal.

Finding out what the problem was had been a relief, in part. But it hadn't fixed it. His mood swings had been unbearable. Unpredictable.

He frowned, remembering. Yelling at Cassidy. He'd *yelled* at her. He'd never been like that before.

He pushed the guilt down, and got up from his computer, realizing he was hungry. And right then, there was a knock on the door.

He frowned. If it was Lydia, he would be glad to see her. If it was his mother…he'd be glad to see her, too, but he would be unprepared. Still, it was reasonable to suspect that it might be one of them.

He crossed the small kitchen and opened the door. And there was Rory.

"Hi. I brought you dinner." She was smiling in that determined way she'd done earlier and he couldn't figure out how to return it.

"You didn't have to do that," he said.

"I wanted to."

He stared at her. "My sister send you?"

"What makes you say that?"

"You didn't deny it."

"I did have lunch with your sister today."

"It all becomes clear. She called me, and she was furious because she didn't know that I was back in town."

"I'm sorry. I didn't know that they didn't know. I wouldn't have said anything if I did." She looked at him. "It's…a lot of stuff. I can bring it in."

He snorted. "Come in."

Rory had been fourteen when he'd left. A kid. Then, as now, she had freckles all over her face. She hadn't grown any since then, either. She was short and petite, and with a finely pointed little face, sculpted cheekbones and a nose that turned upward. She'd been stick thin back then; he remembered that.

But now he noticed she had a petite but luscious figure, and her limbs were what could only be described as willowy. She was… For some reason, she was a certain kind of beautiful that got right under his skin in a way nothing else had for years.

She made him ache and he didn't like it.

"I brought you a potpie," she said.

"Thanks."

"It's hot. I'll cut it for you, and then I'll get out of your hair."

"I know how to cut a pie."

"Yeah, I know. You had some of my pie last night. I'll just serve it for you because it's a little tricky when it's hot."

He stared at her. She didn't have a very nurturing or mothering sort of energy, but she was sure as hell giving it a try. A testament, he thought, to the friendship that she had with his sister.

"So, what have you been up to, Rory?"

What he wanted to do, the only thing he really wanted to do, was haul her into his arms and see if she was as soft as she looked. But he couldn't do that. So he decided to play small-talk games. To see if he could.

It was so hard for him now. He wasn't that interested in people anymore. He didn't know what that was a side effect of. His brain injury, or just generally being in kind of a shitty place in life.

Either way, he didn't care. But he was supposed to go to town tomorrow, and there was going to be a banner. And he had decided to move back here, and that meant he had to get better at playing this game. He had to try and find it in himself to do this sort of thing. So why not practice on Rory?

She'd been easy to talk to back when she was a kid. Or she'd done a lot of talking at him. Either way, she seemed like an easy port in his mental storm.

"Oh. Well. I haven't done much. I mean, the property management, yes, and we opened the farm store. But I…" She scrunched her nose up. "I didn't go to school." For some reason, he felt like that was an incomplete comment, but he didn't press her on it.

"I didn't go to school and I am leaving here at the end of the month."

"Leaving?"

"Yeah. I'm moving to Boston."

"That's a long way. You have a…a boyfriend or…" Was this how small talk worked? He hated it.

"No. I have a job. And a place to live. I'll be managing an old apartment building. It's a little bit different from what I've been doing here, but I'm sure that I can do it. And I'm looking forward to it."

"That's a big change."

"It is," she said hurriedly. "It is. But I'm more than ready. It's been a long time coming. But anyway, yeah. That's… I'm leaving. And you're back."

"Yeah. I am."

"You're going into town tomorrow for…"

"The parade that isn't a parade?"

Rory looked concerned. "I don't know that it isn't a parade."

"My sister said it isn't."

"I'm sure she doesn't think it is. I'm just saying I'm not entirely convinced that it isn't. That's all."

"Why is that?"

"You know how people get. They're very zealous about you."

He didn't know how to respond to that. That had been true once. And he'd taken it as his due. But he didn't deserve all that. Not now.

If they knew the real story. That he wasn't one of the strong ones.

"I don't want that," he said. "I didn't come here for that."

"Isn't it nice? That people are happy to see you?"

She took a knife out of the drawer, and cut into the potpie. Then with a big scoop, she got the crust and all the filling out onto a plate.

"Who are they happy to see?" he asked, a strange, bitter feeling churning in his gut. "Me, or this weird fantasy they have of me from when I was a high school football star?"

She handed him the plate, and the fork, her eyes meeting his, something lost and helpless there, and he didn't do anything to make her feel better.

"Thank you," he said, taking the plate.

He said it with a finality he hoped might see her out the door.

But she just stared at him. "What's the issue, you don't want attention or…?"

"No," he bit out. "I don't. I didn't save anyone, I'm not a hero. I got injured in a bomb blast, there's no act of heroism there."

"You survived," she pointed out.

Part of him had.

And right then it was like something snapped inside him. All the angry and ugly flooded him. Poured out. "Let me tell you something. While people sit around and barbecue and sing 'God Bless America,' young men and women are out there dying. There is nothing… aspirational or uplifting about it. There isn't a music montage. It's not a damned parade. Not a day of it. It's a convoy through hell. And everyone wants their heroes to come back as shiny as when they left but…"

She reached out and touched him. Put her fingers on his wrist.

The touch was like getting burned and he jerked his hand away.

Her face went pink, her eyes glittering. "I think… I think people are just happy to see you, Gideon. No one needs you to be something you're not."

That fire in his gut turned on the wind, rage transforming into something more dangerous.

Damn he was such a mess.

Letting his rage spill over onto Rory before taking the time to lust after her was evidence enough.

"Don't pity me, Rory. I mean it. You don't need to take care of me, and I'm not fragile." He moved away from her, and took a bite of the pie. "Thank you. For dinner. I'll see you around."

He wanted her out of his house. He didn't like the way she made him feel. He didn't like that tightness in his gut. He didn't like that attraction, the beginnings of arousal that he felt.

That was far too strong a reaction to any woman, much less his little sister's best friend. Much less a girl he'd last seen when she was fourteen, and who even now looked far too freckled and fresh-faced and young.

He didn't want to feel this angry. He didn't want to be home.

He was afraid to be anywhere else.

"Oh. Okay. I…"

She looked wounded. It was probably for the best.

"I'll see you later, kid."

Because whether he wanted to or not, he would. He

was here now. Back in his hometown. Where everyone thought they knew him.

The worst part was...there was an ache in his chest when he thought of that parade. A deep impossible need. He wanted to be their hero again.

Life had been so much better when he was the hero.

Everyone thought he was a hero because he'd been a soldier.

Because he'd played a good game of football. But they didn't know him.

Sometimes he worried that he wasn't the good guy anymore.

Sometimes he thought he might be the bad guy.

CHAPTER FIVE

RORY STOPPED WHEN she and her sisters got to the main street of town. They had parked up at the other end and were walking to the grocery store, enjoying the warm early afternoon air that was going to turn heavy and hot by the time four o'clock rolled around.

They might own their own farm store, but they still had to eat processed foods. They weren't animals.

There was a banner stretched over the road.

"They *are* having a parade."

"I told you they were," said Fia.

"I sort of didn't… I mean I said it, I knew it. But…"

She kept thinking about Gideon as he had been last night. He'd said he didn't want this. He'd been…so dark. So angry. It was such a contrast to who he'd been before.

There was a time when she'd thought she'd known him.

When she'd chattered to him while he drove her and Lydia to school. When he'd been in high school and they were in middle school, he'd taken her every day. And she still couldn't quite tell if he even really remembered who she was. The first time it hadn't seemed like he did.

Last night, it seemed like maybe he did know her. But he didn't seem happy to see her.

He was entirely different to the person he'd been back then.

The man he was now…

Maybe he wouldn't come to town. She had to trust Lydia to know what was best for her brother. Except… Lydia didn't know him now, either.

He was wounded. Deep. Even if there weren't scars that she could see on his body.

She wanted to help. But she didn't know what help looked like for him right now. He was here. He'd chosen to come back home.

They went all the way down to John's grocery store, and perused the aisles.

"PowerBait?" Quinn asked.

Her sister's out-of-left-field question burst her deep thought bubble. "I'm good, Quinn. Thanks."

Quinn grinned.

"How is Levi?" Fia asked.

Quinn practically beamed. "Oh, he's great. We're great." Quinn had of course moved in with Levi recently, after her endeavor to get road access from his ranch to their store had turned into something unexpected for the both of them.

Quinn was happy. And Rory was happy for her sister. Even if the change in Quinn's life made Rory feel weird about the lack of progression in her own. Even if it had been something of a trigger.

Quinn had managed to do things Rory hadn't.

She'd had no trouble being away for four years at school. And she kept her focus the entire time.

Quinn knew who she was.

Quinn also knew that none of them needed Power-Bait.

"I do want Pop-Tarts," said Rory, grabbing the cart and taking it down the aisle that had breakfast food.

She also got some syrup and pancake mix. They were all great bakers, but the truth was, she just didn't think anything was as good as pancake mix where you just added water. They were fluffier, and they were easier. And there was simply no reason not to use a mix when the mix was good.

Even though Quinn lived next door now, she did often still come over for breakfast. Alaina less so, but she lived a few miles across the Four Corners property, at McCloud's Landing. Her husband, Gus, was the oldest brother of that clan, and their responsibilities on the ranch kept them busy. That was the other difference. Alaina worked at McCloud's. Her passion was horses, and it had taken her there.

It isn't a move to Boston, though, is it?

She shrugged off her feeling of guilt. It was funny, to think of Alaina as being distant when she was quite literally on the same property.

And had a baby. She was busy. Just because she didn't always come over for breakfast, or go shopping with them, didn't mean she wasn't around. And it didn't mean that Rory was going to be completely disconnected when she moved away.

One thing about being beige: it wasn't complex.

Her move toward a new life and a new Rory was… Well it wasn't simple, that was for sure. It made her excited and regretful at the same time. Happy for her sisters and a little melancholy that they'd moved on to a place Rory hadn't.

Complicated wasn't her favorite.

She was in the middle of a lot of complicated right now, for someone who had never really dealt in that before.

"You're scowling at breakfast cereal," said Fia. "Is there anything you want to tell us about what Honey Nut Cheerios did to you?"

"No," she said, moving away from the box.

She wasn't really a cereal girl. She liked pastries, pancakes, or at least a full two-egg breakfast. Otherwise, she might as well just have nothing.

"Well, anything else you want to tell us?"

"I'm good. I was just thinking about moving."

"I don't like to talk about you moving," said Quinn.

"I know. But it's happening in a little less than a month."

"And were you feeling particularly sad about leaving us for the city life while standing in John's looking at the array of goods on offer?"

"Actually, yes. I was."

"It's the PowerBait," Quinn stage-whispered.

"You don't have to go," said Fia. "No one will think less of you if you change your mind."

"I'm not going to change my mind."

They took all their items and went to the front of the store. "Hi, Fia. Hi, Quinn." John paused and he looked over at Rory. "Hi."

He didn't know her name. John, who knew her family well enough, who had known all the girls since they were children, remembered everybody's name but hers. And this was the problem. This was the absolute problem.

"Rory," she said, finding her voice, some strength, from somewhere deep inside her that she had never really tested before. "My name is Rory."

John turned red, and she banished that feeling of guilt that she'd made him uncomfortable. He made her uncomfortable. He hadn't remembered her. Beige sweater.

They finished paying and went outside. She felt a little bit shaky from the exertion of the last few moments.

"What's wrong?" Fia asked.

"I'm going to leave. I'm going to…start a new life somewhere else, and the people in my hometown barely know who I am."

"It isn't like they socialize with us."

"Easy for you to say, Fia. People remember your name."

They walked down the street and put their groceries in the car.

"Let's have some lunch," said Fia.

"I ate at Becky's yesterday."

"Yeah, and when you're in Boston, you'll have options. Look forward to that. Today, we have Becky's."

She made a big show of rolling her eyes and stamping her foot as they walked into Becky's, and then felt immediately embarrassed. "Sorry. I didn't mean to make a scene."

Both Quinn and Fia looked at her like she'd grown another head.

"A scene?" Fia asked. "That wasn't a scene. *This* is a scene. 'What light through yonder window breaks? It is the east.'" She held her hand out.

"You know what I mean," Rory said.

"Rory, that was the most least dramatic thing."

"How can it be the *most least dramatic*?"

"You know what I mean. You think that you're being pushy, or silly, but really, you're barely showing anything. You are the most—"

"You're *adorable*," said Quinn quickly.

"Thank you, Quinn," said Rory, feeling annoyed. "But I don't need you to lie."

"I'm not lying. You are adorable. But, it takes somebody perceptive to sense a shift in your moods. It isn't like any of the dining patrons knew that you were being overdramatic about anything. Because you aren't overdramatic."

She scowled. "Well, I'm trying to inject my life with…" *Drama* was maybe the wrong word.

Drama reminded her of having beer poured on her. Or of her diary being passed around…

There was no need to start thinking of The Diary Incident.

So she didn't.

Her sisters were wonderful. She loved them so much. But being insulated by them wasn't helping her break out and she just…needed something.

"I'm trying for a little mild reinvention. So maybe when I come back and visit from Boston, you'll get a respectable foot stomp out of me."

They were seated at a table near the window, and that was when she noticed that across the room were Lydia, her mother and Gideon.

And suddenly, the manager of Becky's was over in that spot and held up a big metal pan, which she then banged on with a wooden spoon. "Now, everybody look over here."

She could see Gideon tense, could see him get stone-faced.

You couldn't go making loud noises around a veteran. Even Rory knew that, and she didn't know any veterans except for…Gideon, she supposed, and she didn't know much about his situation, but she knew enough not to go banging pots next to his head.

He was clearly unhappy.

But everyone in the restaurant looked at him.

"Hometown hero Gideon Payne is back. Gideon got a Purple Heart for outstanding acts of bravery in Afghanistan. And, of course, his dinners will always be on the house. Heroes don't pay."

Everyone in the restaurant cheered.

"Of course, the banner outside is meant to mark his return, and there is going to be a procession of classic cars acting as a parade. Gideon, you're welcome to ride in one of the convertibles. With the top down."

"That's very kind, Sarah," said Gideon, his voice sounding strained, and nothing like she recalled from back before. He couldn't smile. Or chose not to, she wasn't sure. "I don't think I'll ride, but I will wave to say thanks for the procession." He frowned. "And the hamburgers. The free hamburgers. Thanks."

He didn't appear to be having flashbacks or anything. Which was a relief. But no thanks to the pot-banging. Though maybe he didn't have flashbacks. She didn't know.

"How fun," said Fia. "We get to see Gideon's parade."

"He doesn't *want* a parade," said Rory.

"Who doesn't want a parade?" Quinn asked.

Well. Rory did. Kind of. Maybe. She wanted to feel special. And she didn't.

But Gideon didn't want one and shouldn't someone care about that?

"He looks uncomfortable," Rory said.

"That could just be indigestion. He had the chili fries," Quinn said.

She winced. "Bad move."

"Indeed."

They got their hamburgers, which they knew were safe, and she looked over at Gideon's table. Lydia waved at her, and she waved back, which drew Gideon's attention. He didn't acknowledge her. His face stayed set like stone, his posture rigid.

She'd put her hand on him last night. She'd been in his kitchen.

He'd driven her to school every day.

He was acting like none of that meant anything.

Maybe it doesn't?

Well, that would be on brand for her.

She went back to eating her food. They finished around the same time as the Paynes, and when they filtered outside, there wasn't just a procession of cars, but a brass band. She grimaced as everything unfolded, and a kid standing down on the street corner unleashed a handful of balloons. And Gideon stood there unsmiling.

The band crashed symbols, and she winced. They shuffled together, and that meant that she was standing right beside Gideon. And in spite of herself, she moved closer to him.

"I'm sorry about…all the noise."

He was watching the proceedings with a blank look on his face. He had been polite in the restaurant, but he wasn't going to pretend he was enjoying this.

Or maybe he couldn't. She hadn't seen him smile since he'd returned. He always looked…distant. Like he didn't want to be here, or was surprised he was.

"I don't mind the noise," he said.

"Oh, that's…that's good."

"Yeah."

"Everyone is happy to see you."

He didn't respond to that.

When the parade of cars was done, the kid at the end of the block was left looking up sadly at the balloons, as if it only just occurred to him that balloons weren't boomerangs, and when you released them, they didn't come back.

And when she turned her attention away from the kid to where Gideon had been, Gideon was gone.

She turned and started to walk in the direction she thought he might have gone in, but Lydia approached and grabbed hold of her. "Well, that was…not good."

"Yes," Rory agreed.

"He isn't even the same person anymore, Ro. I don't know what to do."

She had been thinking a similar thing, but she felt immediately defensive. "Nobody asked him if that's what he wanted. You know that's why he ended up coming and laying low for a few days."

"I know but…everyone is excited to see him. Why can't he… Why can't he pretend to enjoy it?"

"Because he can't pretend." Rory knew it. Just from the little bit of interaction she'd had with him, she knew that.

Lydia looked contrite. "I know. Nobody has ever once offered to throw me a parade. They never even come close. So I guess it's hard for me to imagine getting treated that special and not caring." She grimaced. "I think that's part of my issue with all this. I don't want him to not be him. I also always wished I were him, a little bit. Don't get me wrong, I had it good. I always have. But he… He's Gideon Payne. Everyone pales in comparison."

"I get that," Rory said. "I don't think it's not caring. But it wasn't *for* him. It was for everybody else here. Because if it was really for him, then they would have asked what he wanted, right?"

"He would've liked it. He liked it when they sent him off the first time."

"He was eighteen. And he isn't now. Do you want the same things now that you did when you were eighteen?"

"Some of them," said Lydia.

"I don't. When I was eighteen, I just wanted to be safe. I went to college, but what I wanted was to not be uncomfortable. And I don't want that anymore. I'm completely different. Inside. Now I'm working to figure out how to be different outside. It's okay to not be the person that you were."

She didn't know why she was defending him. Or why she was acting like she knew. It was just that she kept seeing his tortured expression from yesterday, the blankness from today.

He was…he was quite frankly the most amazing person she'd ever known back when she was younger.

She'd had a crush on him. But more than that, she'd been awed by him like everyone else was. Seeing him like this now did something to her. Something beyond words.

He had been formative to her. She'd never felt important. But during the drive to school, he'd made her feel like she might be. He'd listened to her. He'd let her talk his ear off. And maybe he didn't really remember it now, but she did.

She didn't want to just leave him in this state. And somehow it felt inextricably linked to her own shift. She needed change. He did, too.

She wanted…she wanted to help. It was more than an item on a list. She'd seen his desolation. It mattered to her.

"Okay. Point taken," Lydia said. "I won't be grumpy at him. It was just… I was excited to spend some time with him and everything kind of intruded."

"Well, you should go over to Sullivan's Point and have a visit. The cabin is isolated. It might be a good way for you guys to catch up."

"Yeah, maybe," she said.

"I could talk to him…"

"I send you to have one conversation with my brother and suddenly you're an expert on him?"

There wasn't any heat in Lydia's words. She could just see that maybe she was confused and a little bit exasperated.

"You two were always close before."

"Yes," said Lydia. "Before. He used to be easy. He was the kind of person that made you feel like no time had passed since you'd seen him. And now it's just obvious that I haven't seen my brother in a couple of years. And that maybe we don't have a very close relationship. And I don't know him very well. The way he was before, he made everybody feel like they knew him. He was magic like that. And now he's…he's not that."

She could see that. And she could understand why it was upsetting. To feel like maybe you'd misread a relationship your whole life.

"I guess you just have to figure out how to meet him where he's at."

Rory didn't know where that had come from. Except she knew what it was like to not fit. And for no one around you to try and make room for the way that you were. She knew what it was like to feel just a little bit off. To not even have the capacity to be a statistic, because she was far too strange.

And it would've been nice if somebody would've just gotten to know her. Would've taken the time. To see that she was more than quiet and awkward if she had time to warm up. That she was more than glasses and scrawny limbs and tripping over her own feet.

It would've been nice if somebody would've tried to rearrange themselves a little bit, so she didn't have to do all of it.

Maybe that was what he needed. To not have to try to jump to reach people's expectations. The expectation was that he was a man who wanted a parade. He could be a man who deserved one, and not have one. He could not want one. It didn't mean there was something wrong with him. It just meant he was different.

"Hopefully I'll see you around Sullivan's Point."

"We have to do dinner in Mapleton before you leave. Something to celebrate."

"We will. I'll text you some days and you can tell me what works best for you."

"Sounds good. Then I can make a reservation."

"Okay."

She separated from her friend and walked toward her sisters, who had already headed back toward the car. It made her sad to think about how Lydia didn't feel close to Gideon.

She had always felt close to her sisters, even though she was sort of the odd one.

And she supposed she should be thankful for that. She hoped that moving away from them wouldn't dampen that closeness.

"I don't want us to lose touch. Because I need to be with the people who can tell me I'm not being a drama queen even when I feel like I am. It seems important."

"You're never going to get rid of us. Not that easily," Fia said.

"I don't know. I'm the beige sweater of the Sullivan family."

Fia laughed. "That is ridiculous. You are not the beige sweater, Rory."

"John didn't even *remember* my name."

"Well, what does that have to do with you? That's about him."

But she wanted the people around her to see her differently. So it didn't matter why. She decided that tomorrow she was going to devote a portion of the day to her list. And she was going to tackle it in earnest. Because it was important. When she was alone, she took it out again: *Throw a tantrum.*

All right, maybe that one wasn't especially aspirational. But she was a little bit disappointed by how not dramatic her earlier tantrum had been. She was aiming for reinvention, and that reinvention was going to start here.

CHAPTER SIX

GIDEON SIGHED, feeling weary.

The whole experience with the parade had been fucking awful.

The worst part was being in the middle of the crowd and feeling like you were on a different frequency. He could see the people around him, lit up with excitement and glee, and he could not bring his own internal frequency up to match their energy. Couldn't make himself smile when he didn't feel like it. He couldn't find Gideon Payne. Not the one that these people knew.

Maybe he'd been an idiot coming back here, but he honest to God hadn't known what else to do. His family was here. But even they seemed a little bit unnerved by him. Off-put. He supposed it was fair enough.

Lydia had called last night and he hadn't answered. He felt like a dick but he was burnt out on people right now.

He'd just gotten done placing a big order for zip line equipment that had been complicated and had required him to get on the phone with customer service and he just…didn't want to deal

And now he had to hire a manager.

He could only hope that he managed to meet all his financial goals so that the budget held together. Because if he had to do all of this himself, he just didn't know if he'd last.

He'd thrown himself into the deep end here. But he had an anchor. He'd rather do this than twist around drowning in the shallows—and God knew he'd been close to that.

But he had a video interview with a woman in ten minutes for that job, and then beyond that he had to go out to the property and talk to the current owner about some different contingencies. Which meant he had to get a handle on himself.

He made himself a coffee and sat in front of the computer.

He didn't especially like computers. But they sure made everything easier.

He clicked the link to the meeting, and there was the woman he was intending to hire, looking sparkly and fresh. She was probably five to ten years older than he was—he felt like it was difficult to tell once everybody got to a certain age; genetics and lifestyle were either with you or they weren't.

He had been looking pretty good for his age until he got blown up. That aged you a bit.

"You're Monica?"

"Yes," she said.

"Great. Let's get going."

He had a list of questions, which he stated pretty matter-of-factly, and tried not to be impatient when Monica editorialized on every question.

"So, what your responsibilities would be…"

"I was just…"

He looked up, feeling irritation begin to rise in his chest. "I'd rather if you didn't interrupt."

"I'm sorry," she said, fumbling with some papers in front of her. He felt like a dick. He had sounded like such a jerk, and he hadn't meant to. It was only that he was doing his best to hold on to his train of thought, which wasn't usually a problem, but sometimes in situations like this where he had to keep track of a lot of details, it all felt a little bit slippery. In general, he didn't have memory issues. But that was in general. There were times when he got thrown off, and apparently giving job interviews was one of them.

But he didn't say that. He just pressed on.

And by the time the interview was over, he could feel that the energy had been sucked out of the interaction.

It reminded him of trying to do much of anything with Cass in the end.

"Great. Shit." And now he was late for his other meeting.

He grabbed his phone off the counter and headed out the door, and right when he got in the truck, his phone rang. It was Cassidy.

He didn't know what it was going to take to not have a physical reaction when he saw his ex-wife's name on his phone. Not that she called often. For a long time, she had done things through lawyers. But sometimes he wondered if she liked to call to hurt him.

No. That wasn't fair. Cassidy had never done anything to hurt him. It had been an untenable situation, and it was mostly of his making.

"Yes?" he said, picking up the phone.

"Did I call at a bad time?"

"No. Not a bad time. Just headed out."

"Can you talk while you drive?"

"Yeah," he said.

"Just finalizing everything with the sale of the house. And I need you to send over some bank details so you can have some of the money deposited."

"I don't want it, Cass. I don't need it. I got my payment from the military."

"Don't be a stubborn cuss, Gideon Payne. I didn't divorce you to take everything from you."

She'd divorced him because she didn't love the version of himself he'd become. He would rather, if he could, hate her. If she had turned into a greedy, maniacal shrew like his sister seemed to imagine Cassidy had become.

Not that he'd given Lydia the information she needed to fully understand his role in the breakdown of his relationship with Cass. But that was just…shame he couldn't figure out how to live with. And he really was trying to live.

He'd promised Cassidy a different life. He'd been a different man, and she had married *that* man. They'd been a happy young couple with a full life ahead of them and he had sold her a dream. And then that dream had turned dark, fractured. Ruined.

"I told you…"

"You bought the house," she said. "You bought it. So take your half. It's not fair, Gideon. It's not fair for you to try and be honorable now when we both know you weren't at the end. I married a war hero. And I divorced one of those men that you promised me… You promised me you'd never be like that. But you weren't a hero, not for me, and now you're trying to give me a gesture when it's too late. I don't want it."

Her words stung, but they were true.

He'd been so prideful as to think he could never be

one of those old soldiers. Sitting in the gutter holding a sign, tethered to a bottle, prescription or booze.

Yeah, he'd thought he was better than that. He'd been such a prick.

But he hadn't thought so then. He'd thought he was special. He'd thought they were special and they'd shared that thought. This idea that they were special in some way. Golden. That was why he'd thought he could do all those tours and not die. That was why he hadn't worried about a bomb, bullet or pain pill.

Because he was Gideon Payne.

And dammit, all that had meant something. In Pyrite Falls, Oregon, it had meant something. In his own mind, it had meant something. That he was living some kind of charmed existence. That he was immune to human weakness, to these kinds of petty traumas.

How very basic and boring to get blown up on a battlefield.

How weak to not be able to recover from that.

To become one of those homeless men in a gutter, shaking from withdrawal because the VA wouldn't renew his prescription yet.

His house, his wife, his pride, none of it mattered. Not when the only thing he could think of was finding a way to get relief from all the pain wracking his body.

"I'm not being a hero. I just don't need anything from you. I let you down, Cassidy. I realize that. I'm not mad at you for leaving me."

"Be mad at me," she shouted. "Yell. Do…do something. I…"

"I can't do that for you. I can't make you feel good about all that. I don't hold it against you. Maybe you should let that inform how you feel about it. I'm not trying to be a hero. I promise you that. I gave up on the idea that I was a hero a long fucking time ago."

"You didn't use to talk like this."

"I didn't use to feel like this," he said. "But I do now. I do all the time. So, sorry if you like the idea that maybe I transformed into a hero again after I left that house, but I didn't. I'm still a miserable asshole. So feel well justified in your choices."

He could give her this, at least. Separation. Feeling like she didn't owe him, or whatever was driving her now. She was right—he wasn't a hero. Why try to be principled now?

"Just give me a place to send the money to."

He rattled off his dad's old address. "You can send a check."

"Gideon, I wish it hadn't turned out this way."

He gritted his teeth and closed his eyes. Right then, he wondered if she wanted him to be angry so she could remember why she left. And not just remember the things that she liked about him once upon a time. So that she could remember he was also the same guy who'd lost his shit trying to assemble a simple piece of furniture and had ended up throwing a screwdriver into the wall. Yeah. She probably wanted to remember that.

He was better now. He was.

He wasn't perfect, but he was better than that. That had all been…trying. Trying to pretend that he could go back to being the man he was. Without missing a beat. That had been a hell of a game, and it hadn't helped in any way. In the end, he'd realized that. It hadn't helped at all.

"I hope you're well."

"I'm getting remarried."

It was like the bomb had gone off in his chest. He didn't love Cass anymore. Not in the way that he once had. He didn't feel nothing for her. She'd been his wife for eight years, after all. You didn't just not love that person. But he wasn't the husband that had said vows to her, and when she told him that he'd changed too much, he'd known for certain it was true. He couldn't fit into that life anymore, so he couldn't fully miss her, because he couldn't miss all the things they'd once done. She loved going to parties as an officer's wife. Had loved the status that it gave her within the community.

Her dad was a big deal in the military as well, and being the daughter of somebody high-ranking and the wife of someone on his way up had given her a lot of cachet at the base. He didn't even have to ask. He knew that she was engaged to another military man.

"Do I know him?"

"Probably," she said.

"Great. Well."

"Stan Hawkins."

"Congratulations." He'd been higher ranking than Stan in the same unit. Well, he'd probably had a promotion since Gideon was gone.

"I hope you're both happy," he said. "I really do."

He didn't sound happy. He knew that, but he couldn't do anything about it, so he didn't try.

"I'll get that check in the mail."

"Good." And he hit End on his phone, and drove mindlessly over to the ranch. When he pulled into the driveway, he got a pop-up notice on his phone that he had an email. He opened it. From Monica Brown.

I'd like to withdraw my name from consideration for the job. I don't think we would be a good fit.

Fucking hell. He'd fucked that up. He hadn't even gotten an employee yet and he'd already alienated somebody. And Cassidy was getting married, and he didn't even…

He hadn't had sex in two years. Two years. And he hadn't even been bothered by that. Because there had been other things to focus on. His marriage had broken up, and that hadn't been about sex. It had been about the dissolution of a life. The detonation of everything that he knew. He hadn't worried about the sex then.

He'd bottomed out after that, and all that had mattered was pills. Not sex. Then he'd gotten clean, and he'd actively worked to keep sex off his mind. He didn't need to replace one addiction with another. And that void in him had been so powerful right when he'd quit he'd known if he weren't careful, he would. He'd lose himself in women's bodies rather than a bottle, but it wouldn't actually fix him.

Not that he was fixed now. He was better, though. But with nothing to numb him, he was growing impatient with the whole thing.

He'd climbed out of the gutter. He'd gotten clean and sober. But it hadn't fixed the things that had brought him there in the first place, and it…

It made him feel helpless. That had never been him.

He couldn't even do a job interview.

He got out of the truck and just about bit his tongue off when Riley Connor, the current owner, came walking up toward his truck. "I'm here to go over some paperwork," he said.

"Good to see you, too," said Riley. "Looks like you're not having the best day."

He felt assaulted by that observation, not because it wasn't true, it patently was, but because he had no defenses. No way of hiding this stuff anymore.

"I'm good."

"All right. So we just need to talk about the well. The capacity's pretty low right now, and if you want to go adding these new buildings, then you're going to have to dig a new one."

"You didn't mention any of that when we were initially talking about the sale."

"Well, it's since been reevaluated."

"Fuck," he said.

"Now, there's no call to go using language."

"This is call for using language," he said. "Because this is not what we agreed on."

"I don't have control over the water," said Riley.

"You fucking have control over what you choose to share and don't. You've already put me off on the close date and this is unacceptable."

He took a step closer to Riley and the man took a step back, going pale. Gideon realized his fists were clenched and that he was closer to the man than he'd realized.

"We'll work something out," Riley said, suddenly intimidated and a lot more tractable than a moment before.

Gideon didn't like that he'd accomplished that through intimidation. He hadn't meant to but he still lost control sometimes. He still couldn't always handle himself.

With rage boiling in his blood, he walked back to his truck and sat there for a moment before firing up his engine. For one second, he thought about figuring out where Rory was. It was weird, how she'd become a touchstone in some ways. She'd been in the forest when he'd first arrived. She'd brought him pie. She'd been at the parade.

No. He wasn't going to Rory.

He decided to drive to Mapleton. It was the nearest town that was any kind of size, that had chain restaurants and the like. He'd spent most of his time in Mapleton when he was in high school. That's where the school was, but it was also where everyone had hung out. At the diner, the Minute Market. It had been where the action was.

It made him laugh now. He'd lived in major cities in the years since then. Hell, for a year he and Cassidy had lived in Dubai.

This was not a city.

But at the time it had felt like that, and he wished… He wished that he could make himself feel that again. The way he felt at seventeen, cruising down the road in his car, high on a football game win. He pulled his truck into the Minute Market. Because he'd always gone there then, too. For a hot dog and a Slurpee. He had not had a Slurpee in longer than he could remember. And he didn't know why he wanted one now. Maybe he didn't want it. He just wanted to feel something. Something other than anger.

He pulled in too quickly, and that earned him dirty looks from some people who were already in the parking lot. He got out of the truck and walked in. There was a pretty woman about his age standing in one of the aisles, a headband pushing her blond hair off her face. She was exactly the kind of girl he would've liked back then.

She looked up at him, and he tried to smile, and she looked away so quickly she couldn't have made it more clear she didn't want him to make eye contact.

Well. The charm was not intact, that was for sure.

He went down the aisle with the hot dogs, got one, then got a blue Slurpee out of the machine. He had never really been certain what that flavor was. He took it up to the counter, where there was a girl working who might very well have been seventeen. Her hair was dyed black and blue, and she had a face full of piercings. "Just this," he said.

"Serial-killer vibes, Daddy. I like it." She smiled at him. And he was pretty sure she was flirting with him. Though he didn't understand a single word she'd just said.

"I'm not a serial killer."

"It's a vibe."

"I don't know what that means."

"Sorry. Didn't realize you were, like, old like that." She rang him up. He had no clue what had just happened. A completely normal woman had not wanted his eye contact, and the other one had called him *daddy*. So. That was the day. That was the fucking day.

He took his Slurpee and his hot dog out to his truck and leaned against the hood. He had no idea what to make of…anything that had just happened. He'd lost his prospective employee, talked to his ex-wife, terrified the guy he was buying his ranch from with his… serial-killer-daddy vibes, and he'd driven out here to get a Slurpee and a hot dog like it would make him the fucking big man on campus again. And all it had done was remind him that he was a stranger in a strange land.

There had been a time in his life when he'd been sure everything would be fine. But he didn't know that anymore. He was very seriously afraid he was going to fail here. That he wouldn't be able to manage the ranch, that he'd alienate his family. Hell, everyone.

It was all unbearable.

And the Slurpee tasted like shit. What the hell had he been on when he was in high school? He dumped the whole thing in the garbage and ate the hot dog in three bites, then drove back to Sullivan's Point. Right as he was about to walk inside, Lydia called him. "I thought maybe I would come up and visit you."

"Not tonight," he said. "I'm not in the mood."

It was like a self-fulfilling prophecy. But if she came to visit him, he wouldn't be able to be pleasant and that wouldn't be any better.

"Oh," she said. And he knew that he'd hurt her, but she was just in a long line of people who'd had a weird interaction with him today. And he was all fed up.

"I'll see you maybe tomorrow."

"Okay, Gideon, whatever you need."

He knew she *wanted* to mean that. He just didn't know if she did. Because obviously she'd wanted him to move back, and she wanted to get a certain thing out of that.

And now she wasn't getting it.

He'd wanted to start over. He'd been so sure that going back to the beginning was his way of finding something. But he sure as hell hadn't found it yet.

He was starting to doubt that he was going to.

He got off the phone with Lydia and went inside,

kicking his boots off. He didn't bother to undress to get in bed.

He had never thought about what it would feel like when his glory days were behind him. Because they'd always been in front of him.

He had always been able to count on his body to do exactly what he wanted to do. And people had always responded to him in a specific way. And now...he did not exude charm. Not in the least. It was funny because it wasn't like a bomb had blown up his face. He looked the same, just with a little more facial hair.

It was something *else* he was missing.

Something inside.

And he had no idea how to get it back. He told himself he didn't want it back.

But there was a reason he was here.

There's glory on the other side if you can just get to it.

He told himself that because it was the only way he knew how to live. He told himself that not because he believed it, but because it was the only thing that had gotten him through uncomfortable times before.

And if it was a lie, that was just fine. Everyone else was disappointed in him. So he might as well be, too.

But in the meantime, he had to keep going.

Otherwise...he really might as well have died back there in Afghanistan. Maybe he should have.

It was a truth his thoughts circled.

Over and over.

He didn't know if it was ever going to end.

CHAPTER SEVEN

WHEN LYDIA TEXTED Rory to let her know she was worried about Gideon, Rory knew she didn't actually have to physically do anything in response to that. But she had felt restless and upset ever since the parade, and time hadn't eased the concern.

That was how she found herself driving to Gideon's house at 9:00 p.m. And yes, she knew that Lydia could've done that. It was just…she felt sympathy for him. She really did. But her frustration with the entire situation was beginning to boil over. He had come here. And he was still freezing his family out. And at the same time, she had seen the genuine pain he was in. But why come here if he wasn't going to try and connect? If he wasn't going to try to work it out?

The lights were on when she pulled up to the cabin, and she could see him through the window, standing in the kitchen. He looked tired. Right then, his expression was unguarded. And she was mobilized by it.

And then, immobilized.

Yes, it wasn't like her. She wasn't the one who took action. She was the one who crumbled when a situation got intense.

The truth was it mattered. Because when she had been at her lowest point, he had been there for her. It had been enough for him that she was Lydia's friend.

And as for her…he had been formative. Her feelings would always be tangled around him. Her entire adolescent experience. He had been the source of hope and joy, despair and humiliation. He had been everything. It was clear to her that for whatever reason, he didn't feel like he was everything now. So maybe he just needed somebody… She let out a long breath, fortifying herself, and then she got out of the car.

Just don't be beige. Don't be beige, Rory.

Well. This wasn't beige. Of course, she hadn't exactly thought any of it through. Because if she had, her anxiety would've stopped her from completing the mission. She walked up to the front steps of the cabin. She managed this property. And that gave her a feeling of confidence, at least when it came to actually approaching the door.

She knocked. He had to have seen the headlights approaching. Or…maybe he hadn't. There were times when she had a feeling he was detached from what was happening around him.

Of course, she didn't know. Because, as was becoming abundantly clear, few people in his life actually knew what was going on with him.

She waited.

It took longer than it should have. She knew exactly where he was standing in the kitchen. But finally, the door opened. "Rory," he said. "What are you doing here?"

For a moment, she was frozen. He looked wild. Angry. Beautiful.

He was still so beautiful it made her heart hurt.

That isn't why you're here.

"Lydia said you weren't responding to her."

"And you didn't think that might be by design?"

"I wanted to see how you were. I was worried."

"You were worried."

"Well, Lydia was worried and…"

"I hadn't even seen my sister or my mother for two years before yesterday. I've been managing all that time, and they can't get in touch for a little bit and they're worried?"

"Something is wrong, Gideon. Obviously."

"Yeah. Something is wrong. I… I'm this."

"What does that mean?"

"Fucking hell, Rory."

"Is it PTSD?"

He looked at her like she was stupid. "Yeah. I suspect there's some PTSD," he said.

"Well, don't be an asshole about it," she said.

He drew back, and she was shocked at the words that had just come out of her mouth. She felt an unfamiliar fire light in her gut. This was not why she had come. She had come to say something inspirational. She hadn't come to get mad. But he was being…impossible. Like a hedgehog that had curled in on himself and turned out all his spikes. He was here. So he must want people to reach him, and then he was acting aggrieved when they tried. It wasn't fair.

"Why did you come here if you don't want the town to throw you a parade? Why did you come here if you're just going to ignore your mother and your sister?" she asked.

"You're not my friend, Rory. You're Lydia's. I don't owe you an explanation for anything."

"That's…that's not fair. You act like you didn't even know who I was when I came up to the door, but you do. You know that…you were important to me, Gideon.

We talked every day on the way to school. You can't say that we weren't friends."

"Yes, I can. I didn't give much of a thought to my little sister's friend after I left town."

His words lanced her chest, because they confirmed all the things that she thought about herself. That she was unmemorable. And she just wanted… She wanted to fight back against that, and he wasn't supposed to be the one she was fighting. She was supposed to be trying to help. But he was tangled in this. In this endeavor that she was in.

And she felt like fighting. Not crumbling. Like she had done when they had passed out the pages of her diary. Like she had done when those guys had spilled beer on her and made fun of her. She had crumbled. She wasn't going to crumble anymore.

It was the Summer of Rory. And Gideon Payne didn't get to make her feel small just because once upon a time he had been her savior.

"Is this what you came here for? To alienate people who love you? Because that seems pretty stupid. It seems to me that—"

"Why do you think you know anything about my life? Where were you when I got injured? Did you call the hospital? Send flowers? Did you come and sit by my bedside?"

The words took her back. Because no. She hadn't. She had been shocked, she had been upset and wounded. She had been sorry that he was hurt.

But she…

You were hurt that he got married. You didn't want to be connected to him anymore. You didn't want to want something you couldn't have. You didn't want to be found lacking again.

She hadn't been brave enough then.

"I didn't," she said. Her voice was thin, her throat aching. "Did you want me to?"

He growled. "I just want to be left alone right now."

"As far as I can tell, you've been alone, Gideon."

"Maybe I deserve to be alone."

"Then why did you come back? I can't figure that out."

"Because I... Because I don't think I want to die," he said finally. "And I think if I'd stayed away, I would have."

The words were like a knife beneath her skin.

"Gideon..."

"I'm sorry." He looked tortured then. She hadn't fully understood. She wasn't sure she did now, but she wanted to. "I don't... Don't repeat that to Lydia. Please."

"Are you okay? I... I don't want to leave you alone."

"I'm not suicidal, Rory. I'm sorry. I shouldn't have said it like that."

"You did."

"How come it hasn't occurred to anybody that maybe I was protecting them from the reality of the last few years? You all think... You all think that I just got better. And I chose not to speak to anybody. That I chose to... What? Get divorced? No. It's a..."

"What is it?"

He looked at her, and she could see that he was at a loss. That he wasn't sure what to say. If he should say something at all.

"I won't tell anybody. Why don't you talk to me? Why don't you tell me?"

"Because I don't like talking about it."

"What good has that done?" she asked.

"Come in."

GIDEON WASN'T SURE what he was doing, inviting Rory in like that. Because he hadn't talked to anybody about this. Because he hadn't been honest with his mom and sister about the extent of his traumatic brain injury. And he sure as hell hadn't told anybody what had happened after. And thank God, Cassidy hadn't, either. He didn't know if it was because she was protective of him, or of that image.

He could see it in Lydia's eyes, too. He had yesterday at the parade. She'd been embarrassed. That he couldn't be himself. That he couldn't put on the show that she wished he would. And he was embarrassed, too. He understood that. But Rory was... Well. She wasn't his wife. She wasn't his sister. His mother. And she was here.

Today had just been a shit show. He had been the worst version of himself with every single person he had interacted with and he had continued it with Rory. He had driven down that highway hoping to find a piece of himself, and it was like grabbing at a shaft of light. He couldn't hold it. He could just stand in it for a moment, trying to get some of the warmth reflected down into his bones. But he didn't feel it. She was right. He had come back here, and now he acted like he didn't want anyone around. But the truth was part of him had hoped being back here would lock something into place that was missing, and that hadn't happened. He was grieving that, maybe.

But the man he was searching for, the man he used to be, was dead.

He wasn't going to be able to get him back.

Rory sat perched on one of the stools next to the kitchen counter, and he stood back on the other side of the island, leaning against the counter, his arms crossed.

"How annoyed was Lydia that I didn't appreciate the parade?"

She shifted. "I don't think she was annoyed with you. I think she was sad you couldn't enjoy it. Does that make sense?"

He lifted a shoulder.

"I should appreciate the gesture. Once upon a time, I would've appreciated the glory." He shook his head. "I miss caring about that. Sometimes. It made life easy. You need a hit, you go do something that impresses people. And now I just... I don't give a damn. I don't know where that went. I don't know if that explosion blew it right out of me, if it made me realize that real glory has too high a price, or if... Or if it just feels shitty when there were only two of you that lived through that explosion, and everybody else's Purple Hearts came back with a casket. And you just know... All you had to do was stand just a little to the left because that's where my friend was, who isn't here now. There's no glory in being lucky. And there's no sense in it, either. While I deserve a parade."

"Maybe they got parades, too." She looked hopeful, and he almost felt bad telling her the truth.

"They call that a funeral procession, Rory. That's what it is."

"Sorry. I... I spoke out of turn."

"No, don't be sorry," he said, his voice getting hard.

"I can't fucking stand people being so careful around me. It's either all this bullshit hero's welcome nonsense or people acting like I'm a grenade with the pin pulled out, and if they make a wrong step, I'm going to explode on them, and I'm sick to death of it." He put his head in his hands, just for a moment. "I'm sick to death of it being true."

He let silence lapse between them.

"It's not loud noises, you know," he continued.

"What is it?" she asked, softly.

"I know for some people it is. Fireworks and shit like that. Not for me. It's heavy metal music."

"What?" She looked at him, bemused.

"Yep. I had my headphones in under my helmet. Blasting Metallica. When the bomb went off, I didn't even hear the explosion. It was just that music, grinding in my ears while we were thrown to hell. While everything came apart around me. Like a soundtrack. And you know…it's a…lucky thing that I wasn't closer. Because obviously there's no surviving that. But when I went to the hospital, what they saw initially was a concussion. Along with all the broken bones. But when it didn't get better, they did some CT scans. When the bomb went off, it was like someone had taken my brain and rattled it around my skull. It was like years of boxing or playing football. But the impact happened inside. It's…"

"You have a traumatic brain injury."

It was a relief that she'd said it. That she knew what that was.

He needed to say this, because he felt like he was being poisoned from the inside, and it was that feeling that drove him to want to numb things. And that was just so dangerous for him.

He had to talk. Like a confessional, and she was here.

He didn't believe in signs or the divine so much these days but she'd been the first thing he'd seen when he'd come back to town. And she was the one here now.

That mattered. He needed it to.

"Yeah," he said. "Like I said, they didn't figure that out right away. It wasn't until… You know, for a long time when you are living with something like that, you think it's because the whole thing was shit. Right? It was shit. I didn't have my work anymore. I didn't have my position anymore. I didn't have my crew anymore. I thought that I felt like shit, that I couldn't smile, but I didn't want to be around people because what I had been through was shit. But it turns out it was my brain."

"Why didn't you tell anybody?"

This was the hardest thing. Because it was a mix of his own damned ego. Not the one he had now, the one he'd had then. He'd been that all-American boy. He'd been a hero. He'd taken pride in all of it. He'd bought into his own press. Been the grand marshal of his own parade.

He'd believed he was great because other people had told him so. He'd believed he was special. That was a hell of a thing to admit, even to himself. Like he was special by virtue of his birth, his looks, his height, his ability to throw a football. It had all been decimated in that bomb blast.

Then he'd learned the truth. About life and himself, in one world-ending moment.

And he needed to say it. To say this.

"Because a legend is supposed to be invulnerable,

Rory. And I'm not. I don't like this version of myself. I'm not proud of it. I know Lydia wanted me to come and stand there and look at that parade and smile. Take it as my due. Be the guy I was before. I wanted that, too. Maybe that's the reason I don't want to see anybody. I thought being here might fix something. I just brought the same bullshit with me."

He studied her. His little sister's friend, trying to see if he had lost her admiration for him.

Maybe that was why he'd had to say it.

To see what sweet pretty Rory, who'd written a love poem about him once, thought about him now.

He saw pity there. He didn't like that. He'd never been an object of pity before. People had envied him.

"If people can't accept that what you experienced changed you, then they're the problem," she said.

"What makes you an authority on that, Rory?"

"Because I don't think the people around here are infallible. How about that? Because I've always been invisible. But I definitely felt like I was more than that. Because I think people like what makes them comfortable. Whether that's to let somebody like me fade into the background, or to make somebody like you an uncomplicated legend. But that doesn't mean there can't be more to you. Just like there's more to me. At least I hope so. At least there better be."

"Yeah, but you're talking about being more than what they think. I'm talking about being less. You can see that I'm not exactly thrilled by the idea."

"Why does this make you less?"

"Have you enjoyed my company since I came back?"

She blinked. "Not really. No."

"Thanks for that," he said.

It was funny, though. Because although she had been young back then, she had always been somebody he had an easy time talking to. She had been effervescent, and nerdy. He had never understood why she hadn't been able to be herself in school. But maybe… Maybe there was something to that. Maybe it was not unlike him. Like right now. He hadn't talked to anybody like this in a long time, but for some reason sitting with her he was able to.

She had always been one thing with him and Lydia, and to hear Lydia tell it, she'd been quiet and filled with anxiety at school.

He'd never had anxiety in his life, until his body had turned against him.

He sort of understood now.

"Listen, I can't guess at what you're going through. And as somebody who has long wished that they could show a different part of themselves, I know that it isn't as easy as wanting to. But I… I'm working on changing. You told me back then that I was meant for bigger things than this place. I failed at that. At going and making something bigger. Even though I really wanted to. I got scared. I came home. I quit. Because it's really hard to break patterns of behavior when they've kept you safe. So yeah, I get that just because you don't like the way that you've been acting, doesn't mean you can just change it. But the truth is you are aware. And you wish it were different. And that means that someday… I think it can be."

There was something comforting about this. He didn't necessarily believe her, but it reminded him of something. It reminded him of that time back then even more than his drive to Mapleton had earlier.

"Tell me. Tell me about your plans."

"I…" She looked down. "I don't know. I am leaving. I'm moving to Boston. I took a job. I tried to take the safety net away from myself. I tried to make myself a little bit more brave."

The geographical cure. He had tried that moving here. She was trying it moving to Boston. Did it ever work? He had the hope that it did.

"I have this list of things in my head that I failed at. And before I leave, I want to succeed at them. I know your reputation feels like an albatross. I get that. But when I look at you, that's not what I see. I see someone who is admired. And for good reason. I want… I don't want to go out of here as Rory Sullivan, the least memorable Sullivan sister. The most beige human being on the planet. I want to be remembered. For doing something interesting. For being surprising. I want… Maybe I want to be a legend."

"Except you already know, Rory, the problem with being a legend is that you aren't really a person."

She laughed. "I mean, it's like I said before. Everybody thinks that I'm boring. And I don't feel like I am. Not in the deepest part of myself. I know it's not going to actually change me. But I don't know, don't you want to be able to choose the way people see you?"

"I never had to think about it before. But yeah. I guess I do now. I wish I could be my old self, but it's not that simple, because I'm not. I'm angry. About everything. I don't know how to stop being this angry."

He told her about his day. How he had scared Riley, how he had alienated the woman he'd intended to hire as the manager.

"Okay. That's a bad day," she said. "But it's not who you are."

"Who do you think I am?"

"I think you're all these things. You're the guy who basically rescued me back then, and the war hero, and the man you are now."

He wasn't sure he liked that. Because it was true. Whether he wanted it to be or not. Maybe that was part of his problem. He saw this thing he was now as an intrusion. An imposter. And maybe it was just…him. Maybe he had to figure out how to work with it rather than hoping it would magically change. And everything would go back to being how it was.

"You should call Lydia," she said.

"I can tell that I disappoint her," he said.

One thing he hadn't seen yet on Rory's face was disappointment.

But right now he saw something he hadn't expected. Kinship. "When I left college, I know I disappointed Fia. I know what she wanted was for me to fly the nest and find what I was looking for. I felt like she was disappointed in me, because I was disappointed in me. She was disappointed *for* me and there's a difference between the two. Even if it doesn't feel like it then."

"There's a difference between dropping out of college and losing your career, marriage and everything else."

"I've never had all that much to lose," she said softly. "I guess that's the consequence of living a really big life. Your personal stakes were really high."

Her words hit a spot inside him he hadn't known was there. Something hungry for an affirmation that didn't feel empty. Didn't feel directed at a man he used to be, but the man he was.

"I don't know if it was worth it," he said.

"Then I guess it's a good thing you aren't done."

The moment stretched between them.

You aren't done.

A year ago, that would have felt exhausting.

Right now, it almost felt like hope.

Rory stood up and started to head toward the door.
"Rory," he said.

She turned to face him, and he felt the impact of
her like a punch to the gut. Because when she looked
at him, she really looked at him.

Not who he'd been.

Who he was now.

"Thank you," he rasped.

"You're welcome," she said, and then she walked
out. And while she left him alone, he didn't feel quite
as alone as he had before.

CHAPTER EIGHT

THE NEXT DAY, Rory wandered into the woods, clutching her list. Her chest was still sore from her conversation with Gideon last night.

His issues felt...big. They made her own seem so insignificant.

It was beautiful and dark beneath the trees, a shield from the summer heat. She walked down toward the creek, where there was water rushing fast and strong. It was always cooler down by the water. She kicked her shoes off, pulled her dress up past her knees and sat down on the bank. Then she propped her notebook up on her knees and stared at it.

I guess that's the consequence of living a really big life.

Gideon had lost a lot. But he'd been a lot. It was almost embarrassing to sit across from him. To listen to his story. His pain. To only have leaving college as her example of something she'd failed at.

She sat down beneath a tree and pulled out her list. *Climb the damn mountain. Get a makeover. Get a kiss. Throw a tantrum.*

She closed her eyes. What did any of that even mean? He had lost so much. He had lost more than she'd ever had.

And she hadn't wanted to tell him Lydia had made comments about being upset with his current state.

But she knew that Lydia just didn't understand, and he had asked Rory not to tell, so she couldn't make Lydia understand.

Of course, he had also said she wasn't his friend.

But she felt like maybe she *could* be.

That same familiar feeling that had been dogging her for months now, that sense of needing to break out of her own skin, was so intense she couldn't breathe now. He needed somebody who could actually offer him something real. She had tried. But she felt like she didn't deserve to be telling him those things. She felt like her own issues and complaints were so small compared to his.

She was just awkward. That was hardly the same as a traumatic brain injury.

Well, awkward and had once had beer poured on her when she was expecting a kiss.

That kind of stuff got in your head.

Get a kiss.

Rory stared down at her notebook and felt her heartbeat pick up.

She'd been thinking—way too hard—about the things that held her back. From the humiliation over her Gideon crush to her dad's abandonment to that horrible frat-boy experience.

She was bruised by those things. She had very good reasons for being gun-shy about a lot of things. At the heart of all of it was the truth that the people around her had given her no reason to trust.

If your classmates were happy to invade your privacy to make you the butt of a joke, how could you trust anyone at school?

If your dad could carry on a secret affair and then

leave without a backward glance, how could you really trust anyone?

If even a stranger who didn't know you, or that you were the biggest nerd at your school, could pick up on the same things the kids from your hometown already knew and turn you into the butt of a joke again, then how did you trust the problem wasn't you?

It was all valid.

But she was tired of letting it control her. Tired of letting it make her weak and scared and too much the same.

She was letting them keep her in a box she didn't want to be in.

And maybe part of this whole legend thing was showing them.

She didn't want that to be the biggest part. But it was part of it.

She was twenty-seven and she'd never been kissed. That was ridiculous.

So she needed to get a kiss.

Any kiss.

She didn't need to be romantic about it.

That seemed like a good goal. Because it was a particular sticking point for her and most especially kind of a hang-up.

Better still if she could come into Smokey's bar looking wholly unlike herself and snag the best-looking man in the room...

Without even trying, a vision of just such a thing swam before her. But when she approached the man sitting on the barstool, he had shaggy dark hair and a beard...

She squinted her eyes shut.

No. She wasn't going there. She wasn't reverting.

She could only allow herself to be so pitiful. Not anymore.

She'd been publicly ridiculed once for daring to fantasize so far out of her league. She'd known him, and liking him, going to sleep dreaming of him, had felt special.

Until it had been used against her, like the cruelest weapon.

She understood why the kids at school had laughed at it.

Gideon was the best-looking guy in town, in several towns in the area in point of fact. He had been legendary in this neck of the woods.

And he had been whispered and giggled about by every girl around.

He could have anyone he wanted.

Everyone knew that would never be her.

She liked to think on some level she'd known it, too, but having a huge big secret fantasy had kept her going and she hated that her ability to think that way had—for a long while—been taken from her.

That experience had changed her.

When she had dreamed of going to college, it had been a lower-tier school in a place she thought seemed vaguely interesting. But it was something she knew she could have. She'd stopped believing she was going to aim for the heights.

When she had thought she was going to get a kiss at that party, it hadn't been with the best-looking guy there. It had been with one that she'd really thought was probably in her league.

That was what had set her back so far.

She had never seen herself going for Gideon.

She felt she was too pragmatic for that. And yet she had still managed to get herself into a situation where the whole thing had been a joke. Because she was a joke.

She didn't even think she was particularly homely. That was the thing. She knew that so much of the way people perceived looks was in the presentation. She just didn't know how to present herself.

Her sisters did. They were good at it. They naturally put together clothing that created an aesthetic and she just couldn't access that.

Her mother had always been beautiful. But once their father had left, she had just shrunk away into this shell of her former self, and it was like all her confidence, all her joy, was gone.

Rory had never especially wanted to experience such a thing, but additionally she had never really felt like she could ask her mother for advice. Not when her mother was in such a dark place. And Rory had been a teenager. She hadn't known how to handle that. And she had never really… She felt rudderless. Like she didn't have a guide. Like she didn't have the kind of help she wanted.

She wasn't going to blame her mother, though.

It didn't do to blame women for the fallout of men's actions.

And anyway, it was fine that she didn't know how to be shiny.

The real issue was that she also didn't know how to show who she was.

Who is that?

She managed to make conversation just fine with her sisters. It wasn't like she couldn't talk to people— she could.

But she felt like there was all this burning bright

potential inside of her, and she didn't know how to dig it out from beneath the anxiety. The fear that she was doing things wrong.

You don't even like to try, in case it all goes badly.

Right. Well. It was true. She preferred to quit than to try and fail.

So this was Rory's List of Failures. Maybe she would fail at all of it. Again.

What a strange, painful growth endeavor.

She wasn't sure if she was happy about it.

She looked up, suddenly overcome by a strange sensation that she wasn't alone. And there he was. Just like that first day. All in black. The most beautiful man she had ever seen.

It was funny now. Realizing that she hadn't had that reaction to the stranger. Just to Gideon. Gideon, the only man who had ever seemed to create that kind of response in her.

But he was more out of reach than ever. And besides, she was leaving.

"What are you doing out here?"

"I've taken to coming this way," he said. "I like the solitude."

"Me, too."

"I guess that makes for less solitude," he said.

"I guess." She set her notebook to the side and stood, brushing dirt from her skirt.

"Thanks for coming by last night," he said. "I'm sorry if I wasn't… Well. I'm sorry that I wasn't very pleasant."

"You're fine, Gideon. Will you stop apologizing for having moods?"

She was surprised by the tone in her own voice. If Gideon looked surprised, he didn't show it.

"You're about the only person that feels like I don't need to apologize for my moods," he said.

"Then everyone else is a jerk," she said.

He chuckled. "I don't think that's true. But I appreciate you trying to be on my team."

"I don't know. Maybe I'm just on my own team. Like I said last night, it isn't like anyone in town has a super high opinion of me."

"Well. They should. Not just everybody would come storming up to my house, pounding on the door."

"I guess not."

"I scared Riley all to hell," he said. He looked down. "I guess that was kind of useful. Because I got out of having to pay to dig a new well. Though my ex is sending me a pretty big check so…"

"For what?"

He looked regretful. "Oh. Selling the house. I didn't want to take any money from it."

"I thought you were a legend, not a martyr."

"Very funny. Is that a martyr recognizing another one?"

She wrinkled her nose. "How am I a martyr?"

"You came to my house last night at the behest of my sister. You were kind of throwing yourself on the pyre there."

"I wasn't. I was concerned. You…" She wrinkled her nose. "When you stood up for me in front of the school, that kind of changed my life. Or at least, I wanted it to. I don't want to get into comparing my petty embarrassments with the stuff that you've been through, but they were hard things for me. You saying that I was meant for something more than this place, it really mattered to me. I wasn't going up there for Lydia. I was going up there for me. I'm not martyring myself to anything. You drove me to school every day for years. I care about you in my own right."

"Well, that's kind of you, Rory."

"I don't know that I'm being extra kind. I... I get not feeling like you fit in your life. It's why I'm moving to Boston."

"To get away from everyone here?"

She huffed a laugh. "To get away from who I am here. It's what I've always wanted. I tried when I went to college. To embrace something different. But I hated it."

He frowned. "And you think you're going to like it now?"

"Yeah. I do. I want to like it. I don't know if that makes any sense. I didn't know what to expect when I was younger. I was just confidently going out to the world like everybody did, and I wasn't thinking about myself out in the world."

"I think that's everybody at eighteen to an extent," he said, leaning against a tree, crossing his muscular arms over his chest. His forearms were big and well-defined. In addition to being covered in ink. That ink did fascinate her. She didn't know men with tattoos. The guys at Four Corners were a bit more clean-cut than that.

Not that this wasn't clean-cut. It was... Well, it was interesting. That's all.

"I guess so. Though it's never really seemed like that to me. The people around me have always been so resolved about what they wanted, and if they wanted it, they could do it. I wanted to do that, and then I just... I failed."

"You failed your classes?"

She shook her head. "No. I never really had trouble with school. It wasn't the classes, it was the people. But it's different now. I am different. Or I want to be. And I know that I gave up a little bit too early last time. I thought about it a lot. And I wonder how much of life is that sometimes you have to be willing to be uncomfortable."

He nodded slowly. He pushed away from the tree and walked down to the riverbank. He kept about six people's worth of space between them but sat down parallel to her. "Yeah, there's something to be said for that. I don't know that I'm great at the discomfort part. But, what I used to be good at was waiting for the glory on the other side. In football, you're going to take some hits, but that's what you wait for, you wait for the trophy. Here's the thing, I was great here. And I knew how to be great here. Then I didn't exactly get scholarships to college, did I?"

"But you were the best."

He turned toward her, lifting his chin slightly. She wondered if that would have been a smile before. "Biggest fish in a rain puddle. Yeah. I went off to the military because that felt like something I could succeed at by working harder. And I was willing to be uncomfortable for the glory on the other side. That was how I got through basic. That was all good. War isn't a game, though. Some guys took it that way. I think they came out of it better. Or they're dead." He looked bleak when he said that.

"I'm sorry. I'm sure it's…awful. It's not failing out of your first semester of college."

"I don't play those games," he said. "Everybody's

hard is hard. That's the thing. We all have the life we have. Sitting down and whining about the fact that you had it hardest doesn't do anything. It doesn't mean anything. It sure as hell doesn't fix anything broken. No. I don't play that game. There's no value in it. None whatsoever."

"I'm still allowed to feel a little silly, though," she said.

"I can't stop you. But I'm not interested in it, either. Does it do anything to help me?"

That was a good point. And it was, in effect, making it about her.

"Okay. Then I won't do that."

"Good. You're teachable. You'll end up somewhere in the world."

"I hope so," she said.

Silence settled between them.

"I get why I feel out of place now." He looked at her like he was really trying to see her. She didn't think anyone had ever done that before.

"Why do you feel like you're wrong, Rory?"

"Well, you may recall in middle school I was so skinny I think the nicest nickname I got called was Pimento Toothpick. Because you know, the red hair. And I had huge glasses, and braces, and I tripped over my feet when I tried to run. The only thing I was ever a champion of was the awkward phase."

"I don't remember that," he said. "I remember you talked a lot, and I liked hearing you."

She went still. "You did?"

"Yeah. It was always fun driving you and Lydia to school. You read a lot, both of you, and you talked about books and movies. I never had time for movies, and I didn't have time for books. I was always at football practice or track, or…making out with a girl. I would never have admitted it, but I liked hanging out with both of you. You didn't treat me like I was special. You were both…annoying sisters."

"That was almost very nice. Until the annoying part."

"I mean that in a good way. I didn't think you were weird. You were…the most normal part of my life."

She lowered her head and couldn't hold back her smile, even if it was a little rueful. Her being normal was good to him. She looked back up and caught his gaze and her heart slowed, then sped up. She looked away again. "All these things other people seem to be able to do so easily, and I can't do them. I couldn't climb Grizzly Peak when I was in tenth grade."

"It's a shitty hike to take high schoolers on."

"You probably did it at the front of the pack."

"Of course I did. For the glory on the other side. I can't tell you if I remember anything about the hike except that I got there first. That's not better. That's just… I wasn't the best on accident. I needed to be the best. It's what motivated me to do anything. Maybe that's why I don't want the parade now. Because it reminds me too much of that guy. Who wanted to do the most dangerous thing. Who wanted to do something in the fastest time. Who wanted to drink the most shots of whiskey. Who didn't listen to danger. Didn't give a fuck about it. Because I thought I was bulletproof. I wasn't. And now I can never get back to the way that I used to think about things."

"Are you telling me that nobody has it together?"

"Yeah. That's what I'm telling you. It's just that some people hide it behind shields that the people around them like better. But when you meet up against something that defeats you? All you have is what's inside, and then you're left with all the stuff you never dealt with. All the bad things about who you are. It's not the best, Rory."

She stared at him for a long moment, and something started to open up in her chest. A sense of longing so deep she could hardly breathe past it.

His gaze went dark, and he looked down at her mouth. For a second. Barely a breath. She took a step toward him and he jerked back like she'd threatened him with a loaded weapon.

"Don't," he said, his voice hard.

Oh. Oh, she'd shown him that she was attracted to him and he was horrified by it.

Great. Just great.

"I have to go. I have things. Things to do," she said.

"You don't have to leave on my account."

"No. It's me. It is."

It *was* her. It was her staring at him and realizing how handsome he was. It was her being unguarded when she really couldn't afford to be right now. And not with him. Never with him.

It was her being a fool. That was all.

So she walked away as quickly as possible, and she knew she was doing another one of those things that seemed abrupt and strange, but she couldn't help herself.

You're running away.

You're not different.

She wasn't running away. She was protecting herself.

Because she was doing new things. And she couldn't bear to be hurt in the same old ways.

CHAPTER NINE

RORY HAD RUN away so quickly she had left her notebook and pen sitting under the tree.

He didn't notice until after she'd run off, because he'd been watching her run from him.

She'd run like he was terrifying. After the whole incident with Riley yesterday, it was…

Shit.

So now he'd scared Rory. Great.

The one person he'd felt like he could talk to at all. Maybe that had been an illusion he'd been clinging to because nothing else felt…

Like her.

He picked up the notebook and the pen, and he stared at them. It was pretty. Gold-edged pages, a midnight blue cover with mushrooms and small animals on it. It was whimsical.

She had been a pretty whimsical kid. The way she'd talked about her favorite books like every fictional person in it was her best friend.

And now… She was pretty. She was able to put on a bright, cheery facade when delivering gift baskets. And then today, there had been such a deep sadness to her.

He knew about the middle school thing because he'd done what he could do to offset the bullying that had been about her crush on him.

What he hadn't realized was how much it all still affected her.

He'd been golden back then. Everything had been. But for her… Her building blocks had felt wrong, and he had no idea what that was like. He knew what it felt like to be wrong now.

But his whole life had changed with a catastrophic blast. Hers had been a series of setbacks that had taken any fledgling confidence she might have had and cut it off down to the base of the stem. She had confidence. But it was new. Fragile. It kept having to try to come back in spite of all of it.

He was standing in rubble.

His whole life he'd been confident. His whole life things had been easy. He'd wanted something, and he'd gone out and gotten it, and people had been proud of him. His mom, his dad, his sister, the whole town.

Moving through the world had felt simple. Easy. Now it was like wading through a waist-high swamp.

He was constantly overwhelmed by what he couldn't do.

He couldn't make his scars go away. He couldn't make himself give much of a shit about pleasing people, even while he watched the consequences of being such an unpleasant person destroy connections part of him wished he could build.

He couldn't fix his brain. He couldn't take back the way he'd been in those last months with Cassidy.

Yes, he had worked himself out of that space. He had changed some things. But those things would be changed forever.

He knew some things about himself now that he hadn't before.

It was easy to think everything that had happened after the blast was caused by war. What he couldn't escape was the fear that this was in him all along. If the only thing that had kept him from embracing all the worst parts of himself had been the accolades he'd gotten for being good. And the minute that was gone, so was his desire to be *good*.

He'd never taken drugs. His future had been too important to him. He'd never gotten drunk. He'd never done anything like that. He'd had no reason to want oblivion. His life had been perfect.

Then he'd been given a prescription for opioids. Pain pills.

And he'd found the addict inside him who had always been there, just waiting. Waiting to get that first hit.

He'd lived for the praise of other people. Then he'd lived for the relief the pills brought.

When it came right down to it, he didn't have any practice living for himself.

He started to walk back toward the house, and he looked down at the notebook again. He shouldn't look at it. But then, why not?

He was sitting there wallowing in the evidence of his own narcissism, so he might as well do it. It was probably a list of things to put in gift baskets. His probably said: *no wine*.

He opened up the notebook and realized he really shouldn't have done that when he saw the list across the top. *The Summer of Rory.*

Climb the damn mountain.

He knew what the mountain was; she'd just told him about it. Did she really worry about stuff like that? That idea of being brave for other people? A hike that she hadn't finished in high school?

Yes. She does. There was no hike you didn't finish in high school, but there's plenty you haven't finished now.

His eyes skipped down to: *Get a kiss (kiss from a stranger?).*

That same uncomfortable tightness he'd felt when he looked at her pretty freckled face that first day assaulted him again.

Get a kiss. *Any* kiss? And why?

In spite of himself, he could imagine himself giving her that kiss. But he wouldn't want to stop. She would be so soft...

Hell. No.

A list like this suggested a sweetness he didn't want to corrupt. Not at all.

Get a makeover.

She didn't need a damned makeover. She was the most beautiful thing.

Throw a tantrum.

That made him laugh. She was a sparky thing, too. He would bet she'd be terrifying if she decided to throw a tantrum. He almost wanted to see it.

There were notes down at the bottom, too.

Go to Smokey's? (post-makeover?)

Surprise the locals > new look > go out > get kiss? > go from zero to legend (like Gideon?)

He nearly dropped the notebook.

Zero to legend.

Hell, he knew how to do that in reverse.

But this felt...this felt like something he could help with.

He could see what all this was. It had something to

do with all the things that she had just been telling him. Feeling like she'd been afraid all her life, and wanting to fix it. Wanting to change the way that people saw her.

Hell, he needed that, too.

He had come here to change himself. The first person he'd seen here was Rory Sullivan. And she'd felt like an angel.

She wanted to climb a mountain? Go out to the bar? Well, hell, he could help with that. Maybe it would be…a connection to who he'd been then. Maybe it would help him find a part of himself. The guy he'd been back then when he'd defended her against her bullies.

Something closer to a hero than he'd been for a long time.

He needed *something*.

And Rory's list felt like something. Rory felt like something.

He was going to grab hold of it. Because why the hell not?

SHE'D LEFT HER list down at the creek, but when she went back to get it, it was gone. And that filled her with a sense of dread.

So much dread.

Because that list was embarrassing.

And it was giving her major middle-school-trauma flashbacks to think about him finding it. Would he wallpaper something with her list?

Get a kiss.

Maybe with a stranger.

That moment when he'd felt like he might be that stranger popped into her head and she nearly died of humiliation then and there.

No, no, no, no.

He wouldn't wallpaper anything with it. She knew that.

Of course, just because he found the notebook didn't mean he read it. But for some reason, she just had a feeling. Because it felt like her. Because it felt like school. Because it felt like something that would happen to a girl who was just such a loser.

Who was not now and never had been the cool kid.

Oh, because it had happened to her. And she still wanted to melt into the floor whenever she thought about it.

Great. Just great.

She drove up to his house, her heart thundering hard.

She didn't know if she was angry or worried… She didn't even know.

She sighed heavily and gripped her steering wheel. Bracing herself. Then she got out of the car and walked up to the front door, knocking firmly. He opened it.

"Did I leave my notebook?" she asked.

His face was completely neutral. "Yes."

"Did you read it?"

His expression didn't shift. "Yes."

She felt everything inside her crumple up. He'd seen her…her deepest shame in that list. All the things she wasn't. All the things she wasn't brave enough to be.

He'd seen she needed a list to gather the courage to go on a hike and kiss a man.

"Great. So. You know now that I am sad." She closed her eyes and put her hands on her head. "If you're going to make fun of me, just go ahead and do it."

He said nothing. And she finally screwed up the courage to look at him.

His blue gaze had gone serious, and the way he looked at her—into her—felt far too intimate.

"No," he said. "Because I'm not in middle school. And what you wrote isn't funny."

"Oh…"

"It's not sad to make plans. It looks like that's what you're doing."

"I am," she said insistently. "I'm working at leaving an impression."

"Leaving an impression?"

"The other day when I went into the grocery store, John couldn't remember my name. I have lived here since I was a kid. He couldn't remember me. Because that's how I am. Nobody remembers me. I'm not interesting, I'm not… I'm not trying to be whiny. But I just wanted to leave behind something bigger than myself. Like you."

"I'm a *legend*," he said. "You mentioned that in the notes."

She cringed.

"Yes," she said slowly.

"Rory, I…" He looked stunned just then, like he'd run out of words.

"What?"

"You put that you wanted to go from zero to legend. You're not…nothing. Just because this town doesn't see it."

"I know," she said, but the pinching in her chest called her a liar. "I mean, I mostly know. But when I come back home to visit, I just want the story to be different than it is now. I want to leave on a high note. I want…"

"You want a parade."

"Kind of," she said, her heart tripping over itself.

"I decided to move back here. To buy back the ranch. I have plans. A lot like you have plans to move to Boston. But I don't know what to do about…me." He cleared his throat. "I want to help you."

She panicked a little just then. Her heart fluttering rapidly.

The kiss.

He wanted to help her.

He—

"Part of my endeavor with my ranch is going to be to lead hikes. If you want to climb a mountain, I'm the person to help you with that."

"Oh!" She laughed. She couldn't help herself. Because…of course he hadn't meant with the kiss.

"And you want to go out," he said.

Her mouth snapped shut. "Makeover dependent, but yes."

"You don't need a makeover," he said.

His face was so serious then, something in his gaze hot, and she found she was having trouble breathing.

"I feel like…for the kind of going out I want to do…"

He nodded. "If you want to change how you look to fit in at the bar, that's one thing. But don't feel like you have to change because something is wrong with you."

But there had to be something wrong.

"I'll take you out," he said. "I'm not going to be able to help you become the life of the party, though I vaguely remember it. And maybe…"

"If I'm with you, we're going to attract attention."

"That is true. But I… I need to get used to it, and you need to make a splash, so…seems like it'd help us both."

"Yes," she said. "Okay." She was starting to feel not

so upset now. Not so terrified. This was a pretty reasonable solution. This could cover a lot of her problems. But when she imagined going out with Gideon, she imagined dancing with him, maybe. Having his hands on her. She coughed. "You don't happen to know anything about rope climbing, do you?"

"What?"

"Never mind. That's silly."

"I do…"

"I don't want to climb a rope. But it is something else that I quit. Something else I didn't finish."

"Well, it's stupid to expect a bunch of students with no physical training to just go climb a rope. There, you have my two cents on that."

"Thank you," she said. "It is stupid. I was never going to be good at that."

"You've gotta stop thinking that way. It's not about good at it or bad at it. Did you get what you wanted out of it?"

"What?"

"In the real world, there are no points for a good attitude. It didn't matter if I did some grim march out in the desert with a smile on my face, Rory. But I got out of it what I needed. Who gives a shit if you like climbing the rope? Who cares if you did it? Did *you* want to?"

"No. But we were *supposed* to."

"Sure. But what was the consequence for not doing it?"

"I failed PE."

"And does that have a direct impact on where you are now?" he asked.

She thought about it. She could see where he was

going with this. A bad PE grade had nothing to do with where she could or couldn't get in her life.

But that wasn't the point.

"It does. Because what I learned was that if it was too hard I didn't have to try. I could quit. And unfortunately, that was a lesson I internalized. It was bad. On a lot of levels. I became a quitter. And that's the problem. I let all of that stuff make me a quitter. You're right. It's about learning to be about that end goal."

"Just, trust me on this, Rory, you don't want it to be a parade. I feel like what you're headed for is not the destination you want to be at."

"That's easy for you to say. People were voluntarily throwing you parades for your entire life." She closed her eyes. "I'm sorry. It isn't fair of me to say that anything is easy for you."

"No. You're right. For a very long time, I had it easy. I was a golden boy. I was everything that everyone could have asked me to be. And I loved it. I got whatever I wanted as a result of it. You are right about that."

"Maybe I have to have the parade part before I can have the other parts. Before I can have the lesson. I don't know. Maybe I need this."

He sighed. "Okay. Rory, I'll help you. But I'm... I'm going to need your help, too."

The words, so stark and so very unexpected, made her breath freeze in her lungs. She wanted to help him. She wanted it more than she wanted anything on that list right now and that wasn't supposed to be how it worked.

"Tomorrow night," he said.

"Tomorrow?" Her heart jumped. She didn't know what she'd been expecting, or why she'd thought it might not be so soon. She was leaving, after all. She needed to get this show on the road.

It was just she was better at planning, at dreaming, than actually doing.

"Yeah, we'll go to Smokey's. You can help me figure out how to be…charming."

"Maybe you missed part of what my issue is. But some of what's happening here is that I don't know how to be charming."

"You recognize when I'm *not* being charming."

"That is true. So what do I do, like *evaluate* you when you talk to women?"

He looked at her. "You could do that."

That felt like a swift punch in the stomach, and it shouldn't. He had notably not offered to kiss her. He was offering to take her out for another man to kiss her.

For some reason, it made her heart feel just slightly dented. Just slightly.

"So I'm…your flirting coach," she said.

"I didn't say anything about flirting," he said.

"Oh. You said you wanted to be charming, so I just assumed."

"Are you offering to be my wingman, Rory?"

"Well. I could be. I mean, you're kind of being mine."

"I haven't dated for a while. But my ex-wife is getting remarried, so maybe that's my sign."

"Oh. I'm sorry I…" She suddenly felt a little bit ashamed. Like she had stepped into territory where she wasn't invited. Because, of course, he'd been married. And, of course, it hadn't ended well. Or rather, it had *ended*, which she knew was counter to what people wanted when it came to marriage.

"Don't be. I'm not. I'm glad she's moving on with

her life. She should. There was no fixing us, and she wants a husband, so she should have one." He cleared his throat. "Not sure I'm headed that direction, myself."

That struck her as being desperately sad. He was too good of a man to be alone forever.

"I could be your *friend* coach."

"My friend coach," he repeated.

"Yes. If you need help making friends."

"I thought you also had issues with that."

"I do." She frowned. "But I have had a friendship with your sister for a whole lot of years. I know what I want in a friend. Either way, the rule applies. I can be your scowl monitor."

"My scowl monitor."

"Yes. I can let you know if you're being too scowly."

"How? A birdcall?"

"No," she said, feeling annoyed. "Not with a bird-call. But maybe like that... What do they call it? A safe word."

"That isn't what a safe word is for, baby."

She looked up at him, and for a moment, the world slowed down. His blue eyes were intent on hers.

Baby.

Safe word.

Lord.

She shook her head too vigorously, trying to do something to disrupt the tension that had gripped her by the throat. "No. You know what I mean. I mean a code word."

"Well, now I like safe word."

The way his voice skated over that word, rough and deep. She did not know this version of Gideon. Not back then and not now. Of course, he'd never once said anything sexual around her when she was younger, and even though she'd heard that he was amazing in bed, she'd never been able to put too much graphic thought into it then because she'd been too innocent.

She might be untouched, but she knew things.

Enough that just his voice gave her thoughts that were so graphic she wanted to hurl herself off the side of the mountain to get some distance between them.

"Okay, we'll have a…a safe word for if you get too grumpy." She was proud of herself for saying that. Rather than flinging herself over the side of a mountain.

"Pick one," he said.

She felt almost certain he was doing this to her on purpose. "It has to be something that we aren't saying in regular conversation."

"Snowy plover," he said.

"What is it with you and birds?"

He shrugged. "I like birds."

"What is there to like about birds particularly?" she asked.

"Quite a lot. They're interesting. They're smart, very teachable, many of them recognize human faces."

"That's scary, that's not interesting."

She thought maybe he was messing with her. But she really couldn't tell. "You know, if you're joking, you might try smiling."

His face suddenly went blank. "It's like I've forgotten how to do that mostly."

She'd been trying to tease him, and she'd stepped on a philosophical landmine. Great.

"I'm sorry."

He shook his head. "No. It's your job. You're helping me." He grinned. It didn't reach his eyes. That made her heart feel bruised. Seeing him try like this. "Operation Smile More is happening."

She nodded. "Then I'm happy to assist with Operation Smile More."

"Tomorrow night."

"Tomorrow night," she confirmed.

"And think about that safe word."

She felt her face getting hot again. "I will."

She grabbed her notebook and turned around, heading back toward her car. And she realized, with no small degree of absurdity, that she had a date with Gideon Payne.

CHAPTER TEN

"I'M GOING OUT."

"Really?" Fia asked, looking at her keenly. "With who?"

"With Gideon, if you must know."

"With *Gideon*?"

"It's not a date-*date*, don't look at me like that. But…" She'd been thinking a lot about this. It was going to look like it was a date. And that…that was going to make her seem like she might be something special. Though she was supposed to help him talk to women so no one could think they were together.

But no one would.

"I am going as his wingman, kind of. And he's kind of mine."

"I don't understand any of that."

"You had to be there. I'm supposed to think of a safe word."

"Rory… Are you sure that he thinks of you as a wing-man if he wants you to have a safe word?"

"It's not *that kind* of safe word, Fia."

Fia narrowed her eyes. "Is there another kind?"

"It's a code word. If he's acting too grim. And he's going to have to say it if I'm too boring, or too weird, or too…"

"Why do you think that about yourself?"

"It's how everyone has always treated me." She wasn't getting into The Beer Incident. Or The Diary Incident.

"It's not true. People are just… Kids are jerks. If you're basing this off the way people treated you in high school, then you just have to stop."

"It's not *that*. I wish it were just that. But it's like I'm… In middle school I was an object of ridicule, but now I'm just…furniture or wallpaper at best. I'm tired of it."

"Nobody thinks of you as wallpaper."

"Fia…"

"You're sweet and funny. And just because you're like that in a quiet way, does not mean that you're boring, or wallpaper. It doesn't. It isn't fair if anyone made you feel that way."

"A lot of people have made me feel that way."

"Have I?"

"No." She ground her back teeth together. "I don't know, there was something about being the age I was when Dad left, and Mom was just so…grief-stricken. And I needed help with things, and I didn't feel like she cared."

"Rory," she said. "That was her. Her stuff. It wasn't about you."

"I don't know how to get dressed up."

"I didn't know that you wanted to dress a certain way, or different than you do."

"Yes, I desperately do. I don't know how to be like you. You always looks so put together and pretty. Quinn is so sharp you can't ignore her. Alaina is a bombshell. And I'm none of those things."

"You are adorable. I'm annoyed that anybody gave you the idea you weren't."

She sighed. "It's just, all the markers in my life seem to indicate that I'm not interesting at all."

"Come on. We're about the same size, even though I'm two inches taller than you. I can find you something to wear."

She found herself getting ushered into Fia's room, which was funny because generally Fia guarded her bedroom at all costs from intruders of any kind.

Her sister's room was always a little bit haphazard. There were quite a few dresses slung over the armoire and even a few on the floor. There were about four pairs of shoes in various places about the room—they weren't paired up together.

Fia was so together and type A about most things. Running the house, the farm store, the ranch. But very much not her bedroom.

Maybe it was just a bridge too far. She organized all these other things, and she couldn't possibly organize that as well.

It was fair.

"So…what are you after?" Fia asked.

"I need to look a little bit shocking. Where the people in town almost won't recognize me. And I am kind of like a rom-com where the heroine takes her glasses off and then she's pretty."

"You don't wear glasses anymore," Fia pointed out.

"I know. The contacts were shortsighted on my part. If I had kept the glasses, imagine how much easier having a big transformation would be."

"Right. Well. So what you're saying is…you want a makeover, but you still want to be you."

"I don't have to still look like me. If you have enough

makeup to pile on to make me look like someone else, go for it."

"I don't think that's body positive," said Fia.

"I don't feel very positive about myself overall, or did you not get that from this interaction?"

Fia sighed. "Fine. I'm not going to argue with you. I'm not going to try to make you feel better. I'm just going to put your makeup on for you."

She ended up putting on a blue dress that was buried in the back of Fia's closet. Rory had certainly never seen her sister wear it. It was very fitted and came above the knee, the neckline was scooped and it had thick tank-top straps.

She didn't like wearing things that were so tight, because she was still sensitive about…everything. And her legs were still skinny.

But the color suited her, and Fia did a good job on her makeup.

She made it coordinate and made Rory feel something close to confident. Mostly because she actually did look like somebody else.

Get a makeover.

She'd done it.

She could check that off her list.

By the time Fia got the glossy red lipstick in place, she might as well have been a sexy stranger.

Sexy. Maybe she looked kind of sexy.

"And these," said Fia, holding a pair of high-heeled shoes, which Rory slipped her feet into, and then winced.

"These are like torture devices."

"And your legs look eight feet long."

"Uh…not sure about my knobby knees getting that much attention."

"Your knobby... I don't even know what to say." Fia looked at her critically. "Take your hair down."

"Why?"

"Because it's pretty. Show it. And please be careful. I don't know exactly what you're planning on doing."

"I'm not planning on doing anything," she lied.

Because if some man wanted to make out with her in full view of the bar, she was going to take him up on it. And if it felt good, and she liked him, then maybe she was going to have to give him her virginity, because again, the idea of going to Boston weighed down with that was...not the best.

"Be safe and watch your drink."

"I will. Thank you. But you don't need to worry about me. I have literally spent all my life being cautious, I'm not going to suddenly go out and get *not* cautious."

"People do," said Fia. "And I get that you're going out with Gideon... Is there something to that? Or are you hoping for there to be?"

"I told you. I'm his wingman."

"No, I get that. But are you sure that's all?"

Even Fia was a little worried about Rory losing sight of reality.

"He's Gideon Payne," she said, feeling incredulous and annoyed, because...he was still the most beautiful man she'd ever seen.

She was only human.

But she also knew that he was completely out of her league, and she was never that stupid. She couldn't be. She looked pretty tonight. Because she didn't look like her. And it wasn't about the way her features were arranged or the way her body was shaped. There was just something about her that seemed to be fundamentally average.

It was that spark. That specialness. She was trying to manufacture it out of thin air. It reminded her of Girl Scouts. Trying to start a fire by rubbing two sticks together, but not having any real tinder for it.

"Rory, I get that you see yourself as someone invisible, but trust me, you aren't. You're underestimating yourself."

"Nothing in my life has ever made me think that I was a hot commodity."

"You were an easy target because you were easy to hurt. And that isn't at all your fault. It's about the people who took advantage of that. I don't know everything that happened when you went away to college, but I know something did. I get that it was horrible and upsetting. But whatever someone said or did, I need you to know they weren't speaking for everyone. Not everyone looks at you and sees a soft target, or an ugly duckling, or any of the other things that you seem to think. But you know, men and other people around you, they probably know you *do* feel that way about yourself. They know that they don't have to reach for you. They can just bend over and pick you up off the ground. They don't have to be good to you, and they don't have to treat you well."

"No offense, Fia," said Rory, feeling instantly defensive of herself, "but it isn't like you've had any relationships in the last decade."

Fia pitched up the corners of her mouth into a tight smile and nodded. "That's fine. You can say that if you need to. But just for the record, if you have to open the sentence with *no offense*, you should assume that offense is going to be taken."

"I didn't mean to be unkind," said Rory.

"No, I know. I'm giving you advice. To go with your makeover, okay?"

"Okay. But I'm fine. I'm doing something. You have to trust me. I know that you're protective of me because I have had so much trouble with certain things in the past. But I need to stop protecting myself. So I need you to chill out, too."

"Hey, I provided the high heels. I'm supporting you. I just don't want you to be walking into anything you're unprepared for."

"I'm listening," said Rory. "You don't have to worry about me. I'm with Gideon. And you can trust him."

"Oh, Rory. I don't trust anybody."

She said it with a slight smile on her face, but Rory felt the weight beneath that.

She was going to his house, and they were driving from there. So she said her goodbyes to Fia, realizing that she wasn't going to get anywhere with her sister at this point, and drove her car over to Gideon's.

By the time she pulled up, he was already out of the house.

He was wearing a tight black T-shirt and similarly snug jeans, and everything feminine inside her wound itself up into a swoon.

He was just so…so beautiful.

She was the one who had gotten the makeover. She shouldn't be held captive by the sight of him. By this man who was a wholly different creature to the one who had left. To the one who had captured her preteen heart.

He was out of her league. She knew it.

As out of her league as he'd been when she was in middle school.

She needed to learn. She needed to remember.

She was Rory Sullivan. She was too weird for somebody like Gideon. Except her heart beat faster as he took a step toward her when she got out of the car.

"We can take my truck. I'm the designated driver."

"All right. Should we… Should we not go to a bar?"

She realized that she should've asked about that. She was so bad at this.

"I'm fine. It doesn't bother me to be around somebody else drinking."

"Okay."

Maybe she'd misunderstood why he didn't drink.

"I don't buy into the alcohol lie anymore," he said. "That I'll feel better if I take the drink. Hell no. I personally know I'll end up feeling a whole lot worse."

"Okay." But she promised herself not to order anything alcoholic.

He was staring at her, and there was something cold and hard behind those blue eyes of his.

"Did you come up with a safe word?" she asked.

"You didn't like it."

"It's fine. I'll use it. Snowy plover it is." She took a breath. "So… Snowy plover."

"What?"

"I can't tell if you want to yell at me or…"

"I don't want to yell at you," he said, his face still set in stone.

"You look a little bit like maybe you want to cancel the evening."

"I don't want that, either."

"Then you're looking a little bit too serious."

She watched as he made a concerted effort to relax the muscles in his face.

"Is that better?"

"It's going to have to do. I accept that as an effort."

"Well, thank you. And when you're acting out of pocket, I'm going to say *termite*."

She scowled. "Why termite?"

He looked at her with that same inscrutable expression. "I don't know. I think it's funny."

"*You* think that's funny."

"I do. Both are funny."

She couldn't help it. She laughed. Helplessly, even though it was ridiculous. He was so taciturn and he just radiated fury all the time, and yet he thought animals as safe words were hilarious.

Even if he couldn't quite express it.

"I don't like it," she said. "What lady wants to be a termite?"

"You're too hard to please."

"I... I'm too hard to please. Ah. Well. That's *ridiculous*. I'm not the one that wanders around being grumpy all the time."

"I'm not grumpy all the time. That's the problem. Well, I am grumpy a lot, and often don't know how to... dig back out of it."

"Okay. I'm sorry. Termite and snowy plover, because they *amuse you*, because we need to court your amusement tonight."

"Court my amusement." His eyes moved over her, and there was something frank and open about his assessment of her body. She had never in her life experienced anything like it. At least not that she'd been conscious of.

She wasn't supposed to dream about him. Not the man he'd been. Not the man he was now. Both were off-limits. One, because he always had been and he didn't seem to exist anymore.

The other because…

She didn't have a reason.

Right then, with his blue eyes on her, making her feel like she might be beautiful, she didn't have one.

"You look good," he said.

"Thank you," she said, despising that her voice trembled a little bit. She should try to pretend she was used to compliments. That, she supposed, would make all this more believable. That she was interesting. A siren. A vixen.

With him, she couldn't be.

Because she wasn't that good at playing pretend.

She needed to get it together a little bit. Because she needed to exude at least a modicum of confidence when they walked into Smokey's.

She got into his truck and closed the door firmly, folding her hands in her lap. He got in beside her, and she was struck by how good he smelled. Masculine and spicy and clean.

Her breath left her lungs.

She hadn't appreciated just how much she didn't think about desire when she thought of her goals or when it came to this whole endeavor. Whether it was getting a kiss or losing her virginity, it was all about external things.

But he made her heart beat faster. He made her think impossible things.

He made her want things.

And she didn't especially like that.

Because that made this feel so much riskier. It was one thing when she was out to show the naysayers. It was quite another when it involved him. And her feelings were and always had been so tangled up with him.

Good, bad and impossible.

She was relieved when they pulled into the parking lot, but also afraid.

Relieved because she could get out of this confined space with him. Afraid because it was showtime, and they hadn't done a dress rehearsal.

"Are you okay?" she asked. Because it was easier to focus on him. On the way that she had noticed his discomfort with the parade. And on the fact that when they walked in, they were going to draw attention. In a way he didn't want, and in a way she wasn't used to.

"Just fine," he said.

"How do you know when you're fine and when you're not?" she asked, a genuine question and not just one designed to deflect from her own difficult emotions.

"I'm not battling uncontrollable rage?"

"Oh. Well."

"I know soon enough when that's going to happen. I can usually remove myself from the situation in time."

She looked at him, at the stark lines of his face. "I wasn't afraid of you."

"That's nice," he said. "Many people are terrified of me."

"I'm not trying to be nice. It's true."

"You never saw me throw a screwdriver through the wall."

She couldn't imagine the Gideon from thirteen years ago doing that. She could imagine *this* one doing it.

There was so much in him. Vibrating beneath the surface. It had to come out somewhere.

"Did you throw it *at* anybody?"

He shook his head. "When I was still hospitalized, sometimes I'd lose track of where I was. Then, I could be a little bit dangerous. After that, it's just... I get angry. Quicker than I used to. Everything seemed like a joke to me back before. And now sometimes things don't when they should. I don't like struggling with anything I..."

"Nobody does."

"I'm not used to it," he said.

"Sorry. It must be terrible to know how the rest of us feel all the time."

She wasn't making fun of him. If she had always felt competent and popular and easy in a group, she would hate to lose that.

Lost.

He was lost.

He'd been one thing all his life, and he didn't have it anymore, and the understanding in that moment was so deep and real and harsh, she nearly wept with it.

"All right," he said. "Let's go in."

They got out of the truck, and her heart was pounding hard. She looked at him and tried to see if he felt the same. He had that same look she'd seen on his face in the woods. The look of a predator. The look of a soldier.

He was beautiful even then.

And it felt like a secret, to see him like that. Because she knew that no one else had seen that, not here.

"We're going into a bar. Not war."

"Snowy plover?" he asked.

"Snowy plover-*ish*."

"I'll relax."

He did his best. And without thinking, she linked her arm through his, and they walked into the bar.

As soon as the door swung open, she had some regrets.

Because every eye in the place turned toward them. Stared at them.

There were a couple stares of open malice.

She also realized that people thought they were together. Her touching him didn't help.

She hadn't initially considered that because she had thought it was laughable that anyone would think they were together. But now that she could float above them and see them in context, her in that mini dress and high heels, clinging to him, she realized how it would seem.

She slowly released her hold on him because she was supposed to be helping him pick up other women. Her touching him wouldn't help with that.

There were women aplenty in there. All dolled up in dresses that were tighter and shorter than hers.

Maybe she had failed in this assignment, even trying her best.

No. Everybody has different tastes. It's okay.

She remembered what Fia had said. That people saw her the way she saw herself. That part of her problem was she held herself in such low esteem.

Maybe it was true.

She lifted her chin. She didn't think so.

Or, at least she wouldn't from now on.

So she sauntered, or she did whatever walk the high heels would allow, into the bar and went and sat down. He came and sat down beside her.

"I'll have a soda water," said Gideon.

"I'll have a Coke," she said.

Sheena, the bartender, was an absolutely stunning woman. She had tattoos on her left arm, a twining vine with flowers. She looked edgy and mysterious, and like she'd pair well with Gideon.

Rory ignored the tightness in her stomach.

"On the house," Sheena said, grinning. "Heroes don't pay."

Gideon looked tense for a moment, and she was about to give him a *snowy plover*, but then he managed a smile. "Thank you, Sheena."

"You're very welcome, Gideon."

"There," she said. "That was friendly. And you remembered her name."

She didn't ask if it was because she was a beautiful woman with curves like Highway 101. Because she wasn't going to act petty like that.

"I did," he said, after a beat.

"Okay, there are a lot of people in here."

"Yes, there are."

"So, should we go talk to them or…"

"I think we're going to have to focus on each other," he said.

"What?"

"It's unavoidable. We have to dance with each other. I'm going to have to test out my flirting skills on you. And you can try yours on me."

"Why do we have to do that?" she asked.

"Because everybody in here thinks we're together."

"I didn't mean…"

"It's better this way. If people think you're with me… Well, that raises your mystique, doesn't it?"

The problem was he was right. She wanted to badger him about his ego, but there was no ego here. Just Gideon knowing full well how his reputation worked in this town.

"Did it ever occur to you that other men might not want your castoffs?" she asked.

"No. Because in my experience, they do."

"I just don't know what it's like," she said. "To go through life with this much confidence."

"Yeah that's...not really so much what it is anymore. You know now that I terrify people without even trying."

"You're not scary," she said.

"Many people think I am," he said, darkly.

"You don't have to be offended by the fact that I don't think you're scary. You're not in military fatigues carrying a weapon, I might find you vaguely more threatening then, but even so, I wouldn't be your target so..."

"Fine. I get it. But I am just saying, most people think I'm a little bit scary."

"And you don't want them to."

"No. Not especially. I need to be able to hire people, I need to be able to run my business. I'd like to be able to go out like this. I want to be...something like normal someday. Or at least, normal enough."

Silence lapsed between them, and her chest ached. She wanted something she'd never been.

He just wanted to feel like himself again.

"All right then. I guess we'll have our drinks, and we'll dance."

"All right."

He looked at her, his expression going intense, and her breath froze in her chest. Then he reached out, slowly, and tucked her hair behind her ear.

Right then, everything in her body gave thanks to

Fia's demand that she take her hair down. Because then he pinched a silken strand between his thumb and forefinger and drew them down a curl. He looked at her like she might be magic. And even though she thought he was wrong, she felt it somewhere, shimmering low in her belly.

The spark in his eyes wasn't like ice now, but it had warmed to something like a blue flame.

"You look beautiful."

He'd said it earlier and it had been like a balm. But here it was something else entirely. A bridge to a whole new place.

To *insanity* maybe.

She had to remember that he was flirting as practice. For all to see.

"You're doing a pretty good job," she said, her throat going tight. "If this were a math quiz, I would probably give you an A."

He laughed, and he looked almost shocked to be laughing, and that did something to her. Warmed her. He was laughing at her for saying something offbeat. He thought it was funny.

She should've known that he might. After all, Lydia found her entertaining; that was how their friendship worked. They had off-kilter senses of humor, and they liked that about each other.

So, of course, it stood to reason that Gideon might also like it.

"Well, thank you for that. I appreciate it. Makes me feel warm inside."

"I was hoping that it might."

"You have no idea."

He was performing. But it still felt nice. And they were drawing attention, which was what they wanted.

"Dancing?"

"Yeah," she said.

But when he whisked her off the barstool, she wasn't prepared. She wasn't prepared for what it would be like when he took her hand. Wasn't prepared for what it would be like to be caught up in his arms. Pulled up against his hard chest and…everything else.

People were dancing, but she felt like they were the only two people in the whole bar. Maybe the only two people in town.

She'd never experienced anything like this before.

She'd had a crush on him, yes. And then, she'd tried to find a guy to make out with when she was older, and none of it had been this.

The reality of being the focus of his attention.

But it wasn't the same.

When he'd looked at her before, his gaze had been easy. There had been something engaging and soft about it. And it wasn't that at all now.

It was hard and sharp, and she felt like he was cutting through her, felt like he could see things that she would rather he didn't.

It was something she could hardly breathe past, hardly think past. And maybe she was supposed to say something for now, because this didn't feel easy or fun or just a little bit flirty. It felt like something else altogether. And she felt undone. But she didn't want to say anything, because she didn't want to disrupt the moment.

Because suddenly, right now, she felt like a woman

who could go to Boston and be anything. She felt powerful. She felt strong.

In his arms, she felt like maybe she was beautiful. Maybe she was worthy of this. Maybe she could have this.

If her middle school bullies could see her now...

She looked over into the corner of the bar, desperately hoping that those bullies were there somewhere. Sadly, they weren't. But Rory liked the idea that they *could* have been.

This felt like a victory. Because his arms felt like magic, and she never wanted him to look away. Never wanted him to break the intensity of his gaze.

His hands were large and hot. His body was so hot. That was one of the things she hadn't fully counted on.

They were just dancing, swaying out in the middle of the floor, but it was more physical than she had imagined this kind of thing might be.

She supposed that spoke to how naive she was.

She felt like a layer of that naivety had been peeled away.

Just now. Just being held in his arms.

Maybe that didn't make sense. She was past sense now.

"Do you come here often?" she asked.

"I'm going to let you in on a secret," he said. "Women don't have to work hard to get a man if what they want to do is hook up."

"Then why can't I find anyone to hook up with me?"

"Because you haven't wanted anybody enough to do it."

"What?" she asked.

"I know that I haven't been around in recent years.

I haven't watched all your interactions with men. But what I've seen of you recently, Rory, is that if you want to do something, you do it."

"No. That isn't true." She shook her head. "I'm a quitter."

"That's what you think. But I haven't seen that."

No, he'd said she was beautiful. He made her feel like maybe more was possible than she'd imagined.

He always had.

"I didn't climb the mountain. Or finish the rope climb," she said, her voice soft.

"Yeah, I know. But did you want to?"

"No," she whispered.

"That's the problem. You didn't want to. You didn't want to, so you didn't. Now you do, so you will. I'm not saying that there wasn't some personal growth that you needed. You told me that yourself. You wanted to be comfortable more than you wanted to go to school. And that's fine. But now you're ready to have some discomfort, and I think you're going to tolerate it just fine."

His words reached down deep to something wounded in her. Eased an ache there. He made it sound like it wasn't she who had been wrong. That she'd just been in the wrong places, doing the wrong things at the wrong times. He made it sound like she could make anything happen if she really wanted it, and that she could forget about the rest.

He was here, saving her, just like he'd done then. And he thought he was broken. But he wasn't. He was different. Like a bronze statue that had gone back into the fire and been reformed into something else. But the heart of him was still the same.

"Do you want to know what I think?" she asked, her voice almost coming out a whisper.

"What?"

"There's nothing wrong with you. If that was flirting, then…it worked. Okay?" She felt fluttery and hot. "Because that was the nicest thing anyone has ever said to me."

"I don't think, somehow, that most of the women in this room would agree."

"Well. I've never been like most anyone in the room."

"I appreciate that."

"Do you? I never got the idea that you did."

"The reason I appreciate it is because I'm not like everybody else in the room now. I used to be, though. And I'm finding the transition a little bit difficult. If you can show me the way, then maybe I won't get lost."

"I think you're leading," she said, heart thundering wildly.

She wanted to kiss him.

The thought stopped her short, like hitting a brick wall.

She wanted to kiss him because he was beautiful. Because she wanted him.

Not because he was a stranger in the woods, something tied more to fantasy than reality. She wanted to kiss him because he was Gideon. And all the reasons she'd had before for not doing it seemed like they didn't matter. Seemed pointless.

She wanted it.

And that felt like enough.

But she wasn't sure she was brave enough. At least not yet.

The song ended, and they went back to the bar. She felt like her heart was in her throat.

Some women came over and started talking to him, and she felt toxic, raging jealousy well up in her chest, and she hated that. Because all jealousy was a sense of heightened inadequacy, and she was well familiar with that and didn't enjoy it in the least.

"Sorry," said one of them. "I don't think we've been introduced to your girlfriend."

"She's a friend. Rory Sullivan, her family is part of the Four Corners crew."

One of the women looked interested.

"How does that work?" she asked. "I've always been so curious."

Rory cleared her throat. "Well, it works because we all run it as a collective. We have a common goal, and we pool our money and resources to help each other. It makes it so we cover any shortfalls. Makes it so that all the branches are functioning. Recently we opened the farm store…" She studied the woman closely. She still looked interested.

"We opened the farm store. And that's bringing a lot of new revenue. It's been a really exciting time."

"It sounds like it," said the woman, and she sounded like she meant it, which was incredible as far as Rory was concerned.

So much for making people think they were together, though. He'd dropped that as soon as those women came over.

And she tried not to feel acidic about it, because what was the point?

She turned away from them as one of the women put her hand on his bicep, and as she did a man approached her. He was tall, though not as tall as Gideon, muscular, though not as muscular as Gideon. Handsome, but not… Well. He wasn't Gideon, was the thing. But he was a nice-looking man, and probably a little bit closer to her age.

"Hey," he said. "Thought maybe you were attached, but it doesn't seem like you are."

"I'm not," she said.

"Good to know. So, you're from around here?"

"Yeah, I'm…Rory Sullivan."

"No shit," he said, his brows lifting. "Rory Sullivan. *Rory Sullivan*. Mike Heater. We went to high school together."

"Oh," she said.

Mike. Mike who had photocopied her diary, *Mike*. That Mike.

Her bully was, in fact, in residence.

"Do I look that different?" he asked, grinning.

Well, yes, because he was looking at her, and he was smiling. Which was a weird experience.

She should be thrilled with that, she supposed. This was the point of what she was doing. She wanted people to see her differently. She wanted attention.

He was looking at her like she was beautiful, and her only experience of that before this one had been with Gideon just recently. But it felt so different to have Gideon look at her. It had felt warm and exciting. Wonderful.

This was…satisfying in a way but also made her feel a little bit edgy. Not in a fun way.

It didn't matter, though. She'd never thought she was going to build lasting connections. She wanted to be a legend. It was different.

"*You* look amazing," said Mike, not waiting for her to answer his question.

"So do you," she said, doing her best to use that same casual tone.

"I'm in real estate now," he said.

Well, she hadn't expected that.

"Oh. That's interesting."

She wasn't interested. She didn't need to be. She needed him to be interested, and he was. How big of a triumph was it? Rory Sullivan chatting it up with Mike Heater.

He was interested in her. He'd approached her. It made her feel...powerful in some way.

"Listen, if you'd like to go get some dinner sometime..."

"I'd love to," she said, forgetting everything in that rush of actually getting asked out on a date. "Oh. I'm moving. At the end of the month."

"That's okay," he said. "A casual dinner is even better."

Maybe that meant sex. Maybe.

She didn't know what she thought about that. It felt weird. This object of pain being the one she could potentially...

She needed to think more about what she wanted out of sex. In her mind now, it was much more than about doing something to prove she could.

She thought of what it had felt like to dance with Gideon. And she couldn't help but stare at him. At his strong profile. The broad set of his shoulders.

Dancing with him wasn't about proving anything.

It was the heat of his touch, the solid muscular body beneath her hands. Being close to him. Breathing his air.

"Yeah," she said, dragging her gaze away from Gideon.

Because he was still chatting up those women, and so why shouldn't she do this? She should. It was the point of them going out, after all. It had been the point the whole time.

"Great. Can I get your number?"

"Sure."

She gave him her number, and then he offered to buy her a drink, which she accepted. But just another Coke.

"So, he's not your boyfriend?" Mike asked.

She wanted to laugh. Because why would she have accepted a date with him if she was there with her boyfriend?

And why would she be letting her boyfriend chat up other women?

Did he not recognize Gideon?

"No. He's not," she said, shaking her head. "He's a family friend. And he just came back into town."

"That's good. If your boyfriend was flirting like that with another girl…"

"Well, if I agreed to go to dinner with another guy, then we would have some serious problems, wouldn't we?"

"I suppose so."

She was glad that she was getting some attention, but she also very weirdly wished she were talking to Gideon again, and that was kind of a mess.

They stayed for just a little while longer, and then Gideon turned to her. "You ready to go?"

"Yeah," she said.

"How about Friday?" said Mike.

"Yeah," she responded. "Sure."

"See you then."

When they walked out to the truck, Gideon looked at her. "You have something to report?"

"I guess I have a date." She opted not to tell Gideon about her history with Mike, since that history was linked to Gideon in ways he didn't know. "I guess coming in with you worked. It made me seem a little bit interesting. Notorious, maybe."

"Well. Glad I could help."

"You didn't seem to have any trouble talking to those two women."

He shrugged. "Yeah. It was fine."

"Just fine?"

"I didn't want anything else out of that. I just wanted to be able to have an interaction and have it not go south. I get that might not make sense to you, but…"

"No. I do get it. I have a date. I've never been on a date before."

"You haven't?" He sounded shocked, which made her feel soothed in some ways.

"No."

He opened the passenger door for her, and she climbed up into the truck. He went around to the driver's side. He got in. He started the car and began to back out of the driveway. "And that guy is going to be your first date?"

"I went to high school with him."

"Interesting."

"Why is it interesting?"

"I only mean that… Nothing. Never mind."

"What?"

"I thought you were aiming for something a little bit more *notorious*."

But for her, it was notorious. She'd come in here and she'd… Well, she'd been different because she felt different, and Mike had responded to it. It was like Gideon had said. She'd wanted it, so now she'd done it. It made her feel bold. Like anything was possible.

"It's a small town, that's kind of the origin of all my problems. Everyone here knows me too well. But my makeover must've worked because he was pleased enough to see me. And believe me, in school he never noticed me unless... He was a popular guy."

"And you want to go out with a guy who's just now noticing you with mascara on?"

"Maybe I needed the mascara to signal some availability. Or to look...dateable, I don't know."

"You look great," he said. "But you didn't need all that. You're just as pretty without it."

Her stomach felt hollowed out. Why was he saying all this?

She cleared her throat. "If I didn't know better I'd think that was flirting."

Was she flirting? Was she just high on her power because she had been asked for a dinner date, and now she thought she could punch this far above her weight?

"It's just the truth. It's not flirting. I don't know that I succeeded in doing anything like flirting tonight."

"But you think you can..."

"I don't know. I'm trying to figure it out. To relearn talking to people when I don't feel like it. To relearn being out when I don't necessarily want to be."

"You liked it before, didn't you?"

"I never really thought about it before. I was out because people wanted me to be. I was around people because they wanted me to be. I wanted to get laid, so I flirted. I wanted to win a medal, so I fought. I don't know. It just seemed like everything was much simpler then. You would think that having your brain rattled around inside your skull would make you less of a deep thinker, not more of one."

Her fingers itched, and she realized it was because she wanted to reach out and touch him. Wanted to soothe the lines on his face. Whatever this thing was that had been building between them, she wanted to take it deeper.

But she kept her hands at her sides.

"You had a near-death experience. It's not surprising it made you reevaluate things. I didn't have anything of the kind. I'm just getting older, and watching the people around me change. My sister Fia is making this successful business. Quinn is getting married. Alaina has a baby. I just… I was watching everybody do something meaningful with their lives and I wasn't. I was just the same me. The same nervous, scared *me*. And I didn't want to be anymore. I can't imagine how much more almost dying would do that to you."

"I don't know that it was the almost dying so much as everything that came after it." He paused for a moment. "It wasn't an easy road to recovery."

"Your wife left you." She hadn't meant to say it like that. Like an accusation. But how could that woman have left him like this? It hurt her to think about. Made her chest ache.

"Yeah. She did. Well. I'm the one that physically left. Because she stayed in the house. But she…she asked me to go. And I did."

"I'm sorry," she said. "She should have…"

He shook his head. "No. She shouldn't have. She expected something different. I *promised* her something different." He cleared his throat. "I met her at an event on base. Her dad's an officer. Kind of a cliché, I guess.

But she was the daughter of a high-ranking military man, and she was attracted to military men. The Army brats get into what they know."

"If she knew, then how could she divorce you after you got injured?"

He let two curves in the road stand between her question and his answer. "Because she looked at her dad, and saw a man who had endured the same things and come out strong, unchanged. Because for me the injury wasn't the end of the story. Recovery is a whole different thing. Okay?" His voice was getting short now, and she could tell he didn't want to keep going. "Hey, do you want to do that hike?"

"What?" The change in subject was so abrupt she nearly got whiplash.

"We'll do the hike. I'll take you up to hike, and we'll camp."

"Oh. Right. It is like a two-day thing, isn't it?"

"Yeah. It is. I got all the equipment. I've been getting it all set up for the new property."

"Then yes. I'd love that. You can help me climb the mountain, and I can get you started on your outdoor business. Though I imagine pretty much everybody you're going to take out is going to be more competent than I am at this whole thing."

"Remember, it's about what you want to get out of it. What do you want in the end?"

"I want to *not* quit."

"Then that's all you have to do. Not quit. Remember, there are no points for a good attitude."

She smiled just a little bit. "Okay. I'll remember that."

CHAPTER ELEVEN

HE NEEDED TO get his head on straight. He was feeling off-kilter after last night. He hadn't cared at all what any of those women had said. All he could think about was how beautiful Rory had looked.

The way she felt when he touched her. When they danced. The way she made him feel.

It wasn't the dress—though it had been enough to bring a man to his knees. It was something about her. Something about her that was pushing up against a wall he'd built up inside himself a long time ago.

And she'd been pushing at it since the moment he'd seen her in the woods.

She was... She was getting to him. And he really couldn't have that. Because there was a whole host of good reasons why he had built up that wall. And it wasn't just about keeping out affection. It wasn't just about keeping another person out.

It was about keeping them *safe*.

He didn't know quite what made him decide to go buy the rope. He already had a set of weights, but they'd been left behind back in Georgia, and he really didn't have the urge to go collect them, not given the circumstances he'd left under.

So yesterday he'd bought another set, to go with the ropes. And at that point, he'd figured why stop there?

He talked to the owner of his family ranch about setting up an obstacle course early, and he'd agreed, seeing as he never left the main house to go on to the rest of the property.

He was in the process of moving out anyway and would be gone for the week, coming back in between visiting his new property in Northern California and coming back to this one.

And Gideon had an idea.

It wasn't just an excuse to spend more time with Rory.

He gritted his teeth and drove the truck down to the Sullivans' house.

The Sullivans' house was much like he remembered it. Except there was something a little different. It was brighter. There was a clothesline out on the lawn filled with frilly dresses, and chickens running around underneath. There was a big weeping willow and some fruit trees. A large barn stood not too far away, along with some gardens that had high fences around the perimeter, no doubt to keep out deer.

It was neater, more orderly, and also somehow a bit more whimsical.

There was a large chandelier hanging from one of the trees in the front yard. It seemed silly. There was no reason for that. Yet, it looked beautiful.

Normally, he wouldn't think of anything like that. Normally, he wouldn't pause and look at all these details.

But there was something strange about part of him feeling like he was back in the past, while he absolutely couldn't deny he was also in the present.

There were memories here, and they weren't terrible. They made him feel good. Comforted in a way.

"Just as long as Fia doesn't skin me alive," he muttered as he walked up to the door.

He opened it and was surprised to see not just Fia, but Rory and two other sisters he didn't know in this present time. He knew one of them had to be Alaina, and the other was Quinn. He just didn't know who was who.

"Good morning," he said.

"Good morning," said the four redheads staring back at him.

"I was wondering if Rory was up for a little field trip."

"Oh," said Rory. "Well. We're eating pancakes."

"So you are."

He looked into the room, which was cheery and brightly painted, and the dishes on the table were mismatched, orange and teal and cockatiel-yellow.

They had coffee mugs that had probably originally been intended for tea. Bright pink and green, ornately shaped.

They were an explosion of color, the Sullivans were.

They were gloriously put back together, he could see. Trying their very best to take control of this life they had been left by their parents.

He didn't know the details.

He just knew that they weren't here anymore.

And he knew what it was like to try and piece something back together when an essential ingredient was gone.

They had done it cheerfully, so there was that.

"Come have some pancakes," said the youngest-looking of the group.

"Uh... I don't know about that."

"Come on," said Fia. "If you're going to kidnap our sister for the day, we might as well get to break bread with you."

"I'm Quinn," said the smallest one.

"Gideon. Gideon Payne."

"Oh, we know who you are," said the other one, who had to be Alaina, he figured, by process of elimination.

Alaina and Quinn had rings on their left hands; Quinn's was just an engagement ring, while Alaina had a wedding band as well.

Rory was looking muted, and a bit stubborn.

"So, you and Rory went out last night," said Fia.

"No," said Rory. "Not like that. We went out as friends. Because I am trying to leave Pyrite Falls a little bit better than I have been living in it these past few years. I'm trying to make a splash."

He nodded. He wasn't exactly sure what he was doing with his face.

He looked over at Rory. She mouthed, *Snowy plover.* He smiled.

The other three women blinked. He had a feeling his smile wasn't overly successful. Damn. For a second there, he'd thought he'd actually managed.

"So you're moving back," said Fia, trying to transition things, clearly.

"Yes. And I am taking over my family ranch. Though doing something a bit different with it."

"Always good to know that we don't have more competition coming into town," said Alaina cheerfully.

"I'm not sure that anybody is a real competitive force against Four Corners."

"Levi is," said Quinn, smiling. "He is my fiancé."

"And he's…a rancher?"

"Beef. But it's *wagyu*. Very specialized."

"Well, I'm not that attached to beef. My land is going to be turned into an outdoor recreation facility. That's what I wanted Rory to help with today."

All eyes swiveled to Rory. "I was not consulted about this beforehand. Don't you want pancakes?"

"Right."

He went into the kitchen, grabbed his own plate and put three pancakes on it. The butter and syrup were on the table, and he was liberal with both before he picked up the rest of the conversation.

"Right. So… I'm going to start setting up an obstacle course. I think eventually there's going to be some zip-lining, I'm going to lead hikes, there's going to be cabins and campgrounds and things like that."

"I think that's a great idea," said Alaina. "The only thing similar to that is the equine therapy facility my husband runs, but that's more specialized."

"Equine therapy?"

"Yeah. It's really successful with people who have experienced trauma."

She was looking at him a little bit more meaningfully than he might've liked. Or maybe he was imagining it.

"Is that right?" he asked, his tone neutral.

"Yes. We've had great successes. With people who have been in abusive relationships, kids who have come out of foster care, veterans."

Yeah. She had been looking at him with meaning.

And the truth was he wasn't wholly disinterested in the thought.

"Interesting," he said.

"It's great work. But you know, it's not a holiday place. So I think it would be really great to have something like that in Pyrite Falls. Good for all of us. We are not a tourist town the way that Copper Ridge or even Mapleton are. People just don't think of us for that because it's so small. But a rustic getaway, that's a great idea. Something that makes use of the natural beauty."

"Well, necessity is the mother of invention and all that." He realized that there was no context for that statement. "I'm starting over." He regretted saying that.

"Oh," said Quinn. "Why?"

Rory looked taken aback by Quinn's direct question. Though Gideon realized he didn't actually mind answering.

"My military career is over, marriage ended, so it was time to do something else."

"Oh, I'm sorry," said Quinn, who did look slightly embarrassed.

He realized it didn't embarrass him. Which was interesting. He wondered if that part of him was broken.

"I'm going to have you consult on the obstacle course," he said to Rory. "Because I thought given your newfound stance on risk-taking and bravery…"

"I never said I wanted to do an obstacle course."

He looked at her. Just her. "I have a rope climb."

"I didn't end up adding that to my list."

"It's never too late to alter your list, Rory."

"What list?" Fia asked.

It was the oddest thing. In that four-line exchange, he'd forgotten anyone else was there.

"Nothing," said Rory. "Anyway." She took the last sip of her drink and stood up. "Are you ready?"

He was only halfway through his stack of pancakes. "Sure," he said.

Then she all but hustled him out the door.

"You should've called first."

"I don't have your number."

"They're going to think this is weird."

"Why is it weird?" he asked.

"Nothing. Well, no, something. Because, of course, people don't think men and women just hang out."

"You're Lydia's friend."

Something that looked vaguely like hurt filled her eyes. He frowned. "I didn't say that to hurt your feelings."

"No. It didn't hurt my feelings… No. It's fine. Why would that hurt my feelings?"

"You look hurt."

She looked at him for a long moment. "I don't think anyone has ever cared if I look hurt or not."

"Surely your sisters do."

She closed her eyes. "Yeah. I have a bad habit of acting like they don't count. I tend to focus on all the people I don't even like that much, anyway."

"I think we all do that."

They walked toward his truck. "I do understand if you're busy today," he said. "If you don't have time to do this, you don't have to."

"My job is pretty free-flowing. I have rental stuff to check on, but not every day, and I've been phasing that out because I'm leaving."

"That's understandable. So what you're telling me is you have a lot of free time."

"Yeah. So sure, I'll come and check out this obstacle course thing."

"Oh," he said. "It's not up. I thought you might want to help with that."

"I didn't say I wanted to become a builder. I said I wanted to become a legend."

"You want to climb the mountain, right, Rory? If you want to climb a mountain, you gotta build some strength first."

"Oh, my gosh."

"You know I was in the military. I can be your personal drill sergeant."

"And what do you get in return?"

He looked at her. And the first thing that echoed inside him was *more time with you.*

He couldn't explain that.

Not even to himself.

But there was something easy about Rory when people were so rarely easy for him anymore.

"I find it hard to believe that people were ever mean to you," he said as they drove out to the main highway.

"Why?"

"Because you're so easy to talk to."

"I'm not, historically. I've gotten very good at it in the context of being the manager of these different cabins and rentals. I don't know, it was sort of my attempt at fixing myself, I think. But I don't have a lot of close friends."

"I liked you when you were a kid. You were always telling me about something interesting. You talked a ton on those car rides. I just don't understand why people didn't like you at school."

"I couldn't talk like that there. Lydia has always

made it easy. You always made it easy. I never felt like I had to adjust myself to talk to you. Either of you. I get excited about something and I want to talk about it endlessly, and you just never thought that was silly."

"I don't understand, isn't that most people? They like to talk about what they like. Especially when you're thirteen."

"I think the problem was I was never interested in the thing that everybody else was. Maybe the problem was just me. I was the perfect person to pick on. Skinny and a brace face and usually wearing a dress that would look better on a prairie than on a middle schooler."

"I feel like I see people wearing those all the time these days."

"Well, I was wearing them before they were cool, let me tell you that."

"Do you ever wonder if maybe people just pick someone they know they can hurt?" She thought it was her, and in some ways it was, but he'd been in the military. He knew about bullies. What he wanted her to know was that the flaw was in those people, not in her.

She blinked rapidly. "I don't know. Do you really think people do?"

"I'll tell you something about being an officer in the military. I had to identify early who was going to break. And in basic, I would break them quickly. And mercilessly, because you had to. Either they were going to be able to recover from that, or they weren't, and then you had to figure out what to do with them. You couldn't send somebody fragile out on the front lines. So, the sooner you broke them, the bigger favor you were doing for them. Now, middle school is not the military. But yeah, I do think some people know exactly who they can break. They didn't break you, though, did they?"

"Sometimes I feel a little like they did."

"You seem whole to me."

They pulled onto the property, and this time he felt calmer. Maybe because he wasn't just coming off a phone call with his ex-wife.

They drove past the main house, out to the spot where the trail ran through the trees.

This, he thought, would be a great place for the course.

He went to the bed of the truck and started to get the different things he needed out.

Rory hung back, watching him unload items, including the set of weights.

"What's that for?"

"Personal training," he said. "I'm not gonna send you up a rope without doing some reps."

"No way," she said, rolling her eyes.

"I thought maybe it was a good idea. At least, maybe it's a good idea for me."

She wrinkled her nose. "Your muscles are huge."

He did not tell her that was because when you had addictive behaviors, sometimes you replaced unhealthy ones with healthy ones. At least then you weren't in a gutter.

"I have a pretty fixed routine," he said. "It includes a lot of lifting things."

Sometimes running until the edges of his vision got black because that's what happened to him now, and sometimes running till he wanted to vomit because no matter how far he ran, it still felt like something was chasing him. But he wasn't going to say that.

"Do you roll tires around the backyard?"

"Sometimes," he said gravely.

He grabbed the rope, and the mounting equipment, and looked up at one of the big pine trees in front of him. It would be as good as any.

He pressed the edge of his foot against the tree, and launched himself upward, getting a firm grip on the trunk with his thighs, one arm wrapped around the base.

"What are you doing?"

"Hanging the rope."

He started working his way up the mostly branchless trunk.

"I thought you were *injured*." She sounded worried. He didn't hate that.

"Just in here," he said, tapping the side of his head with the rope.

She smacked her hands down at her sides and made a literal squawking sound. "That's *not funny*."

"It's funny to me."

It was also not true, but scars on his skin didn't limit his mobility.

She wrinkled her nose and shaded her eyes with her hand. "What exactly… What are the exact injuries?"

"I am a moody son of a bitch," he said. "I didn't used to be. They say traumatic brain injuries can change your personality. Which I think we can both agree it did."

"Not *that* much."

He stopped. He looked down at her and saw her staring up at him. He noticed he could still see her freckles from this vantage point. The wind ruffled her red hair, and he was suddenly very aware of the way her T-shirt molded to her breasts.

They were small and perfect. Beautiful.

So was she.

He had no idea why he was thinking about her breasts in the middle of this conversation. That could be the head injury. Quite possibly.

"You don't think so?"

He remembered keenly how it had felt to hold her in his arms as they danced last night.

He just hadn't been able to muster up much enthusiasm for the women he'd been talking to.

That in and of itself didn't surprise him. He'd been celibate for going on two years, and sex wasn't more than a faint memory.

And he just hadn't cared.

Hadn't missed it. Hadn't minded.

He had wondered if it was one of the things that had broken in him.

Chemical castration or something. Not that he was impotent; he just didn't give a shit.

But when he looked at her…

Yeah. When he looked at her.

And he wasn't exactly sure what it was. If she was this breath of fresh air from the past that made him feel more connected with a part of his life when he had been in control, or if it was her. Now.

Past Rory had nothing to do with sex.

Present Rory shouldn't have anything to do with sex, either, and yet, when he looked at her, his body didn't seem to get that memo.

She was appealing to him, but it was about more than looks. There were a lot of beautiful women out there.

But none of them were Rory. She was captivating.

And there was something about the vulnerability in her. The way she shared it with him.

It allowed him to share different things with her.

Not everything. There were some things he didn't want to share with anybody.

But he just felt more rested around her than he did around most other people.

She didn't act like she expected him to perform. Like she expected him to behave a certain way.

She just seemed to be okay with him.

There was a weight he could put down when he was around her, that otherwise he only ever let down when he was alone.

It seemed natural. But he knew the secret was in the way she shared herself.

"I have a few short-term memory issues, but not as many as I used to. That's improved. I also have difficulty concentrating when things are too chaotic. Like if it gets too loud around me, and I'm trying to look at something, everything gets blurry. That's why I like things quieter now. I like to give myself a lot of time. Going to get all this stuff for the obstacle course is a good example. I have to give myself time. To choose things, to think about things. I wouldn't want to be climbing this tree right now if there was an entire crowd of people here, as an example."

"I'm fine?"

"Yeah," he said.

He continued on up the tree and got to the part where there were some big sturdy branches for him to begin to use as stepping stones. Roy let out a strangled sound, and when he looked down again, she was covering her eyes.

"Rory, I spent a collective six years in war zones. I

only got blown up the one time. If the pine tree takes me out, then I had it coming."

"I don't want it to take you out while I'm right here."

"You can catch me, right?"

"You want me to be your flirting coach, you want me to catch you… Some gentleman you are."

"I never said that I was a gentleman."

Even though he was up in the tree, he decided to flash her what he was fairly certain was a wolfish grin.

She made an exaggerated hand gesture from down below, and that made him grin even more.

"So you're going to manage an apartment building in Boston," he said, looping the rope up over a branch and beginning to attach the hardware.

"Yes," she said. "It lets me live in a way nicer place than I would be able to otherwise. And it's what I have job experience with. And it's really amazing that I got hired at this building because I don't have any experience with apartments. But the woman who managed it before me just really liked me, and she thought I had the right countenance to deal with the residents. So… I got the job."

"Have you ever been to Boston?"

"No."

The rope looked secure, and he grabbed hold of it and let go of the tree branch, swinging himself out away from the tree.

Rory shrieked. And then he slowly climbed down the rope.

Things like this made him feel alive. Because he was still great at this.

This physical stuff.

His brain didn't fail him here. And his body hadn't let him down at all.

He thought about the kid that had lost both legs and his arm in the explosion.

Nineteen years old.

And his stomach felt a little sour.

Well. It would be ridiculous of him to not use his arms and legs in light of all that.

With three feet left to go, he jumped down to the ground, his boots making satisfying contact with the dirt.

"That was dangerous," she huffed.

"By the end of the week, you're going to climb that."

"Don't set such lofty goals for me."

"It's not a lofty goal. You can do it before you go on your date."

"You are drinking your bathwater."

"I'm not."

"You said yourself, you're damaged up here." She tapped her forehead once, then moved her hand away quickly, looking vaguely sheepish, but like she was testing out that level of teasing.

He smiled. "Yeah, but I think you'll be fine. You can lift weights while you look at some of the other things that I bought."

"Okay. So what am I going to do for you?"

"Nobody said you had to do anything for me."

"But I should," she insisted. "Because if I need help with my list, then you need help with…"

"Did I scowl today?"

She looked at him. "No."

"You're helping me."

CHAPTER TWELVE

SHE WAS THANKFUL she'd had a heavy breakfast because she watched him work until well past one o'clock without stopping for even a snack.

He put in swinging platforms that hung from trees that you could go between like they were stepping stones.

He also fastened climbing handholds to a big board that he mounted to some trees.

There was a balance beam and a few other easy things for kids.

Or at least he claimed they were easy. She doubted she would be able to do any of these things.

Coordination was not her middle name.

But he seemed to think he was going to have her rope climbing by the end of the week.

Well, it would give her something to talk about on her date, anyway.

"Go ahead. Test out the balance beam."

"No," she said. "It's fine. I mean, it's very low to the ground."

"Are you insulting my balance beam?"

No. She didn't want to make a fool of herself on the world's easiest-looking balance beam.

But she couldn't even walk in a straight line. Something like that was going to take an embarrassing level of concentration, and she didn't know whether or not she wanted him observing that.

"Fine," she said. "Here I go."

Because in the end, her pride got the better of her.

As well as her desire to see him smile again. Which he did.

This whole exercise had been a trial.

Because he was beautiful while he worked. The play of his muscles beneath that tight T-shirt did strange things to her stomach.

And then there were his forearms.

She couldn't say she never really noticed forearms on a man, as she was regularly surrounded by muscular, hard-working men on the ranch. But Gideon's were something else entirely.

A distinct sense of sadness made her stomach feel hollowed out.

Was it *always* going to be Gideon?

Was he always going to make others pale in comparison?

"Stop it," he said.

"What?"

"Stop second-guessing yourself."

The accuracy with which he'd narrowed in on her train of thought, even if he didn't know the exact topic, made her feel like she was gasping for air.

"I don't…"

"Listen. This is boot camp, okay? Summer of Rory boot camp. I'm prepping you to complete that list. Right?" He came close to her, his blue eyes locked with hers, and suddenly her mouth went dry.

He breathed in deep, and she noticed a hitch in that

breathing. And she wondered if it had anything to do with her.

Stop it.

"I want you to repeat after me."

She looked at him, forgetting for a second to get lost in his handsomeness. Because suddenly he was acting like this was a kindergarten class. "Why?"

"Because," he barked, suddenly in drill-sergeant mode, "I'm giving you a mantra, Rory. A *fucking mantra*. And you're gonna say it."

She was staring down the soldier again. This was not kindergarten.

This soldier had that ruthless intensity about him, but she had a little bit more understanding of what that meant now. This soldier who had known that if the men in his care didn't take the training seriously, they could die.

He was intense, but it came from a place of being protective.

Did anyone know the weight that he carried on his shoulders?

"Mantra time," he said, snapping her back into the moment.

"Okay."

"I can do whatever I want."

"I can do whatever I want," she said, her voice trembling.

"I can do whatever I *need*."

"I can do whatever I need." Her voice faltered at the last word.

"I can't hear you, soldier. Say it *louder*."

She took a breath. "I can do whatever I need," she shouted.

"That's it." His eyes blazed into hers. "And no motherfucker gets to tell me who I am."

"And no…" She swallowed hard. "I'm not going to say that."

"Say it."

It wasn't like it was imperative. Like the world would end if she didn't, or a bomb blast would kill her. The fire blazing in his eyes made it clear this was life or death, and she knew it wasn't. But it felt like it.

She squared her shoulders and faced him down. And she found her own soldier. "No… No motherfucker gets to tell me who I am." She was breathing hard, her heart beating rapidly. "Including you."

"Including me." He nodded. "Be whatever you want. Get on the balance beam if you want. But if you don't get on it, don't let it be because it scares you. Because you're afraid of doing a bad job. Who the fuck cares? Get on, try. If you fail, this isn't war. Nobody's going to die. You understand me? The only kind of failure that's fatal is not trying in the first place."

She had a feeling that he was saying that to himself just as much as he was saying it to her, and she didn't know why that felt like it meant something. She didn't know why she was responding to it.

This was something they both needed.

Maybe he needed to feel like he could help her.

Because she thought of everything he must've lost when his military career went away. And she wondered if the purpose, that sense of being somewhere he was needed, was one of the hardest things to lose. She swallowed hard.

It was just a balance beam. And the worst that would happen if she fell was that she fell.

She couldn't get hurt. He was right. This wasn't war. But she was so afraid to try because she was afraid of failing. She had identified as a quitter for all these years, but the truth was she had gotten to where she wasn't even a starter. She was a never trier.

And that needed to stop.

She took a deep breath and walked to the balance beam. "I can do what I want," she said, stepping up onto the beam.

"Atta girl."

"I can do what I need."

"Yeah, you can."

"No motherfucker gets to tell me who I am or what I can do or…or how much I can have."

"No, they don't," he said.

She took a step, wobbled and fell.

She landed on her feet, she was like one whole foot off the ground, but she felt incredibly deflated.

"Back on, Rory."

"I was distracted."

"Don't quit."

She stood for a moment, breathing hard.

"I said, don't be a *quitter*, Sullivan."

The words were like a hot iron poker, goading her forward. "I'm not quitting." She growled, took a breath, and this time, with all her concentration focused on the beam, she hurried quickly across it like she was a rat coming down off a sinking ship.

Except there was no sinking ship.

Because she did it.

Because it wasn't actually hard. And falling hadn't vaguely embarrassed her.

She let out a growl and put her hands on her knees. "Why do I care so much about that?"

"About what?"

"Looking stupid. Because some people made me look stupid… Because…" She swallowed hard. "Because I felt stupid when I woke up one morning and my dad was gone. I didn't know. I didn't know that he wasn't happy. I didn't know he was going to leave." Her eyes suddenly welled up with tears, which was dumb, because she didn't cry about that. There was no use crying over a man who was half so ineffectual as all that.

"Hey," he said, moving over to her. He reached out and cupped her chin, tilting her face up, and it was the strangest thing. Because it was a crackle of lightning electricity that transcended the sadness within her.

"It is just a terrible thing that people let you down and made you feel like you were stupid for expecting them to be decent human beings. You get cynical in the military. Of course you do. You can't do work like that without a little cynicism. But I'll tell you what. I can always trust my family. My parents. Even knowing what I do about the world, I always trusted them. You are not the foolish one. Your dad is. You're not the foolish one."

The words were like a balm, soothing. But also… highlighting how very much she needed a balm. How much of a wound this was.

"That feeling… The feeling just… It kills me. It reminds me of just the worst moments. That sensation of discovering that everything you thought is wrong. That everything you thought is just a lie. That's what it reminds me of." Her eyes stung, her throat ached. "It's dumb. It's just a balance beam. And all I did was fall off in front of you."

"And then you got back on. And then you finished."

"I did."

"And you're gonna climb that rope."

"I don't know if I want to climb the rope."

Except now she felt like she did. Because maybe she would fail.

Maybe she wouldn't be able to do it.

But this time she would try. She wouldn't just sit down and refuse.

And yes, she still thought mandatory PE was stupid. But that wasn't the point. Not right now.

"Okay. I'm going to do it."

"You know sometimes the real issue is that you weren't set up to succeed. Some of it is needing to teach technique, and work on your muscles a little bit."

"I never really thought of it that way." And she hadn't.

But the truth was they hadn't been taught any kind of technique in school. They had just been sent on their way. It had blown her mind when she'd found out that there were techniques to running. In school, they had just sort of sent you careening around the track and hoped for the best.

She had to wonder if there was something truthful in that. Something she hadn't ever really unwound before.

Maybe some people just flailed around the track more convincingly. Maybe there wasn't something quite as fundamentally wrong with her as she thought.

She had always thought the girls who showed up with the perfect hair and makeup when they were thirteen years old were perhaps a different species from her. That they had it together. But, of course, her mother hadn't been showing her how to put makeup on, and partly because she hadn't found it all that important.

Maybe the thirteen-year-old girls who'd had perfect makeup had their own neuroses. Their own problems.

She had always just assumed they were prettier. That they were more clever, or maybe more female.

She had never been the life of the party, but she was a very good and loyal friend.

She had always done well being driven to school by Gideon. She could talk to him and Lydia; she didn't have any problems with that.

It was big, unwieldy groups of people that made her uncomfortable. It was the lack of control in those situations.

Obviously, he had always felt comfortable in them. He had always been assured he would be met with a positive response.

She wondered if that was the secret. If those formative moments decided whether you felt like you were awkward or not. If you were met with applause or skepticism.

She had always been met with skepticism. At best.

And it was weird now to try to disentangle what she wanted, what she was hoping to get out of this gambit, her date with Mike, everything, and feeling like she didn't care about popularity.

She had always told herself she was maybe above them because she wasn't shallow.

But didn't she like Gideon the same as everybody? And wasn't she still consumed by the fact that she couldn't make them all like her? Is that why she'd agreed to go on a date with Mike?

Maybe people were just all the same. Maybe they were all the same and whether or not you were good with a big group or a small group was what determined

if you controlled the feelings of other people. Except…
She must bring up some feelings in *somebody*. She had
always thought of herself as a beige sweater. But if she
made those kids at her school so upset just by standing
there, they must've been pushing her down for a reason.

This was quite the revelation to be having over
thoughts of mandatory PE.

"Do you think that everyone is secretly insecure?"
she asked.

"I don't know about that," he said, frowning. "But
I do think that maybe everybody has that one block in
their Jenga tower, the one that's holding everything up.
And if life removes that, they fall apart. In fact, I would
say that people like me… That's even more true. If you
haven't struggled, then I think you often don't know
what to do when you aren't excelling."

He was fit, healthy, here—all after his life had im-
ploded. If that wasn't succeeding, she didn't know what
was. He hadn't chosen to get injured in a war. But he'd
chosen to do all of this since.

"Well if it helps, from my perspective, you look like
you're excelling. I'm not saying I don't recognize that
you have difficulties. But I'm just saying, even *with*
them, you seem like you're doing well."

"Thanks," he said. "I didn't come here at the worst
point of my struggle. Just so you know. I didn't come
here to lick my wounds. They're pretty well healed up.
Cassidy and I split two years ago. It's just still taken
time for us to deal with the house and all that."

"What was…what was the worst?"

She watched as his expression became guarded.
"This part isn't about me, Rory. It's about you."

"We're helping each other."

"Right now, this is about you."

And by now she knew him well enough to know he was stubborn. He wouldn't share more until he was good and ready.

She cleared her throat. "I've always felt like maybe I was uniquely anxious or faulty in some way. Because people look at me and see a soft target. But I didn't even think of it that way ever. I just thought of it as people seeing a weirdo. And reacting accordingly."

"I think it's more than that. I do think people see threats to their power." He took a sharp breath. "I like to think that I was never a bully."

"You weren't. You rescued me from my bullies, remember? Everybody liked you."

He rubbed the back of his neck. "I'm sure everybody didn't, though. There was probably somebody who felt like they were pushed into my shadow who didn't like me. And I am certain that I wasn't above acting a bit superior when it suited me. I'm sure that I wasn't the best *all* the time. And for a while there, I was kind of living two different realities. Because when I was deployed, I had a community. I had these men I was in charge of. Their safety, their well-being, that was all that mattered. There was the mission, but my personal mission was to bring them home. I told you when we did basic, I identified everybody's weaknesses, and I pushed them hard. But knowing their weaknesses meant that I knew them."

He *knew* them.

And she knew that in that last mission he had lost men.

"So that's what you think? All those middle schoolers just saw all my strength, and they felt threatened by me?"

"I'm not saying that. But I think that's probably closer to the truth than there being something wrong with you. And what I'm really starting to think is that it comes for you eventually. You can't live like that forever. It's not a question of if the block will get removed. It's *when*. You know, you've had things happen, but they happened while you were being built. So you might've fallen over a little bit, but you were only a couple stories up. So it wasn't catastrophic. And you rebuilt from there, and when life knocks you down again, you rebuilt a little further. And a little further. And look at you now? Going to Boston. When that tower crumbled, it kicked my ass. So... I don't know why people do what they do. I'm not an expert in human nature, I wish I were. I can sense things and people, though. And you're strong, Rory. I have never seen you as anything else. You've never seemed boring to me. Why were you such a target?"

"Braces, glasses. Skinny. Redhead. Freckles. Four eyes, carrottop, you name it. Brace face. Somebody once said that my knees probably had their own gravitational pull. Because they were so knobby."

He looked down. "I don't see that."

"Well, they're less knobby now. I have a little bit more weight on my body these days."

"So people had to manufacture something, because there's not anything wrong with you, and there never has been. People are just so damned insecure. Ridiculous."

"Well. There were the poems," she said.

He looked at her, his expression stoic. "Then they

hated you because you had passion they didn't have. You were never boring."

"Did you…did you read them?"

He nodded slowly. "I did. And I didn't laugh."

"I was…"

"You were young. If you'd been my age… Hell, I think I…"

Everything stopped, for just a moment. Because Gideon had been so nice, defending her from everybody, but she had never assumed the poems might have actually been nice for him to read. Or that he even liked them.

Or her.

He straightened, and the spell between them was broken.

"After you do a little working out. After I teach you some technique, I'll tell you more about my stuff."

"Okay. Agreed."

But she was going to be pondering all of that for a long time.

CHAPTER THIRTEEN

AFTER THAT, she spent every day at his obstacle course. She would lift some weights, which she was dubious about being effective, considering she was only going to work with them for a week or so, and she only did a few reps at a time.

But he demonstrated the rope climb for her.

The first time he did it, she just about swallowed her tongue.

He was wearing shorts, which he at some point called Ranger Panties, and they were *short*.

She could see the edge of a scar on his left thigh, and she wanted to keep staring at it. Figure out exactly where it extended to. How bad it was, how deep.

But then she got distracted by the rest of his thighs. And the muscles.

And his butt.

He was so beautiful.

All of him.

When she was a girl, she had liked things like his square jaw, his blue eyes, the way his dark brown hair swooped gently away from his forehead. Now his hair was a bit too shaggy, and he had a beard.

And she liked it.

She appreciated things like his muscular thighs, and that they were a bit hairy.

He excited her in ways that were not juvenile.

Not at all.

He made her wish, just a little bit, that she knew more about sex.

And in fact, it made her want to educate herself, just a bit.

Which was what brought her to Quinn and Levi's house later that day. She felt jittery and a little bit reluctant to reveal too much to her sister, but she and Quinn were close, and Quinn knew what it was like to get caught in Fia's overprotective tractor beam.

She hadn't liked it, and Rory had a feeling Quinn would take her side on this.

Not that she was going to have sex with Gideon. But she was maybe going to have sex. And looking at Gideon, and fixating on his thighs, had taught her that perhaps there were some things she maybe needed to get straight.

Not that she didn't get sex, the mechanics of it and all.

It was just after her incident, she had been so embarrassed that she had avoided a lot of things that pertained to it.

"I was just about to make a sandwich," said Quinn. "Do you want one?"

"Yeah," she said. "I would love one. Thank you."

"No problem."

Quinn bustled for a second, and then turned, gripping the edge of the counter. "Does this have to do with Gideon?"

"How did you know?"

"Because, it was weird the way he showed up the other morning, and now I hear tell you've been over there every day since."

"He's helping me learn how to climb a rope."

"He… What?" She looked at her with round confused eyes. "Is that a euphemism?"

"No, it's not a *euphemism*. But I do have a date on Friday, and it is entirely possible that I will need knowledge beyond the euphemistic re: sex."

"Rory…"

"I went with you to the bar. When we were considering maybe finding a guy. And I didn't say anything to Fia. And I think that you owe me a courtesy."

Quin looked defeated by this truth. "What courtesy? The sex talk?"

"I assume you and Levi have sex."

Quinn went scarlet. "Yeah. A lot. But I don't know that I want to…"

"*Please.* I realize that I have ignored my own education. I went away to school, and some stuff happened, and I came back, because… Basically, I did try to kind of hook up with a guy and it blew up in my face, and I've never gotten over that. Because it just reminds me of all the other times in my life I haven't been good enough. When I thought things were going to go a certain way and they didn't, and I have to get over that. I'm moving to Boston. Who is going to want to have sex with a twenty-seven-year-old virgin? I ask you. I am on the shelf by any definition. I am a spinster. I am going to have to tell people that I've been a nun up until this point to make them think that at least I had a good reason. I wish I did. I wish I had a purity ring. Something that I could tell people that makes it sound like this was a choice and not an accident of my awkwardness."

"Oh, Rory," said Quinn. "I don't… What do you need to know?"

"How bad does it hurt the first time?"

Quinn winced. "I mean, that depends."

"On what?"

Quinn looked left, then right. "Dimensions."

Rory blinked. "Like...a multiverse?"

"Not those dimensions. Physical dimensions."

"Oh. Well. How big is—"

Quinn held up a hand, palm out. "No. One day I will be drunk enough to have that conversation, but I'm not drunk at all, and I am not telling you that."

"Are we talking mini cucumber, eggplant..."

"*Nothing* with the word *mini* in it, how about that."

She thought about her future brother-in-law, who was handsome and tall, and it was probably a very good thing he was proportionate and not mini. "Good to know."

"You know about sex," Quinn said, exasperated. "I don't understand why you're acting like you need the talk."

"You're right. I do know *about* it. But everything I know feels textbook and clinical. Do you just... Do you just go for it? Or should you hang back or..."

"No guy is going to complain if you jump in with a blow job. Trust me. But you have to want to do it. You jump in because you're enthusiastic. I don't know who you're going out with tomorrow, but it doesn't sound to me like you want to have sex with them."

She thought about Gideon's thighs again. It certainly wasn't the date with Mike that had gotten her worried about this.

"How do you know?" she asked.

"I know because if you wanted to have sex with the guy, then you wouldn't be nervous like this. Because if it's right, you know. Because when he kisses you, you don't want to stop. Because passion overtakes everything. Better judgment and inexperience. That is the definition of enthusiastic consent. When your body is shouting yes and you don't want to resist yourself. When your anxiety isn't the most important thing. When the most important thing is having him. And if it's not, don't be with him."

"I do so very much feel like I am letting down feminism in this world of sex positivity…"

"I don't know. Sex positivity seems to be luring a lot of girls into crappy sex. They think they have to just because they went out with a guy. You don't. Have sex with him because you can't not. Because you think you'll die if you don't. But don't have sex with anyone for any less than that."

"That's how it is with Levi?"

"Every time. I didn't even like him. Or I wasn't supposed to. But he overwhelmed me. He made me question all these things about myself, the way that I saw the world. What I thought was important. He taught me things about myself that I never could've learned on my own. I think that I did the same for him. We fit each other. Physically and emotionally. And when passion clicked with that, it was like I couldn't even imagine not being with him. I wanted to throw all caution to the wind. I even absolutely and completely risked Fia's rage."

"We need to get our spinster aunt a man," mused Rory.

Quinn chuckled. "I mean, agreed, but you're going to Boston."

She marinated on that. "I am going to Boston."

"I'll finish your sandwich now," Quinn said.

It was turkey and mayo, which felt sort of inglorious after that sex conversation.

"Gideon is as hot as ever, isn't he?" Quinn said.

"I don't have a date with Gideon tomorrow," she said.

"Why not, Rory?"

The question scraped her out. Made her chest feel sore and hollow.

"Well, I'm leaving, first of all."

"Also true in context with whoever the guy you're going out with is."

"I guess. Except that guy is just that guy. And Gideon is Gideon. And he's different. And it would be different." She looked down at her sandwich.

"What are you doing exactly?"

"I'm trying to prove that I'm not the same person I was."

"To who? And why? I love you. I have always loved you just the way you are. You are such a great and loyal sister. And you're fun and you're quirky. And I love hearing you talk about books, and movies, and your opinions on things. And I like the way you dress. And I don't understand why you've let other people decide those things are bad."

"You're telling me you don't have any insecurities?"

"Of course I do. But it never occurred to me not to be with the guy that I wanted because of them."

"Like you said. It was undeniable, right?"

"Yes."

"You were swept up?" She took a big bite of her sandwich.

"Yes."

"There's no sweeping up happening. He's... He's a

mess. He's a disaster cowboy. He is absolutely and completely not available. And even if he were, I'm leaving. And I guess that is the point. I don't think he's the kind of guy I could leave lightly. I've had feelings for him since I was in middle school."

"You cannot have sex with another guy while you have feelings for Gideon."

She stared at the turkey and mayo. It was very normal. This conversation wasn't. "I'm going to have to. Because I'm going to have feelings for Gideon for the rest of my life. I just have always had them. And when I saw him standing there, I tried to pretend that I didn't. And he was so different, he is so different. What the years have done to him is so cruel, and I still think he's so beautiful. And he is so kind to me. He's just always listened. That doesn't equal attraction. I think I'm like a sister to him. And on top of that, Lydia is my best friend."

She wished she could stuff those words back in. Not just so she could go back and have her sister not hear them, but so she wouldn't have to sit there with them, either. They were too real. Too desperately true.

"Do you think Lydia would be mad?" Quinn asked.

She took another bite of her sandwich.

"No," she said, considering. "But honestly, it's just so far-fetched I can't even wrap my head around what Lydia might or might not be. Anyway," Rory continued. "I just wanted to ask some questions. Or maybe I just wanted to feel like I wasn't by myself. Crazy. Because I feel very alone. You're all with somebody, except Fia. But I don't get the feeling that Fia is unaware of the realities of what happens between men and women."

"No," said Quinn. "I don't think so. I have a feeling

that Fia isn't all that naive. But maybe that's not the best thing."

Rory nodded because she did feel like that was a deep truth.

"Do you ever wonder if she and Landry didn't actually have a big breakup?" Quinn asked.

Rory frowned. "Oh. I… No, I hadn't."

"I didn't, until recently. Until Levi. I thought that her hostility with Landry could only mean one thing. And now I'm not so sure. Because it doesn't seem like a fun tension."

"I figured he broke her heart."

"It just seems like more than that to me. I figured they had sex in high school. Or didn't. And they wanted it but it…seems way deeper than that."

She didn't know what to do now that this new thought had been introduced to her. Because she had to admit, it made her wonder.

But how could Fia keep that entirely to herself? The rest of them couldn't keep any secrets.

She kept having to reevaluate things. Recast them. And it was making her wonder if her take on the world and herself was entirely accurate. Oh, she knew that her feelings were real enough. They always had been.

But she had to wonder if she put a little bit too much stock in the opinions of others.

Even while thinking she didn't.

"Just promise me something, Rory," said Quinn, as Rory finished her sandwich.

"What's that?"

"Promise me that you're not going to have sex just to have sex. Because I just feel like you're rushing to something because you're afraid of what you actually want."

"I'm fine," she said.

She shoved the last bite of sandwich in her mouth and stood up, hugging her sister. "You don't need to worry about me. If I have sex with the wrong guy, I'll get over it."

"Yeah, all right. But is there a reason you're planning to?"

"Maybe I want something bigger than passion. I need to prove something to myself."

"Okay, Rory. I can appreciate that."

"Anyway, my list only says *kiss*. So don't worry. I can get a kiss and still make my goal."

"There really is a list?" Quinn asked.

"Maybe."

"Oh, Rory. You are a delightful little weirdo."

The way Quinn said that made her feel not quite so bad. Made her feel like perhaps it was all okay. To be weird. She'd had the epiphany the other day that she was good with small groups.

But she would really like to be good with a crowd.

Do you? Or is it just how you imagine it would feel to be good with a crowd?

Well. Whatever.

She drove home, thinking about passion, and Jenga towers, and Gideon Payne's thighs.

Somewhere in there, she felt like she could find the truth. She just wasn't quite sure of all the particulars.

CHAPTER FOURTEEN

HE NEEDED A break from Rory. Some time to get his head on straight, and he wasn't going to get it. Between the rope-climbing training and the upcoming hike, his world was pretty Rory-centric at the moment.

And you're solving that by...taking her shopping?

Okay. Maybe he needed a break, but he was pretty consciously not taking one.

They were heading out to Mapleton to go to the outdoor store so they could find everything they needed.

That in and of itself would be kind of a trip.

She had her date tomorrow night. Fine.

Then the day after that they would go on the hike, and that would probably keep her from hooking up with that guy.

Gideon didn't like the look of him.

If Rory had never been on a date before...

Well, that didn't mean anything much about her sexual experience, he supposed.

She had to be twenty-seven. The idea that she might not have been with anybody seemed pretty ludicrous.

He got out of the car and walked up to the front door. Back when he'd picked her up from school, he never got inside. She had raced out the minute he pulled in, and that had been it. They'd driven away for school. But he figured since this wasn't that kind of thing now, he might go to the door.

His footsteps seemed a little bit too heavy on the front steps. He felt like he was surrounded by metaphors he didn't want to explore. So he didn't. He just knocked on the door.

Fia answered. She was pretty; he'd noticed that the other day. Hell, he'd noticed it back then.

They were about the same age, and he'd seen her around town often enough. She was maybe a year behind in school but hadn't gone to the high school in Mapleton.

"Hi, Gideon," she said. "More time with Rory today?"

This must be what it was like to pick a girl up for a date and be confronted by an overprotective father.

He didn't know because every father he'd ever dealt with had been thrilled to have him picking up their daughter.

Fia was clearly *suspicious*.

"Yeah. I'm taking her on a hike up to Grizzly Peak. So we're going to get outfitted."

"I heard that." She was looking at him and there was a glint in her eye that was slightly feral. "It's an overnight hike."

"It is. This is what I'm planning on doing for my business. So we're getting some practice in. Same kind of thing we've been doing out at the ranch this past week."

Her eyes went narrow. "I just want to know what your intentions are with my sister."

He felt like a bomb had detonated in his stomach—and he didn't use that metaphor lightly, because he knew what it felt like when a bomb detonated.

"I intend to take her on a hike."

And that was the truth. His intentions were not, nor would they be, to do anything about the burning attraction in his gut. Because that was a bad idea. A very bad idea.

"Okay. Rory is very *sweet*. And I feel protective of her. Because she has gotten this far without…without… Just please don't hurt my sister."

He thought of Rory's beautiful freckled face. Her upturned nose and wide hazel eyes. That glorious red hair that made his fingers itch to touch it.

That smile that felt like it was for him.

The him he was now.

"I would never do anything to hurt anybody on purpose. But I am kind of a mess. The thing is, though, I know that. So. You can rest assured in that."

"*Rest* is a strong word," she said.

"Whatever helps you," he said.

"Fia," came a very stern-sounding voice that he wouldn't normally have associated with Rory.

"What?" Fia asked.

"Don't be mean."

"I'm not mean," said Fia.

"Why don't you go pick a fight with Landry?"

Fia looked flustered, and then stepped away, and Rory went past her. "I'm ready."

"All right."

"I promise to have her back by dark," he said, trying to give Fia a convincing smile.

Instead she just looked exasperated.

"What was that?" Rory asked.

"I was being charming," he said.

"Yeah, I should've warned you. My sister doesn't find men all that charming."

"Who's Landry?"

"Landry King? He's the son of one of the big families. They have some kind of history, but none of us know exactly what it is."

"How can you keep secrets like that in a place this size?"

"Well, my sister is intimidating. So anyone who knows anything isn't going to spill. She's also very private. Fia has had to carry a lot. Since my parents left, she had to finish raising us. I don't think it was the most comfortable thing on earth. She's amazing. But it's too much for one person. She shouldn't have had to do all of that."

"Yeah. That's not fair."

"It's not."

"I had such good parents," he said when they got into his truck.

"I'm sorry about your dad," she said. "Your parents really were wonderful. Are wonderful."

"I was off doing my own thing. Chasing glory. And… I dunno. Sometimes I regret that. But I was away."

"I think people make regrets out of anything they can when they lose somebody."

He stared at her. "What gives you that idea?"

"I don't know. All I feel is a wall of regret over things I didn't do. I feel like Fia regrets Landry. Something she did do. I just think that whether you do the thing or you don't, whether you were here or you weren't, you find ways to second-guess your life. Especially when you find yourself unhappy with where you're at."

"That's almost profound," he said.

"Maybe it's being in the front seat of a car with you. Reminds me of when I used to give my unsolicited opinion all the time."

"Yeah, you did do that."

He pulled out of the driveway and headed down the dirt road that would take them to the main highway.

"It was the only place I ever did that. Other than with your sister. I guess in some ways you two are the only people I've ever really said everything to."

"Why me?" It suddenly seemed essential to know that. Why she had found it easy to talk to him. Why him? Because she had never idolized him. Not like everybody else. She had never treated him like he was more than human. So what was it about him that made her want to talk to him? Because maybe that thing was still in him. Because none of the hero stuff was. None of the legend stuff was. Maybe there was something he could grab onto.

"I just liked you," she said, looking out the window.

"Because I was great at football?"

"I don't care about football."

"Oh. Was it the track, then?"

"No."

"Then what?"

He looked at her, and at the same time she turned to face him. "It might've been your blue eyes. I don't know if anyone has ever told you this before, but they're very…" She cleared her throat. "Well, they're very blue. That was in the poem, Gideon, you really shouldn't be surprised."

That felt like a sucker punch, and for the life of him, he couldn't say why. A lot of women commented on the color of his eyes. Or they used to. Now it was *serial-*

killer vibes, Daddy. But at the end of the day, being found handsome initially wasn't foreign to him. Rory thinking his eyes were very blue—well, that was something else.

He supposed his eyes were *still* blue. So maybe that was it. He did still have that.

They drove on in silence for a while.

"Where are your mom and dad now?" Gideon asked her.

"Didn't Lydia ever mention it?"

"No."

"They had a hideous divorce. My dad was having an affair. And he left under a cloud of smoke. My mom hung on for another three years, and then she left, too. She went to Hawaii. She's living her best life over there, enjoying the sunshine in the ocean. I went to visit her once. It's beautiful. I get why she's there. She lives in this little community with a bunch of other retired people and they do art and go swimming in the ocean every day, and I didn't ask questions about the different rotation of people that I saw leaving her house early in the morning in the same clothes they came in the night before."

"Sounds like she's having the time of her life."

"And why not? As much as his leaving affected me, as much as it made me feel like I couldn't trust anything, I know that it was worse for her. He was her husband. The father of her kids. She gave so much to him, and to this place. She wasn't a Sullivan by blood. She had moved here from California, and she missed the ocean. The warm ocean, not the Oregon coast. I think she felt like she devoted her life and gave up so much, and then he just ended up leaving. Treating it all so cheaply. She doesn't like coming back. I can't blame her."

"No. Of course not. But it must've been hard to have somebody you love leave like that."

"I admire it, too. It's the thing that I wasn't able to do. I tried. I failed. I understand that you regret not being here with your dad. But I don't think you can afford to put your dreams on hold for anybody. My parents decided to leave. At least I know I didn't stay because of them, only to have them go."

"He was proud of me. That's what Lydia says. He was never sorry I wasn't there because he believed in what I was out doing."

"Of course. That's really… I get it. I get it."

"Doesn't mean I don't question it."

"There's always a question to ask, but sometimes it's just endless. I ask all the time what would've happened if I'd stayed at school, but I can't get an answer to that. There is no answer to that. I can't know. I'm just here now, trying to make a different choice. That's why I'm trying to do this. So that I don't have any more what-ifs. But I'll probably still find more."

"Yeah. Well. I want to believe in fate. Because that means it was predestined or something for me to avoid dying in that bomb blast, but not to avoid the injuries that I got. What happened after."

"I don't know, can't it be somewhere in between? Maybe you're here for a reason. Maybe all that other stuff is just evil. Maybe it wasn't supposed to happen, but you're still here for a reason. Can't it be both?"

He laughed, his chest feeling full of broken glass, but somehow he felt lighter, too. Like he'd finally said some things he needed to say. Even if there was no real answer to it. "Well, since no one has answers to anything that makes any more sense to me, I don't see why it can't be both."

"I don't know what I'm supposed to be doing. I'm just guessing. But I have to believe there's something out there for me. In Boston, I guess."

"Yeah. I guess so. Hey. My ex-wife found another thing she was meant for."

"You mentioned that. That she's getting married."

He nodded. He had forgotten he'd said that to her. Which worried him a little. He didn't think he had too many memory problems, but he would've thought he'd remember telling her that. So maybe he had more than he thought. That was the issue with memory problems. It was hard to know if you had them because if you had no close relationships, there was no one around to tell you what you forgot.

"Yeah. I guess she figured she could get back on track with a husband who could still be the thing she needed."

"That's not marriage."

"Have you been married, Rory?"

"No. As you know, I have never even been on a date."

"Then how do you know what marriage is?"

"I dunno, but I think it has to be more than somebody existing to be the fulfillment of your fantasy. It has to be a little bit more about reality." She looked stricken for a second, and then looked away. "Sorry. I don't know what I'm talking about."

But those words stuck with him. Because hadn't he always been a fantasy? For himself, for other people. The idea of him so much more compelling than who he actually was. He has lived in that space for a long time. It was just that he wasn't able to do it anymore. And that was some shit.

They switched to lighter conversation, her current favorite book series about witches in a small town, and it reminded him so much of the past. So much of a simpler time in life. He wasn't a reader, he was never going to be no matter how many times she recommended a book to him, but it didn't matter. He just liked to hear her talk about it. He liked her enthusiasm for something he didn't care about. That he didn't relate to. He liked that she was a little bit mystifying.

When they pulled into the outdoor store parking lot, he got out his list and handed it to her. "All right. You can be the cruise director."

"That sounds like a lot of work."

"I think you're up to the task."

"I can pay for—"

"No. I'm paying. I'm setting up an outdoor excursion business, so I ought to foot the bill because I can use the equipment. And I can use the experience. So even if it's for you personally, let me buy it."

"I don't want to—"

"I'm not strapped, I promise. I got a decent amount of money from the US government and permanent disability. Not that it's a whole lot, but the ranch will make money, and I also am about to come into some proceeds from the sale of my house. So it's all good."

They walked inside and he grabbed the cart. There were animal mounts everywhere. A bear standing up in the entryway, elk and deer with big racks, and a few little black bears that looked like they'd have only been a threat to a garbage can. It was funny, because that kind of thing had given Cassidy the willies, but it was white noise to him. Every outdoor store in the state of Oregon had much the same look. It was white noise to Rory, too.

She barely even blinked when she went over to a section that had camping lanterns and a taxidermic squirrel was sitting on top of the shelf, staring at them both. Said squirrel had a tiny lantern in its hand.

They got sleeping bags, a tent and all kinds of things that they could carry in backpacks.

Some cooking utensils and some rations.

"I'm having PTSD," said Rory. And then she pulled a face. "I'm sorry. That was distasteful."

"I think it's kind of valid to use that in context with something you experienced in high school."

"No. It was insensitive. I'm sorry."

"It might've been offensive to some people, Rory, but not to me. Believe me, I'm not so protective of that label or experience that it bothers me."

"Okay," she said slowly.

"Don't worry." She was very clearly worried. "It's more important to me that you talk to me like a normal person than start being all careful."

A lot of people talked to him like that. Careful like that.

Cassidy had been an interesting mix. She was often very careful, and then it had dissolved. And there had been careful, careful, *careful*, cruel. And once she had gotten cruel, she'd gone all in. He understood. She'd been trying to find something to reach him. To change him. He did get that. He just didn't want to think about it anymore, so he didn't.

They finished walking through the store and checked out, and if the price tag made his eyes water a little bit, he did a decent job not showing it. At least there was one benefit to his emotions being buried. He could keep the heavier ones under wraps if need be.

They walked out of the store laden with bags. He took the ones Rory was holding, and their fingers brushed. Her eyes widened just a fraction and met his.

And he felt like everything slowed. That happened to him sometimes. Usually because of something bad. But this wasn't bad.

The feeling lodged in his chest—it wasn't panic.

It was something sweet and warm. Something he wanted to save. Something he wanted to hang on to.

She wasn't looking at him like he was a hero. She was just looking at him.

She wasn't afraid. She wasn't starstruck.

Her hands were like silk.

How long had it been since he touched anything soft? Everything had been hard these last few years. Absolutely everything.

And Fia knew that. *It's why she warned you off. Because if all you want is to rest your head on someone soft for a while, it cannot be with Rory Sullivan.*

Yeah. He knew that.

"So. The date is Friday."

Rory blinked. "The date… Oh, yes. And then Saturday we'll head out on the trip."

"I hope you have a good time, Rory."

"I don't know what I'm going to do if you're not there to shout *termite* at me."

"I never had to say it at Smokey's."

"No. You didn't."

"You'll be fine."

"I hope so."

"Would you mind… Would you mind stopping at this

boutique down at the end of the street? I don't need you to go with me, I just…"

"I'll go with you."

Her eyes looked vaguely pleading then.

"Oh, you meant you didn't want me to go with you."

"No," she said. "No. Yes. I don't… I'm a little embarrassed. But I was borrowing Fia's dress the other night, and I don't want to do that this time. I want to have something of my own to wear."

"Sure," he said. "That's completely fair."

"If you want to, you can tell me if it's good. You're a man."

"Yeah," he said, his tone flat. "I am."

"I have terrible fashion sense."

He looked at the loose, flowing dress she was wearing. He would never have called her fashion sense terrible.

She looked like a little relic, maybe, but he thought it was pretty.

"All right, let's go. You don't need to be embarrassed."

"I can't help it. I'm probably going to be."

"I mean, I can't stop you from being embarrassed if you want to be."

"I'm always embarrassed."

They drove down to the end of the street, past all the little shops and restaurants, and through the town's one traffic light.

They pulled over at the curb, and Rory scampered out of the truck.

He followed her in but hung back by the door while she bit her lip and looked around at all the different clothes.

"Can I help?" A woman was working behind the counter who looked a few years younger than Rory.

"Yes please," said Rory.

That was how Rory found herself in a dressing room with an endless array of dresses being thrust her way.

Gideon stayed in his position.

And that was when the torture started.

She came out in a tight black velvet dress that made the heat in his blood something more pronounced and harder to deny.

Then there was something light and wispy that he was sure he could see the silhouette of her legs through.

She tried on a green dress that skimmed her curves loosely but looked elegant.

He was basic, though, so he liked that black velvet one that hugged her curves.

He had never been a man with a particular type. He liked women.

Appreciated softer, more dramatic curves, and a muscular, athletic frame. Enjoyed pint-sized bottle rockets and tall Amazons.

Rory's curves were compact but lovely. She was short, but something about her proportions made her legs look long.

She even had freckles on her shoulders, and he found that sexier than he had a right to.

"She'll take them all," he said.

"Gideon," she said. "You can't do that."

"If your boyfriend wants to pay, let him," said the woman.

"Thanks," he said, and the lady treated him to a little bit of open, frank admiration.

There. He was getting better responses from people all the time.

Rory looked scowly about it, but he took the dresses from her and took them up to pay.

Unlike the camping equipment, he didn't mind the price tag.

Because Rory looked so—

She was beautiful. Like a window into something new and fresh. She wasn't a window into something he'd had before, something he ached to reclaim.

She was like a promise of springtime.

And she was going to be wearing these for another man.

Well. He lost himself there for a second.

He paid, and the dresses were folded up in tissue paper and put into an elegant paper bag.

Rory took hold of the handles and carried the bag out in front of her as they walked back to the truck.

"You didn't have to do that."

"They all looked great on you."

"Thank you," she said. "But…"

"But what?"

"It's just too much."

"Why? Why shouldn't somebody do something nice for you?"

"Why, though? Why are you doing it?"

"What do you mean why?"

"Because unless we were related, or you were my best friend, no one has ever done anything nice for me for nothing. They'd just lure me into a closet so they can trick me into thinking they were going to kiss me, and then pour beer on me."

He stopped in the middle of the sidewalk. "You have to tell me what that means."

She sighed heavily, and stared at a point just past him.

"When I was at college, there was a guy, and I was at a party. And he said that he wanted to make out. And I wanted to make out with him. Even though I was afraid. And I agreed to go into the closet and wait for him. He left me in there alone for almost an hour. And when I came out, there were guys waiting outside and they poured cups of beer on me. And everybody laughed."

"What?" He stared at her, completely unable to believe that was true. What asshole would do something like that? What a… What a fucking idiot.

Rory had been waiting there to kiss him, and he…

It was unfathomable to him.

"I can't even believe that," he said.

"Well, unfortunately, it's true. And it happened. It's just… It's not the first time that I've experienced bullying like that, and I'm sorry, it's just hard for me to believe sometimes that somebody is just being nice."

He took a step toward her, and he felt something feral and fierce rise up inside him. "Rory, if I said I was going to kiss you, I would fucking kiss you. And if I ever run into the bastard who did that to you, I'd kill him."

He felt like he'd said too much. Given away too much. Been too much of the dark thing inside him.

But he hadn't been able to help it.

She looked stunned. Terrified.

Great.

He took a step back. "I'm sorry."

"It's okay."

The entire ride home was silent.

CHAPTER FIFTEEN

"DID YOU DECIDE which dress you're going to wear tonight?"

Rory took a deep breath and tried to squash the butterflies in her stomach.

She was staring up at the rope. Because today was the day she was going to attempt to climb. Which felt like a metaphor, because she had her date tonight.

She and Gideon had been working at this. At the climbing thing. And then yesterday there had been the shopping trip and...

If I said I was going to kiss you...

She was really hoping that she was going to make it to the top. Because it felt somehow inextricably tied to the date.

To the weekend camping trip.

But most of all the date, and she had to stop thinking about what Gideon had said.

There were only just over three weeks left until she went to Boston. She had to get this kiss. She had to climb this rope. She had to climb that mountain. Dammit, there was so much climbing. "I will probably wear the black one," she said, stretching her arms out. "Because it's sexy."

The minute she said that she felt embarrassed heat rising in her cheeks.

"It is that," he said.

Their eyes clashed.

Telling him about the whole thing with the frat boys had been…a moment.

The way that he'd said that to her… The way…

She felt undone by it. That husky promise in his voice. That maybe wasn't a promise. And combined with what Quinn had said to her yesterday, she was just feeling a bit feeble.

Because she had a date tonight with a man she remembered only as an antagonist, who was pleasant enough to look at, but who hadn't lit her up inside by any stretch of the imagination when they had seen each other again last week.

Not like Gideon.

And sometimes she felt like they were hurtling toward something impossible to ignore. And then she thought… She was a grade A coward. She could ignore whatever she wanted. She was great at ignoring things. It was like one of the things she was best at. Along with quitting. Along with avoiding.

"Well, thank you," she said, her throat scratchy.

"The other two are very pretty. The green is nice. But it looks more like you're going on a picnic with your sisters."

"Yes. A picnic-sister dress. I think I'll avoid that since I want a guy to jump my bones."

The way that he looked at her was fierce. "Is that right?"

She hadn't gotten this far with him by holding back, and she felt driven by something now. By the impending date. By what Gideon had said to her. By the restless need she felt whenever she looked at him. By Quinn's warning. By the impossibility of it all.

"I do. Yeah, I mean that. I would like that. Who doesn't want that? Everybody wants sex. It is a fundamental truth of humanity. People do crazy things to get sex. Empires have been destroyed for sex. Helen of Troy. The face that launched a thousand ships."

"I didn't realize that I had signed up for the world's weirdest sex talk. But yeah. Admittedly, people are notoriously poor decision-makers when it comes to sex, but I didn't take you for one."

"I went to high school with him. Maybe it's a long-held fantasy of mine."

"Is it?" he asked.

"Maybe," she said.

"Just climb the rope, Rory."

She let out a long, slow sigh.

Nothing bad was going to happen to her. Now, on that climb they were taking tomorrow, something might happen. They had to hike on an extremely narrow path. And she could fall to her death. She had pretty much gone over that a hundred times.

So, that was a very real possibility. For the rope, though, the odds were she wasn't going to get up high enough to fall and hurt herself. So it wasn't harming herself that she had to be concerned about. It was just humiliation. And what was a little humiliation in front of Gideon?

"You won't think less of me if I fail?"

She hadn't realized she'd said it out loud until his face shifted.

"There is no failure here. I have trained men who were already at a certain level of physical conditioning to do this kind of thing. I'm good at it. But you admittedly don't have rope-climbing experience. If you're not able to get to the top, it's not a failure. It just shows where you are right now. And if you want to keep working at it, you could. But there's no failing. You worked really hard to get where you are, and wherever you are today is just a progress report. Join a gym when you get to Boston, keep going till you're happy with where you're at. This is the problem. You know your own strengths, and you know what you really want. Rory, I think you must've read two hundred books that year that I drove you to school."

"Two hundred and five."

"I bet you some of those people that could whip up that rope in gym didn't read *one*. Count me in that camp. Everybody has their different strengths. And they have to work at other things. I've read more in the last couple of years than I ever have. Mostly nonfiction, but I discovered something that I enjoyed. I'm never going to be as fast as you, or it might take a few more years of practice, and maybe I will be. But it's not inherently better or worse. It's just everybody has those natural inclinations, and you can build them as you want. And no, I wouldn't think less of you if you failed. But you *can't* fail today. Just showing up was already a success."

"Why aren't you a motivational speaker?" She was only kind of kidding.

"Because I've been through a lot of things that are not particularly motivational."

"But you are standing here," she said, not having any idea what he meant, but knowing it didn't matter. Because he was an inspiration all the same.

"Yeah, but I *crawled* over. Across broken glass. So. People don't really like to hear that, or watch you keep on picking glass out of your skin." She was about to say something to that, when he regrouped and changed tone. "Come on. Up the rope."

She looked up, and she grabbed hold of the rope.

She remembered what he had told her, what he had shown her. He used his feet to help, and he said that she would probably need that. Because her lower body would likely naturally be stronger than her upper body.

And so she began to go. Climbing, pulling up with her arms and following up with a scooch from her legs.

Up, and up. Her shoulders were screaming. A week of lifting tiny weights was hardly enough to prepare her to haul her whole ass up a rope.

Thank God it was kind of a skinny ass because it wasn't that heavy to lift.

Halfway, she thought she was going to throw up. Or simply let go.

She felt herself beginning to slip. "You can let go," he said. "I've got you."

And she did.

But it didn't feel like quitting. It felt like something else. Like being okay with a limit. Accepting where she was at.

And knowing that someone would be there for her no matter what.

That he wasn't waiting to humiliate her. To hurt her, to step away, to pour beer on her.

She let go, and she trusted him.

And she landed right in his arms.

HIS HEART WAS beating fast.

He had been a little bit worried about catching her.

Only because he knew it was so critical.

Not just for him—for her.

There was something healing about this coaching he'd been doing with her the last week. But it was more than that.

He could feel himself stitching a bond between him and Rory with golden thread, and in some regards it freaked him the hell out.

Because it just couldn't happen.

But he was holding her now, and he had caught her. And that made him feel like she might be his.

She was soft. Her hair a reddish gold halo in the sunlight.

"Rory," he said, his voice rough. "You did good."

She looked up at him with wide, searching eyes.

"Did I?"

"Yeah," he said.

He touched her cheek, and without thinking drew his thumb down to her lower lip and traced it. She closed her eyes.

"Rory," he said, her name a whisper.

Then her eyes snapped open, and she wiggled out of his hold.

"I've got that date. Tonight. And now I have sore shoulders."

"Did you need your shoulders?"

"I don't really know. I don't know. Because I haven't been on a date. You know. Ever. So, maybe I will need my shoulders. Maybe."

"I hope that you check off *climb the rope* on your list."

"I didn't climb it. I let go."

"You climbed it. You tried. You gave it everything, and you let go when it was safe."

But he didn't feel safe. He felt fucking wasted.

Torn apart.

He had caught her. And that made him want to roar.
Made him want to growl in victory. Because he'd done
it. What he needed to. He'd been there.

But it wasn't a big deal. It wasn't something to feel
triumphant about.

He was still the man who had shattered under pres-
sure. Who had destroyed his own marriage.

A disaster. It had been said.

A selfish bastard. That had also been said.

*You couldn't keep it together for me? Not even for
me? You aren't the man I married.*

And he'd been selfish yesterday, watching her try on
dresses. Saying what he'd said to her.

Catching her. Holding her.

He took a breath and watched Rory as she shook
her arms out.

"I hope you get what you want out of it," he said.
"The date, I mean."

It would be better if she did. Better she did hook up
with that guy. If she got exactly what she was looking for.

Because he had to stop this.

"Well, I'll let you know how it goes tomorrow when
we go on the hike."

"Great. I can't wait to hear about it."

"I can't wait to tell you."

She turned away from him, and he felt like something inside him had torn in half. He couldn't explain
it. Didn't want to.

But he did find it all kinds of inconvenient that he was
suddenly having feelings that he hadn't had for years,
with a woman whose heart he simply couldn't risk.

CHAPTER SIXTEEN

RORY DECIDED ON the green dress for her date. Because the black one just felt too sexy in the end, and she didn't want to lead with sexy. She couldn't explain that. Especially not after what she had sort of thought she wanted from this whole thing.

But the last two days had thrown her off-kilter. The whole thing with Gideon was a knot she was having difficulty untangling.

I would fucking kiss you.

Did he want to kiss her?

The heat in his eyes had been undeniable, but what did she know about heat? She'd been honest in what she'd said to him. No one had ever been nice to her just for the sake of it outside of her family or best friend.

But he was being nice. And then he'd gone and said that and it had been like someone had flipped the light switch on inside her, and she had seen all these things lit up clearly.

Kissing and sex and desire.

When she'd had a crush on Gideon, she'd been a kid. Her crush had not been about sex. It hadn't even been about a kiss.

She just thought he was beautiful. She just wanted to marry him, and at thirteen that had been divorced entirely from the physical—at least it had been for her.

Now it was all rattling around inside her, and she was having difficulty sorting her thoughts out.

She and Mike were meeting in Mapleton at Jack's Grill because she had just thought that committing to driving that far with a guy she had only shared a very brief conversation with was not the best idea.

And she just wanted to have her own car. Just in case.

She had trust issues. She came by them honestly.

Fia gave her the whole be-careful speech, and she waved her off as she went down to the car, and started another drive to Mapleton. It felt like too many back-to-back.

But driving with Gideon had been different than driving by herself, and while she was on the road alone, she had no choice but to replay every interaction she had had with him since yesterday.

They were going on that camping trip tomorrow.

She was obsessing about that. About him. And she didn't stop, even as she pulled into the parking lot at the restaurant.

She got out and walked up toward the front, where she saw Mike standing at the end of the sidewalk. "Hi," she said.

"Hi," he responded.

He leaned in and kissed her on the cheek.

It was warm because his skin was warm, but not for any other reason. When Gideon's fingers had touched hers, it had been like a lightning bolt had gone off through her body.

This was just regular old ninety-eight point six meeting skin of the same temperature.

There was nothing deeper. Nothing that affected her beyond that simple contact.

It was all very weird.

She realized it was vaguely gross to have somebody's mouth on your skin when they didn't light you up inside.

If I said I was going to kiss you...

I would fucking kiss you.

"I thought I might get a hamburger. I mean, they look like they're pretty good hamburgers. I checked the menu online."

Wow. Way to convince the guy she wasn't a weirdo.

"Well. I didn't look."

Check the menu online. How could anyone live with themselves going to a restaurant when they didn't know what they would find? Maybe that was anxiety. But honestly, she just thought it was sensible.

"Well, what else did you think looked good?" he said, seeming to recover from the awkwardness of her introduction.

"The flatbread. The fried cauliflower as an appetizer. I like sweet potato fries."

"Great."

He didn't sound like he thought it was great. He sounded a bit bored, actually.

They walked into the restaurant and were seated by their host. "So, real estate."

"Yeah," he said.

"How did you get into that?"

He started talking in way too much detail for her to ever retain any of the information, and honestly she was never going to care.

It was funny how she and Gideon could talk about anything and she felt like she cared a lot.

"And you're moving to Boston?" he asked.

"Yeah," she said.

It was weird how distant that felt now. And it was closer. It was just that all of these things with Gideon had been looming large in her mind. This mission to become some sort of legend.

It somehow seemed a little bit smaller. Which was silly. Because it was the reason she was doing all this.

"I'm going to be building manager. In the north end. It's this really beautiful historic place, and I am just so excited for a fresh start."

"Yeah."

About that time the check came.

"You're just looking for something casual," he said.

"Yeah. Casual."

Except she knew she wasn't looking for anything. Not with him.

He walked her out to her car, and when she got to the driver's side, she saw the way that he was standing. Looking at her. Expectantly.

Then he started to lean in. And without thinking, she took a step back.

"I had a great time," she said.

"Me, too. Do you want to... You can come back to my place."

"I'm very religious," she said. "And it's important to me that I guard my heart. In this season. And my... My *chastity*. So. I shouldn't. I enjoyed our courtship. Tonight." Everything that came out of her mouth sounded stilted and ridiculous, but she was panicking. And it seemed like maybe the nicest way to let him down. What could he say if it was against her religious convictions to go back with him? It wasn't. And she felt a little bad about that. A little bit like a lightning bolt might hit her. But surely God would understand. She needed to try and extricate herself without hurting his feelings. Or making him mad.

"I...didn't get the impression that you were?"

"I had a conversion experience. Maybe I'll tell you about it sometime."

"I'm good," he said.

He took a physical step back.

"Well. Good luck selling houses. I probably won't see you before I go to Boston."

She got in her car quickly, and pulled out of the parking lot feeling like an absolute idiot.

What the hell was that all about? What the hell had she done?

It was just that she couldn't kiss him. Not for the sake of it. She wasn't going to be able to have sex with him if she couldn't even kiss him.

She had been thinking of those things as something to get over. As something she needed to accomplish. As markers that she was a coward.

A quitter.

But it wasn't any better to do something just to check it off. Just to get back at people. That didn't make her free. That didn't make her anything but that same scared girl doing things because of the bullies in her life. Who were still by extension controlling her.

She hadn't even brought any of that out. She hadn't even taken this opportunity to harm or embarrass him.

She just couldn't care. Right now it was so hard to care because she was spending time with Gideon. Because he was taking her camping tomorrow. So what did any of that matter?

Yeah, Mike and so many of the others had been hideously mean.

Mike had moved on and changed more or less, because while he was a little bit of an opportunist who had been hoping for easy sex, he hadn't been rude or insistent, and at no point had he been mean.

She was moving to Boston. And she was friends with Gideon. They were friends. Except…

If I said I was going to kiss you…

Right. Well. It didn't really matter. What mattered was the future.

And that she learned something.

Maybe Gideon was right.

She was looking for a parade when the big change needed to happen inside her.

She was looking for a parade when it didn't matter. What mattered was what she wanted.

An image of Gideon swam before her.

She swallowed hard.

Tomorrow they were climbing a mountain.

So who knew what else she might find the courage to do?

That almost scared her.

She was scaring herself.

She laughed. In the emptiness of her car, she laughed.

Her own audacity was a little bit disconcerting. And that might be a good thing.

Maybe that was what it was all about.

If she could terrify herself and show up anyway, if she could throw caution to the wind and see where it blew her, maybe that was what might make her truly legendary. To herself.

And maybe that was all that mattered.

CHAPTER SEVENTEEN

HE WAS EXPECTING her bright and early, so when she showed up with her giant backpack already on, and a grim, determined expression, he wasn't surprised, but he was a little bit amused by the intensity.

"How was the date?" he asked while he began to assemble his own pack to put in the truck.

"It was fine," she said.

"Yeah?"

"Yeah," she said. "Just fine."

"Check anything off your list?"

"I don't know that we're close enough to have automatic list disclosure occurring."

"Weird. I thought we were. Considering I bought your dress for the event."

"I didn't ask you to."

"Which one did you wear?"

"Why? The green one."

That made him want to smile. Because the green one was pretty, but not the one he would've picked when he thought she was trying to signal she wanted to be taken to bed.

"Good choice."

"I don't think you mean that."

"What do you care what I mean?" he asked.

"You're so rude."

"Yeah, I know." He lifted his backpack up off the table and gestured toward the door. "That's kind of why I needed the flirting coaching. The safe word."

"Snowy plover."

"I'm not being mean," he said.

He marched her out the door and hefted his pack into the bed of the truck. Then he went up to her and without thinking unclipped the belt from around her waist.

His hand skimmed that spot just beneath her rib cage.

He was suddenly focused on that spot, there beneath her breasts.

His stomach tightened, his blood getting just a little hotter.

Then he grabbed the top of the backpack and pulled it off, putting it in the back.

"All right. Get in."

He knew he was being a little abrupt now.

She didn't respond to that, though. Instead she went around to the other side and got in.

"Here we go. Climbing the damned mountain."

"Climbing the damned mountain," she reiterated.

"But you didn't kiss him."

She looked at him, eyes narrow. "How do you know that?"

"Because you didn't wear the black dress. You wear the black dress if you want something specific."

"Is that what you would wear if you wanted to hook up with them?"

"Probably."

"Fine. I realized that I didn't want to kiss him. I thought it might be nice. He was…legitimately awful to me in high school. And I wanted to do something about that. Change it into another story, I guess. But that's not wanting somebody. And I realized that I want to *want* the person that I kiss. I want that more than I want to write a good narrative. I want that more than I want to laugh at him and say now you think I'm good enough."

"That's good, Rory." His chest felt so tight he could barely breathe.

He hadn't realized how much he hadn't wanted her to kiss him.

"I kept thinking about what you said. About the parade. About how wanting a parade isn't enough. It's not... That it doesn't sustain you. Or whatever. And I get it."

"It just only gets you so far. When I didn't have the roar of the crowd, I didn't have anything left. And even worse, I realized I couldn't handle the roar of the crowd anymore. I don't have the answers. I just know which things I was holding on to didn't have the answers, either."

He felt closer now. With her. Watching her look for answers inside herself. This time with Rory had been the only time in his life he'd connected with someone, and it hadn't been about him being great.

It was different.

It wasn't a parade.

It was better.

"I think I understand that now."

"What did he do to you in middle school? You mentioned other bullying."

She shrugged. "Just normal stuff."

"I would never have known. I drove you every day. Until the diary thing, I had no idea."

It hurt. To realize that he'd been used to hurt her.

It wasn't a happy thing, or even funny.

He was the guy that drove her to school every day. And she'd had a little crush. And that had been used against her because people thought something about him that wasn't even true or fair or real.

"Oh that was just…one of the many things but that was the thing that hurt the most. Because if it was about my knees or my boobs, at least it wasn't really me. But that diary…that was me. It was why it hurt so bad. Thank God your sister is such a good person because we used to make fun of the way girls acted about you, and then I would go home and write these furtive, ridiculous things. She could have been hurt by that. She could have said I was a liar, which would've been even worse than the whole school just thinking I was sad. Or stupid. She didn't. She just understood. She said it was okay. She was so nice to me." She sucked in a sharp breath. "And then you stepped in and you told everyone to stop, and if you'd been anyone else, that would have made it worse but you were you. So they respected you and they listened to you. Maybe that's the real reason I wanted to have a parade. I just wanted… I wanted it to matter the way it did for you."

He was glad he'd done that. It was maybe the only thing he could feel a little heroic about at this point. But it still made him mad that she'd ever been treated that way.

"I don't understand how this town treated you that way. You didn't do anything to anybody. There's nothing inherently wrong with you. Just like there's nothing inherently good about me. It's bullshit. When things fell apart for me, they fell apart. When I couldn't be the best anymore, I just wanted to make it go away. I just wanted… I didn't handle myself well."

Hypocrite.

Yet, he was. He didn't want to share all that yet. All guts, no glory.

Because he already knew what it was like to have a woman look at him like he was the biggest disappointment on the planet, and he couldn't bear it if Rory Sullivan thought he was a disappointment.

Maybe that was his real problem. Maybe he was drawn to Rory because she had looked at him like he mattered. It was more than hero worship.

He was also tired, though, and he didn't want to excavate his entire soul to answer these questions. He just wanted to be with her right now.

And he wanted to keep protecting himself.

"I don't know. But whatever that thing is that you have, Gideon, I just don't. And I've known forever."

"I don't anymore, either," he said.

"Maybe we'll find it here on the mountain."

It was as good a plan as any, he supposed. The mountain might hold some answers. Or maybe it was just a rock. But either way, he was doing something.

They parked the truck at the trailhead and got their belongings together.

He helped her clip her backpack into place and then moved away quickly because he didn't need to encourage the intensity of the feelings that were pounding through him.

"All right, we ought to make it to a spot by sunset. Then we can get the camp set up and make a meal."

"Sounds good. I hope you know how to cook camp food," she said.

"I'm okay at it. We were in charge of dealing with our own rations when we were on assignment."

"Right."

They started up the trail. It was narrow and uneven, big rocks protruding up through red clay. The pines on either side towered above them, scrubby madrone trees interspersed between them, and ferns and other plants that loved the shade clinging to the forest floor beneath all that green coverage.

It was beautiful out here. He had forgotten. He had never really let himself sit in the stillness, in the silence of nature, all those years that he had lived here.

He hadn't done it in the desert; he hadn't done it in Georgia. He was so driven to be around noise.

Around people.

And then these last few years had been like being in a sensory deprivation tank. Cut off from all of it. But worse, cut off from the enjoyment of it. Because it was all there. He could've gone out and found that life again, except he didn't like it anymore. So he was just alone.

But this didn't feel like quiet isolation. It felt like peace. Walking with Rory felt like peace.

Rory stopped and picked a leaf off a branch, then twisted up and tore a piece off. Then another. "A couple of times I've seen a look on your face, and I feel like I know who the soldier is." She tore another chunk out of the leaf. "The man who went out on deployment. You were different. Different than when you left."

She let the leaf fall to the ground.

"Yeah," he said.

He had never talked about this, not to anybody.

Cassidy hadn't wanted to hear about the military, and his father-in-law had told him very seriously that one of the most important things he could do was protect his wife from the reality of what happened overseas. It was what he had done, protected his wife and his children from the gritty truth of war.

It was the job of a soldier to keep civilians separated from the horrors of the big bad world.

You had to do it most of all for your own family.

Gideon had taken that very seriously.

Rory had said something about noticing a difference. Noticing a change. No one else ever commented on it, and he wanted to know more. What she saw.

This change he'd brought back with him overseas, no matter how hard he'd tried not to.

"What did you want to know?"

"Was it different than you thought?"

"Yeah. I thought it would be like a football game. I mean I knew that it was life or death, on some level, but I didn't think that it would be that for me. You can get badly injured playing football, and I never did. I felt like I was golden. And you know, years in different combat scenarios, and it was true. I was always lucky. But I also learned some hard truths. That it wasn't because I was special. Because I watched good, special, *solid* men and women lose their lives out there. I saw death in a profound way that I never had before. And as I rose up the ranks, they were my men. And I felt responsible for every single death. I felt destroyed by it. It's not romantic. It's not about playing hero. And so many men went out there, and they were still playing Army man, you know? They laughed when they took out an enemy, but at a certain point, all I could see was that they were all boys. For the most part. Doing what they thought they had to for the thing they believed most in.

"I could never feel better anymore. And I couldn't

think of why we were there sometimes. Just killing. And being killed. And it started to wear at me."

He stopped for a moment and stared off the edge of the trail. He'd come close to this truth before, but he'd never let himself say it out loud. He'd never even let himself verbalize it in his own mind. Because it hinted at a truth that sat uncomfortably in his gut.

That he might have ended up here even if he'd never been injured.

That something had gone awry inside him before his brain injury.

That he'd started to realize the world wasn't golden, after all.

"I think I was broken before that bomb went off. I shoved all my doubts aside, and I forced myself to carry on. To keep with the mission. It was important. The most important thing. And if nothing else, I felt like I was protecting my family, because even though it was impossible for me to not humanize the people we were fighting, I did know that they presented a real threat if left unchecked. I don't know. But it wasn't a game to me, that much I can tell you. And then… That day, we were all doing a pretty routine patrol. But there were some high-ranking officials from the US who had come to visit a village. That was a dangerous situation, but we had been in it many times before. Me and a few other men decided to go offer protection. We were there without weapons, but it was routine like I said. I still had one earbud in my ear. With my music playing loud. We were keeping an eye on the horizon for insurgents. We didn't expect there to be a bomb in the middle of everyone."

He started walking again, feeling like a heavy boulder that had been sitting on his chest had shifted. The pristine surroundings were at odds with the words that were coming out of his mouth.

"It wasn't the first time I was adjacent to an explosion, or to all the damage that it could cause. Ten years in the military, five deployments, and I had been gone more often than I was home. I had seen all those things. But not that close. Not where it could've easily been me. And it was luck, fate or a divine joke. Just the noise rattles your brain around. Gives you a concussion. But there was the impact as well. I had some burns. Some physical injuries. A good friend of mine lost his arm and two legs. We were lucky. I don't know why. I still can't figure out why. I went home and I just wanted to be myself again, and I wasn't. I couldn't find *me*. I was in pain, and I couldn't make the healing go any faster. I tried… I tried to just be okay. My father-in-law was okay. After the Gulf War and… He was okay. I don't know why I couldn't fucking *be okay*."

Rory didn't say anything. Instead, she came alongside him on the trail and touched his wrist, then slowly moved her hand around so that her palm was touching his, before she wove her fingers between his own. She said nothing; she just held his hand. And they kept on walking.

It burned there. Where she was touching him. But not in a bad way. He'd been burned in a bad way. This was different.

They didn't speak. But it was like the wilderness around them had all the words they didn't have between them.

The birds were chirping, and the wind blowing through the pines made a distinct comforting sound.

It was music, and not the kind that triggered flash-backs.

And more than anything, it was an out-of-body ex-perience to have somebody simply walk with him. Not ask anything of him. Not trail behind, not run ahead. Just walk with him.

"This is the easy part," he said, talking about the trail, but felt like it could mean something more. Even though he hadn't meant to infuse it with a double mean-ing. They were holding hands. They were getting a lit-tle bit too close.

"I know. It gets pretty rough up ahead."

"Yes. It does."

"I think I can handle it," she said.

"I know you can."

He wondered if they were still talking about the trail. She was strong. Stronger maybe than she gave herself credit for. But she didn't need to be strong for him. He couldn't bear to put another woman through that. It wasn't fair. It would be the same shit he'd already been through. He already knew all the places he fell short. All the places he didn't come through when he needed to. He never wanted to do that to Rory. He'd been hon-est with Fia when he'd said that.

But he also didn't want to let go of her hand. Right now, the trail was easy. Right now, they could hold on to each other. Right now, it was okay. And that was what he would hold on to. While he held on to her.

CHAPTER EIGHTEEN

THEY KEPT ON going up the trail, and it narrowed. It got to the place where she had quit last time.

But he held her hand and pulled her up behind him.

"I'm scared," she said, stopping and hugging the wall. She looked down below at the river, so far down, craggy rocks the only landing offered if a person was to slip and lose their footing. It wasn't like it didn't happen. People fell hiking all the time. Her fear wasn't totally irrational, even if she did feel a bit like she needed to find some extra bravery, in the presence of a man like him.

"I've got you," he said.

And those were the eyes of the soldier. Not just a soldier, but the man who had been in charge of a unit. The man who had promised not to leave people behind, but who had, because bombs went off and stray bullets hit people who didn't deserve it.

Because that was the nature of things, even if it shouldn't be.

He wouldn't leave her behind. He wouldn't let her fall.

She clung to him, as they navigated the narrower parts of the trail. Him in front, and her coming up behind as she braced herself on the wall, and then would reach for his hand when she got to a wider spot.

He was calm. Measured. He was exactly the kind of man you wanted leading in a moment like this.

Steady. Certain.

She saw the hero. The substance of the real hero. Not just the moments of glory.

This was the real thing she wanted. Not a parade. She wanted this thing he had. In spite of everything, he carried on. In spite of everything, he was like a compass. Pointing north. Leading.

And when they made it past the toughest part of the trail, she couldn't help herself. She wrapped her arms around his neck and buried her face just there, at the crook between his shoulder and jaw. She rubbed her face against his skin and smelled the sweat, a scent that was uniquely his.

Tears stung her eyes, and she knew she didn't have a right to those tears. Or maybe she did. Because she had done something on her list. She had completed something she set out to do. She hadn't quit.

She had finished.

"Thank you," she whispered. She lifted her head and their eyes met. He reached up and pushed a lock of hair off her forehead, and she shivered. His hold was firm, hot. She wanted to stay pressed against him like this forever. This had nothing to do with the childhood crush.

This was about him. Right now. The man he really was.

In this moment, it was a feeling electrified by her own bravery.

What a wonderful thing.

Finally, he began to loosen the hold he had around her waist, and she stepped back from him.

"Thank you."

"Everything's fine," he said. "You could do it all along. You didn't need me."

"That isn't true. I think I would've quit without you. I would've been too afraid. But you're the kind of person you look at, and you just think it has to be okay."

"Camping spot's just up ahead," he said.

It took a while, but they reached their final destination for the day, without encountering any of the terrain that Rory was worried about. Listening to Gideon talk about his time in the desert, about the bomb, made her feel like her worries were so abstract and unrealistic in comparison.

He was a hero. He had been trying to think that a hero was somebody who didn't react when things were complicated and painful. She thought a hero was exactly who he was. Somebody who saw all the difficulties, who felt them, who recognized that there was a cost to everything. Someone who mourned those who had been in his charge.

Why would anyone want that simple kind of hero they had fashioned him into? She looked at him now, at the strength in his body as he started to unpack and assemble the tent they'd brought, folded up tightly in his pack.

She was fascinated by this man.

Yeah, she'd had a crush on the one she'd known all those years ago, but she hadn't known him. Not more than anyone else. She had fashioned him into what she needed him to be. She had talked at him, making him the object of her fantasy as a middle school girl.

She had seen him as being handsome and nice, and a great listener, because it suited her for him to be those things. She was happier now that he had poured some of his real self out to her.

Happier now that she had been able to walk with him holding his hand.

"Once I get this set up, I'll make a fire."

"Shouldn't I do that?"

"Are you trying to earn a Girl Scout badge?"

"No," she said. "I'm not. But it seems like you shouldn't do all the work yourself."

"I'm gearing up to be a trail guide," he said.

"What makes you want to do that?"

"It's something that I have the skills for. I don't have much of the know-how to be a cattle rancher, and anyway, competing with Four Corners is a dead end. You can't do it. Some people have innovative ideas and ways of doing it, but you have to be passionate about ranching for that to work out. I'm passionate about the land my family has always had, but I don't think I'm passionate enough about cows to try and compete with the massive operation you all have."

"My sister's fiancé is a rancher. Right next door to Four Corners. It's not easy. He kind of introduced us to the concept that people outside our compound don't think all that highly of us."

"Jealousy," he said. "Which again, I don't have, because I don't especially want to be a rancher. But I learned wilderness survival, and this is a good way to keep me in shape. A good way to keep me busy. Moving." He set up the tent quickly and then moved on to making a fire. This early in the season it was still allowed, but once it got overly dry, there would be no open flame out in the woods. The threat of wildfires was too real.

He looked up at her, his blue eyes clashing with hers, and she felt a spark ignite in her stomach. She had no doubt between the two of them there was enough tinder to start a whole wildfire. Something was happening. Something outside of her experience. She knew about attraction. She never experienced it like this.

He hadn't said anything or indicated that he felt the same, not really. Except... *If I said I would kiss you...*

She swallowed hard.

He got a fire going, and then reached into his backpack and took out... Sticks. And hot dogs.

"These are the survival rations?"

"Yeah. They're basic. Perfect. Hot dogs."

"I don't know about that," she said.

"Trust me. It's going to be great."

He had a package of hot dog buns that were only mildly squished, and she was surprised to find a small plastic container that had sauerkraut and ketchup packets and mustard.

She speared the hot dog on the stick and quickly put it up over the fire.

"Don't look like you enjoy that too much," he said. "I'm liable to take it personally."

It took her a second. And then she laughed. Because suddenly she realized that he was thinking of...

She blinked. "Oh, I have no desire to... That is, I'm not angling to spear... I don't..."

"Settle down there."

His voice was just so soothing that she did settle.

She felt like things were reckless between them. Even if she couldn't pinpoint how. Or why?

Maybe it was the way he held her. The way she clung to him.

Maybe it was that.

"To climbing the damned mountain," he said, holding his own hot dog stick up as if it was a glass he was raising in salute.

She lifted her own hot dog out of the fire. "Climbing the mountain."

They tapped them together, and her cheeks got hot.

"Get your mind out of the gutter, Rory."

"I didn't... You... I..."

"You're cute when you're flustered."

And then he smiled.

He was different. Relaxed. Like the hike had given them something, or maybe the walk up had been cathartic.

Telling the story of what had happened that day.

Just maybe.

They assembled their hot dogs, and both drank cans of sparkling water with them.

And then they sat there in silence, as the fire crackled. The stars above were clear and bright, and her heart felt...full.

Finally, it was time to turn in, and only then did she realize that sleeping in a tent with him was...was maybe a little bit more intimate than she had realized. In truth, she hadn't thought about sleeping arrangements. Perhaps intentionally.

She got her bedroll, complete with her sleeping bag, and he got his, as they entered the tent.

It was small. Any tent that could be carried backpacking was bound to be.

"I don't mind sleeping outside," he said.

"No," she said.

She didn't know what was going to happen. But she knew that she wouldn't be unhappy if…

They were pretty silent. The only sound was the rustle of them arranging the sleeping bags. It was dark inside the tent, but they didn't need lights.

She got into her bag, and he into his. She could hear him breathing, ragged.

And then she shifted, turning over onto her side, looking at him in the dark. He did the same. There was space between them and two separate sleeping bags. And even still she was…electrified.

She turned, and moved closer to him, closing the space between them. Then she reached out and put her hand on his chest. His hand came up and trapped hers there, and she could feel his heartbeat raging. She looked up, and he looked down at her, and she could feel his breath against her lips.

"I'm going to tell you something else," he said.

"Okay," she whispered.

"I was burned when the bomb went off. Severely. It took some surgeries and skin grafts and things like that to get me on the road to recovery. It was very painful. Burns are a pretty hideous thing."

She remembered, absurdly, a time when she had spilled boiling water on her hand, just at the fatty part between her thumb and forefinger. She'd had red scalded skin and a giant blister for weeks. She couldn't even imagine a burn that penetrated deeper than that. Couldn't imagine how painful it must be.

"And I just wanted everything to be back to the way it was. They give you pain pills. And for a few hours, you feel better. Functional, almost. By the time I got home, there were all kinds of awards and things happening, because we were considered heroes. We were given Purple Hearts for acts of bravery. And Cassidy wanted to go to everything. It was exactly what she wanted. I don't mean that in a bad way. But it was hard for her to see me so different. Without the energy that she was used to, not feeling up to it because of all the pain I was in. I had headaches on top of it. So I started taking more pills. More and more. And whatever other issues I had, whatever PTSD stuff was happening, whatever traumatic brain injury side effects I had, it was all eclipsed by the pills."

She didn't say anything. She had thought maybe he had an issue with alcohol. It hadn't occurred to her that it could be related to other substances.

"For a while, it made me better. I could do more, I could push past whatever was going on in my head as far as depression or anxiety because it wasn't me. It was like I wasn't there. I was pretty damned vacant. But that didn't matter. I could put on my dress uniform and show up. I could be the soldier that she needed me to be. I seemed unaffected, and that was what she wanted, so I kept pushing. When I realized it was becoming a problem, I tried to cut back. But that just…"

He took a sharp breath. "I would get so short-tempered. And that was when I was trying to assemble some bookshelves in our living room, and I couldn't figure out the directions. I couldn't figure the fucking directions out, and Cass was in the other room and she was on the phone, and she was just talking and talking. I just… I was so filled with fury. And I just stood up and threw the screwdriver right through the wall. Not at anyone. But that feeling of being out of control, the fury building until I couldn't take it anymore… I just went and took more pills. Because at least they made me feel the same. But you lose weight, it's obvious. You start looking like a junkie. And you are." His voice was rough, and he shifted behind her. She wanted to touch him, but she was afraid to move and break the spell. "I was a junkie. I might as well have been sticking a needle into my vein. I was close enough to that. All my life, I felt better than everybody else. And it turns out that when things are hard, I don't know what to do." The last word was tight. Like it had cost him to speak. "I needed crutches. I didn't walk through hellfire on my own. I made the flames hotter. Something happened to me that I had no control over, but I made it worse. And I need you to know that. I need you to know that's part of me."

"You're here," she said, because of all the things it was the only thing that came to her. They were the only words that she could find. "You're here, you're not dead. You're not in the gutter. You're healthy, fit. As far as I can tell, not taking pills."

"No. I've been clean and sober for two years. And I made sure to take everything away from myself. Absolutely everything. Because I didn't trust myself. Not anymore. I didn't want to give myself a new thing to lean on, so that meant getting rid of everything."

"Did you go to rehab?"

He shook his head. "No. Because I would've probably needed to do it through the military to have it paid for. And I had some issues with that. With people knowing. It's a common thing. But I never thought of myself as common. There's a lot of alcoholism in the military, but that's easier for people to ignore. There's a socially acceptable quality to problem drinking. But it's not socially acceptable to have a problem with prescription pills. That's fine. I didn't need anyone to support me. I was killing myself. Plain and simple. I bottomed out when Cassidy told me to leave."

"Why didn't she want to help you?"

He closed his eyes. "She was the woman I married. You have to understand that. She and I were both golden. Absolutely golden. She was the apple of her daddy's eye, the prom queen, the head cheerleader. She was my female counterpart in every way. Top of her class, brilliant in college. Wanted to marry a man who was going places in the military. And we went through life not recognizing that the only reason we were where we were was that we never really struggled. We didn't have to fight. We just walked easily to right where we were. And I remember clearly one day we saw a homeless veteran with a sign. Asking for help. Asking for food. He was skinny. Obviously on drugs. And she said…*it's sad how many of them can't hack it.* And I said…*I don't get it. I've been out on tour, it's shit, but you just deal with it. You get over it. You don't need to be self-indulgent.*" He laughed, hard and fractured. "That's what I thought. That I had some kind of magical inner strength they didn't have. And now I know, it's a thin line separating you from becoming your worst nightmare."

The only sound now was crickets. She didn't speak, because she knew there was more.

"The day I left she said…*you promised me that this would never be us. You became that guy holding the sign. I didn't know I married a weak man.* And I don't think she's right. Not about everything. But I married that woman. And I knew she was that woman when I married her. I was a man who matched her then. I am the one that changed. Not her. I'm the one that changed and I'm the one who had to go."

She felt his heartbeat slowing beneath her fingertips. Almost like he was relieved to have it out.

She wished she could give him advice, but the truth was she was a woman with a very basic list of things she wanted to do because she hadn't done much of anything.

The hiking trail was a triumph for her. He had been to hell and back.

"She sounds like a bitch," said Rory.

And what really shocked her was that he laughed. He tightened his hold on her hand and laughed, the deep rumble vibrating through his body.

"Well, given that I'm the one who caused all the problems, I tend to have a nicer view."

"I don't have a nice view at all," she said. "And I don't have to. She isn't my…my friend."

There was a short silence. "I appreciate that."

"Honestly. When you marry somebody, it's supposed to be through all of that," she said fiercely.

"Addicts hurt people, Rory. We lie. We're erratic. We're unpredictable. Some people want to stay and try to shepherd you through it, some don't. Neither is wrong. That's just how I feel about it. She didn't change, but sometimes she was cruel, and the truth is, I made her cruel. She didn't like that version of herself any more than she liked me, and why should she have had to keep living in that?" He cleared his throat. "Yeah, I sorted myself out. But only after she kicked me out. Only after the safety net was gone. Not everything is black-and-white. I thought marriage was forever, but I thought I was going to be a certain kind of person forever. I'm not. Even if we had fought through to me getting sober, I don't know if we would've worked. She's marrying another officer. That's never going to be me again. I'm done with that life. And it's a life she loves. I'll tell you what, I don't want to be married to somebody I'm dragging down. Making miserable. I need you to know that about me. That I'm not golden, or perfect. That when shit was hard, I folded. I need you to know that I was homeless for a while. And I flirted with the idea of sticking a needle in my arm. When it was getting too hard to get pills because I was visibly and obviously a pill seeker. I need you to know that when I say I hit rock bottom, I was really far down. Because you have a right to know if you're going to put a hand on me. I'm not the guy you wrote about in your diary."

His words were raw and bloody. Painful.

"No," she said. "You're not. I think you're better."

It was his turn to squeeze her hand tight like he was thinking he might fall off the edge of a cliff.

And she rested her head on his shoulder and held on to him like that. Until his breathing went steady. She probably could've kissed him. Here in the darkness. But it felt like an even bigger triumph that he'd *shared*.

And she could wait. Until it was right.

You're leaving. When will it ever be right?

She didn't know. She had a plan. And she was so certain of it. Her list. And now here she was at the top of the mountain, that damned mountain, with Gideon Payne.

And she felt like she just wanted to stay on the mountain forever.

Not because she was afraid of climbing back down. Just because they were here together.

CHAPTER NINETEEN

THE NEXT MORNING, he was feeling a mix of emotions over last night's admissions. He felt wrung out. Lighter in some ways. Angry in others. He scrambled up some eggs in a frying pan over the fire, in preparation for the trek back down, and when she emerged, she looked like she hadn't slept.

"Good morning," he said. He was feeling short and grumpy, and he knew it might not even actually be real. Just his stupid brain.

"Good morning."

She moved over to him, and reached out and took his hand. Then she put her hand on his cheek. Her eyes were searching as she looked at his face. And then she did something completely unexpected. She stretched up on her toes, her fingertips still pressed against his cheekbone, and kissed him.

It was hesitant. Soft. Almost featherlight, and he should've let her leave it at that. Should've let her pull away, but without even thinking, he wrapped his arm tight around her waist and pulled her body up against his. With his free hand, he gripped her chin and pressed his mouth hard to hers.

He'd said all that to her and she wanted to kiss him. The roar that went through his veins was like a triumph. Like a battle cry. He parted her lips with his tongue and tasted her. She gasped, her hands going to his shoulders as she held on to him tightly.

She wasn't pulling away.

He kept hold of her face, his other arm tight like a vice.

And he kissed her.

It had been years since he'd kissed anyone.

Years since he'd been touched.

He hadn't realized how much he missed it. How much he was starving for it.

And it felt right that it was Rory.

Even though he never would've said that if he'd been asked weeks ago.

But she wasn't a kid now.

Not even close.

She made a small noise, and it was like that sound penetrated the fog of arousal rattling around his skull.

He released his hold on her and took a step back, breathing like he had just run a marathon or climbed the damn mountain.

"Oh," she said.

"Sorry," he said. "That was probably more than you bargained for. I… I lost control." He just looked at her beautiful face. How could he not lose control? He couldn't be himself around her.

Or maybe this was himself now. More of a beast than a man.

Driven by elemental need.

"I'm good," she said. "I promise. I'm not upset. I…" She took a step toward him and touched his face again. Like he was a spooked horse and she was trying to still him. "I wanted to do that last night. But… I did feel that maybe there was another conversation that had to go with that."

"And what's that?"

"I've never been kissed before."

Everything in him went still. "What?"

"I've never been kissed before. I had a huge crush on you, and then I was shamed for it. Then my dad left and devastated my mother, confirming for me that men were maybe trash. Then I tried to get a kiss in college, and I was just humiliated. So I have a very bad track record, and I kind of gave up. But that was why it was on my list. It wasn't just about getting a kiss in front of people. It was about actually getting a kiss finally. And not being traumatized by my past. Not carrying that forward with me into my new life."

"Rory..."

"I'm a virgin, obviously. I would like to not be. Before I leave. I..."

He gripped her chin again, needing her to look at him, needing her to hold still. "Honey," he said. "Please tell me you're not asking me to—"

"If you don't want to, that's fine."

She looked small and sad and hurt, and he knew she thought he didn't want her, but that wasn't the issue. Not even close.

"I should not be anyone's first time. Not yours most of all."

"Why not me most of all? Is there really something wrong with me?"

"No," he said fiercely, "there has never been anything wrong with you. You have always been the sweetest, most delightful part of my day here. Always. But there is something wrong with me. I can't do a relationship. I can't. I fucked that up so many different ways. And I just want… I can't do another crutch."

"I'm leaving," she said, looking at him like he was crazy. Maybe he was. "I was never looking for a relationship here. But you know I realized when I went out with Mike… By the way, Mike is one of the guys who made fun of me and made photocopies of my diary."

He took a step back. "You went on a date with *that guy*?"

"I don't know, I thought it might be healing. Or cathartic. But at the end of the day, I realized that I couldn't kiss somebody just because I wanted to get a kiss. And I couldn't sleep with somebody just because I wanted to feel like I had won some game. Like I'd beaten the level that I was stuck on in middle school. I want you. Being with you this past week has made it very clear to me what desire is. And that kiss… I think you melted the soles of my shoes. I just want you. And I feel like if you could be my first…"

"I don't want to help you become a legend by letting you wave bloody sheets around in my name," he said, suddenly feeling irritated when he didn't have a right to be.

He was telling her flat out they couldn't have a relationship, so why did it piss him off to hear her say the same? That she just wanted sex. Sex was all he had to offer, and dammit, he'd been celibate for too long. It wasn't like he didn't think he'd ever have it again. He was so hard right now he thought he might die of it.

He wanted this woman.

But he didn't want to be a notch in her belt because of who he was to the town.

"Nobody needs to know. I realized something else

after I climbed this mountain. After you told me all the things you did. I don't need anyone to know. I don't need them to know anything about me. I'm the only one that needs to know. What I want is to go into my new life with confidence that I'm strong enough to do it. I don't want to regret anything. I wanted to kiss you, so I did, and it has nothing to do with a list. You asked me what I wanted to get out of this hike. I wanted to finish. That was it. Ask me what I want to get out of being with you."

"What do you hope to get?" he asked, his voice low and raspy. "What do you think it's going to get you, to let me lay you down in my bed and strip your clothes off you? To…to let me have you. What do you think that's going to get you? Me, a junkie ex-soldier whose wife left him."

He waited for her desire to turn to disgust. It didn't. Instead, she drew closer to him, and he felt air rush out of his lungs in a gust.

"I want to," she said. "I want to be with you. That's it. That's the beginning and end. Trying to scare me away. You're doing that thing."

He frowned. "I'm not doing anything. It's me. This is just me."

"Snowy plover," she said softly.

"That only works when I'm *not* trying to be an asshole."

"Are you trying to be? Are you trying to push me away?"

He nodded. "Yeah. Because I think you might need to be pushed away."

She shook her head. "I told you. What I want is just to be with you. To have the experience. Don't you just want that for a minute? To just feel good? Up here on this mountain, you make me feel beautiful. I've never felt pretty in my life."

"Fuck everyone that made you feel like there was something wrong with you, Rory Sullivan. I *want* all those things. The only thing holding me back is the fear that I could hurt you. I've already hurt too many people. If Lydia and my mother knew about my substance abuse and the time I spent on the street…"

"What's between us is between us," she said.

"My sister is your best friend."

"*You're* my friend."

He'd had no idea how much he needed to hear somebody say that. How far that went in healing some damaged place inside him. Because his friend from the military, who had never checked on him again, was marrying his ex-wife.

It wasn't Cassidy getting married that hurt. It was the way that whole group, that whole life, had rearranged itself without him, and done so effortlessly.

No one needed him. They didn't even want him. Didn't even miss him.

He was human. That sucked.

"Let's get the camp packed up," he said.

"Are you saying…?"

"I'm not saying anything just yet. We've got a mountain to climb."

THEY GOT CAMP packed up, and headed back down. Rory didn't have time to be shocked and embarrassed by her own behavior because she was nervous about the narrow section of the trail again. She did try to make it as much as possible without actually physically clinging to him.

She couldn't decide then, after they got on the wide portion of the trail that didn't scare her, whether or not she was proud of herself or horrified.

She had gone for what she wanted. She had woken up with the burning need to kiss him like she hadn't done last night. And when he had tightened his hold on her, and taken the kiss deeper, she'd been lost.

And she'd known exactly what she wanted.

Gideon needed to be her first.

Her only.

She ignored that whispered thing inside her.

She wasn't going to be naive. Or that silly. She wasn't thirteen. She knew that kissing somebody, sleeping with them, didn't mean it was going to be forever.

But she wanted him.

And it felt something like fate that they'd been brought here together. That he'd helped her climb that mountain, and shared everything he'd been through.

And maybe they were here for a reason. To help each other through the things that life had done to them.

Just maybe.

But now she was a little embarrassed. Also. In addition to being proud. Becoming a legend in your own mind was complicated. She had meant what she said.

She didn't need anybody to know. It could always be a secret between the two of them, and it would be lovely.

Wonderful.

She wasn't going to beg, though. There were lines. She couldn't beg him. She had too much pride for that. She thought that maybe he wanted her.

There was just too much other stuff.

The way down was easier in some regards, a little bit harder in others, and she winced every time her toes hit the front of her boots. Especially when her brain decided to add a word to that little rhythm. When her foot hit the ground, then her toe hit the boot.

Stupid.

Stupid.

Stupid.

Stupid for kissing him. Stupid for revealing herself that way.

She wanted to hide.

He had rejected her. And she had taken most of the hike to really, fully take that on board.

He didn't want her.

Stupid.

They made it down to the truck, and he moved toward her like he was going to help unbuckle her pack. She did it quickly herself, even though when it fell off her shoulders, she almost fell backward.

Then she hefted it into the back of the truck on her own and got into the passenger seat.

He didn't say anything as he took his own gear off and got into the truck, starting the engine.

He drove her back toward his house.

And the silence between them was so thick and painful she felt nearly dead of it.

He pulled his truck up next to her car, and when he turned the engine off, she scrambled to get out, but by the time her boots were on the ground, he was over there.

He looked at her for a long moment, and then he was moving, closing the distance between them, and he took her in his arms, kissing her like a savage thing. Wild and untamed, and beyond the kiss they had shared on the mountain.

She clung to him, to the front of his shirt, her heart beating hard as his tongue invaded her mouth, sliding against hers.

She didn't know what she was doing, but she knew she wanted this. She wanted him.

The space between her thighs pulsed with need, and she could feel him, hard and insistent against her stomach as he continued to kiss her, deeper and deeper.

When they parted, her lips were swollen, the skin on her cheeks tender from being burned by his whiskers.

"Come inside," he said.

"I would love to."

CHAPTER TWENTY

IT WAS NEARLY DARK, just the faint outline of pink around the mountains, as he took her hand and led her up the stairs into his house.

Rory felt calm. Not worried. Not nervous. Just resolute. Certain.

She had waited a long time to be with anybody.

She should've known that Gideon was always going to be the right one to be the first one.

How many people got to live out fantasies they'd had for so much of their lives?

This was the ultimate in not quitting, she supposed.

None of that really mattered right now, though. She wasn't worried about what was coming in the future. She had him now. She had this. She wanted him. He kissed her like he was a dying man, and she had the cure. He kissed her like she was special. Like she mattered. His kissing her proved he would keep every promise he'd made. That if he said he was going to kiss her, he damn well would.

He pushed her up against the truck, and she sighed.

It was the way he was desperate for her. The way that this wasn't about a list. Or parades or diary pages posted all around the school.

This wasn't recompense for anything. It was just

what they both needed. Here and now. It was what they were both desperate for.

And she wasn't dressed up or made over. She was wearing hiking gear.

She was just…her. She was just her.

And he was Gideon.

But she knew him. Better than anyone did, maybe. He might not be a legend, but right now he was hers. And that mattered more than anything.

He picked her up, lifting her right off the ground like she weighed nothing, and carried her to the porch steps, up through the door. He slammed it behind them and set her down in the kitchen.

"I'm on the pill. Just so you know."

He looked at her like she'd hit him in the face.

"I have been for a long time. Mostly for hormonal reasons, but I have always believed it is best to be prepared when you can be. I mean there's an entire boys club built around that philosophy."

"I don't think that's the only thing it's built around, but yeah."

"The point is," she said. "I have protection."

"Right."

"We can use condoms, too, if you want," she said.

"Sorry," he said. "You surprised me because I didn't think of it. Either way. And I can honestly say that's a first. But it's been a long time for me."

Her heart contracted painfully. She didn't know why hearing him say that affected her so much. Maybe because it made her feel as if they were more alike than different.

"Gideon." She closed the distance between them and put her hands on his face. "We have new lives on the other side of this. I know we do. I need to believe that we do. That your life didn't end with a bomb, and mine can start anytime now. And here, we have this. And maybe it'll be just what we need. Maybe it will be enough."

He nodded. What he understood, what she was saying, was that this didn't mean nothing. It wasn't about just losing her virginity. And it could mean something without her needing it to be forever.

Forever.

That word whispered across her soul. What did she know about forever?

She was a quitter. She was working on being more than that. But climbing one mountain was hardly a cure.

"Tonight, there's nothing but this. You and me," he said, his voice rough. "I don't care about tomorrow. Or Boston. Or Cassidy or the mistakes I've made. I don't care about anything but this."

That was what she needed. She hadn't realized how much.

When he kissed her, parting her lips and going deep, she shattered. It was the most amazing sensation she'd ever felt in her life. He smoothed his hands down her back to cup her ass, and she found herself arching into him, feeling the hard press of his arousal against her.

Tears pricked her eyes, but not because she was afraid, because she was sad.

She realized that she knew desperately little about sex. She hadn't exposed herself to a lot about it because she had always felt like she was lacking in some way, and what was the point of consuming herself with it, of getting wound up and in over her head if nobody wanted her?

She just felt really sad for herself. For the girl that

she'd been all those years. For Rory Sullivan who had let other people define what she could have.

From her parents to her bullies.

But he was right. There was nothing outside of this room, and no room for regrets.

"I am distressingly innocent," she said, separating her mouth from his and pressing her forehead against his brow. "I know some things. But honestly, I have avoided learning too much about it the way that someone who is allergic to sugar would have to avoid a bakery. I want you. I want everything. But you're going to have to teach me. Show me. I'm sorry that I'm not going to be a really good, skilled time. Especially because you've been celibate for a while."

He growled, grabbed hold of her chin, and looked at her with those fierce blue eyes. And here again was a moment where he was wholly unlike any Gideon she had known before this. The intensity, the raw quality to him, and even more, the way he saw her. Now. He was so present. So utterly and completely there. Present in the moment.

It only just occurred to her he wasn't like that years ago. He was always looking for the next thing. That added up with what he'd told her about himself.

The way he was always chasing glory. But she really understood it now. Really.

Because she felt the difference. When he said there was nothing else to him beyond this moment, he was telling the absolute truth. It wasn't hyperbole.

The only thing was this. The only thing was them.

"You could never disappoint me," he said, his voice rough. "I want you to understand that. I want *you*. I don't want sex. I could've had sex at any point. This whole thing that I've been dealing with the last couple of years, it didn't keep me from being able to attract women. Yeah, it might've made it so I had difficulty flirting in a conventional sense. But believe me when I tell you, there's always somebody out there who wants to warm your bed because they need a place to stay for the night, or is willing to suck you off to get some of the pills that you've got. I didn't want that. If I wanted sex, in the most basic way possible, I could've had it anytime. I didn't. I never felt the need for it until you. Okay?"

"Okay," she said, feeling shivery and needy and altogether undone.

"Rory, when I saw you in the woods that day I thought you were an angel."

He kissed her then like she was a revelation, and she believed it. She believed it with her whole body. She believed it with all that she was.

Maybe she was desperate. Maybe.

But she didn't think so.

She was done telling herself to stop dreaming big. She was done telling herself not to want the things she wanted most.

There was a lesson in this. He was the original source of her desire, and he was the one she was having now.

She had always told herself that Gideon, as a dream, was too much.

Then why was he *hers*? Why was he trembling almost as much as she was as he kissed her and kissed her until they were both breathless?

He moved one hand up to cup her breast, slid his thumb over her nipple, and she gasped.

She had never been touched so intimately. Of course she hadn't; she had never even been kissed.

And she realized, with that well of anxiety rising up within her that was just so damned familiar, tonight was going to be nothing but a scroll of firsts. Touches, tastes and kisses. Her first time being possessed by another human being.

She had thought of it as a checklist item. As something simple. Lose her virginity.

It wasn't. It could never be. Maybe that was because it was with Gideon. But whatever the reason, it felt infinitely complex, infinitely awe-inspiring and infinitely terrifying. But she wanted it all the same. Wanted him.

She clung to him because if she didn't, she was going to melt right down to the floor.

Then he moved his hands down to push them up beneath the hemline of her T-shirt, which came off neatly over her head, his movements smooth. He might not have been with a woman in a while, but that he had been with one, with several, was evident in how easy his motions were as he divested her of her clothes. Her bra was next, and he managed it with the kind of finesse with which he did everything physical.

And she was bare in front of him, her nipples tight and hard because of the cool air, and the intensity of his gaze. And then he put his rough hands on her untouched, untried flesh, and she arched into him. Her need welled up within her, desire like she hadn't experienced overtaking her entirely. She wanted him. She wanted this. There was no room for doubt inside her.

Not when there was Gideon. In front of her. Touching her, tasting her. He kissed his way down her neck and along her collarbone and moved his mouth down to fasten it to one tightened bud. She was unprepared for the intensity of the arousal. The sensation.

She cried out, arching against him, her entire body shaking.

"I want to touch you," she said.

She began to pull at his shirt, getting it up over his head, the revelation of his bare torso almost more than she could bear.

His muscles were well-defined, covered by hair. His stomach rippled with strength. But there, just at his side and around toward his back, was fire-damaged skin. Rough and discolored. He looked at her, and turned around, showing her the extent of the damage. Then he put his hands on his belt, his button and zipper, and he pulled his jeans down.

She was caught between the shock and eroticism of seeing a naked man for the first time in her life, one that was thoroughly aroused by his desire for her, and what he was showing her. Where the burns and the shrapnel wounds extended down his hip, down to the top of his knee. It was such a significant portion of his body to have been burnt and damaged.

No wonder he hadn't been able to cope without help. No wonder. No wonder he hadn't…

And she hated Cassidy right then.

She'd never met the woman, and she never wanted to. But how could she look at him and see this pain and not understand? How could she want that symbol back more than she wanted him? This flesh and blood man who had put his body on the line for his country, for something that he believed in. This man who really was a hero. And who was altogether dear to her in ways that she could never quite express.

How could anyone turn their back on him? What she saw only made it seem miraculous that he had lived. That he wasn't gone. That he hadn't succumbed to the horror of it all, because she couldn't blame him if he had.

If that was what it had done to his body, him, one of the survivors, then she knew there was more he'd left out. Because those who had died... The horror he had witnessed that day.

She reached out and she put her fingertips on his hip. On one of the deep gouges there. She looked up at his eyes. "You're beautiful," she said.

And he shuddered, lowering his head.

It was her turn to grip his chin and hold him steady so that she could kiss him. So that she could press her bare breasts to his chest.

He stepped out of his jeans, his shoes and everything else, completely naked. He wrapped her up in his arms and held her tightly. She was still wearing her own jeans and hiking boots but was only dimly aware when he stripped them from her body.

It was incredible. This need. This desire. Coursing through her. Arcing between them.

She wanted him.

And everything that came with him. The scars, the baggage. All of it. Because he wouldn't be the man before her without them.

And she might've had a crush on Gideon Payne, the golden boy of Pyrite Falls, but the feelings that she had for the man in front of her, this damaged, half-feral man, went so much deeper.

They kissed until she was slick with desire, until her body felt hollowed out with need. They kissed until she was trembling. Until she thought she might expire from it. They kissed until she thought she would be undone. Wholly and completely.

And then, when she was slick and ready with need, he took her back to his bedroom.

It was Spartan. Unsurprising, since he wasn't planning to stay. But she had expected some evidence at least that he lived there. But she realized, and nearly laughed, that it was his military precision.

It was still like barracks.

She was suddenly hungry to know more. About that life. About the ways he had transitioned between having a home and a wife and being overseas.

She wanted to know what his plans with Cassidy had been. Had they wanted children? Had they tried to have them? Had they eaten dinner together every night? Had coffee together in the morning? What had domestic life looked like for him, and what had his life in the military looked like? She had known this man for years, and yet it felt like she didn't know him at all.

There were so many years between his leaving, and this one. She knew what had made him the feral thing before her, but there were other steps. She wanted to know who he'd been in that life that had been blown up along with the rest of him.

But then she couldn't think anymore, because he laid her down on the bed and kissed every inch of her body. Because he opened her thighs wide and settled between them, and then he looked up at her. "Remember what I told you? If I said I was going to kiss you, I'd fucking do it." She nodded, wholly incapable of speech. "I'm going to kiss you now, Rory. I'm going to kiss you right here." He kissed her inner thigh, and she shivered. "And here." He kissed her again. "And here."

This time, he landed directly at the heart of her, moving his tongue through her seam, penetrating her deeply. She gasped, arching up off the bed. She wasn't dumb, she knew about oral sex, but she hadn't known that it was quite so...

He licked into her again, and she gripped his shoulders.

Yeah.

She hadn't realized you could do *that*.

He pulled her toward him, clasping his hands over her stomach as he drew her down more firmly against his mouth, moving upward to suck that sensitized bundle of nerves between his lips before he went back down.

He made a savage, satisfied sound as he ate her, and she was lost. She forgot to wonder about the past, and she didn't wonder about the future. Because now was all that mattered. Now, with Gideon's mouth on her.

She grabbed hold of the sheets, balled them up in her fist and flexed her feet out, trying to root herself to the mattress. Trying to get a hold of something. Anything.

She felt lost. Utterly and completely lost. In this. In him. In all that he was.

She moved her hips in steady rhythm with his tongue. And then he unclasped his hand and put it between her legs, pushed a finger inside her as he continued to tease her with his mouth.

Then he added another, the stretching, stinging sensation foreign.

"Gideon," she said, a plea. For what, she didn't know. For him to stop, for him to keep going.

Definitely for him to keep going. Need was tightening inside her, her climax building.

She might be ignorant of sex, but she knew how to furtively bring herself to completion.

This was not the same. This was slick and graphic and wonderful. It was debauched and beautiful, and she couldn't have asked for anything better.

"Come for me," he growled.

And with an order like that, she could not resist.

She had no desire to resist.

She shattered, her internal muscles tightening around his fingers as she found her release.

She breathed hard and heavy, feeling like she had just run a marathon. And then she looked at him, and he was hard and huge and wanted her.

She reached out tentatively, curling her fingers around his erection.

She bit her lip as she tested his heat and the strength of him. He closed his eyes, his breath hissing through his teeth.

"I want…" She scooted forward, lowered her head and flicked her tongue across the tip of him.

The sound he made was short and tortured and he reached out and grabbed her hair, pulling her head back hard. "I won't last if you do that."

"But I want you."

"The world has tested me enough. You can test me later. But now… I just need you. I need to have you."

And she didn't want to resist him. So she didn't. She let him wrap his arms around her and pulled her body against his. She let him ease her down so that she was lying on her back and he was settled between her thighs. He kissed her, long and deep, put his hand between her legs and pushed two fingers inside her again, slowly and rhythmically moving them in and out.

He was much bigger than that. But she knew that he was trying to prepare the way.

"It's okay," she whispered.

He gritted his teeth, the veins in his neck standing out as he pressed the head of his cock against the entrance of her body. And slowly, very slowly, he entered her.

It hurt. But it was a wonderful kind of hurt.

She had felt wrong and lonely and like parts of her didn't line up with anyone or anything for most of her life.

But Gideon Payne fit her. This man who felt alone, ostracized, who felt like he'd been abandoned, fit her. And she fit him.

And when he was fully seated inside her, he pressed his forehead against hers and stared into her eyes before kissing her, deep and long.

She shivered, her internal muscles rippling as his tongue slid against hers. As her need began to build, past the discomfort, past the pain.

And when he began to move, the slick friction, the feeling of his possession, began to heighten her arousal. Pushing her back toward that sweet, sultry place of release.

She locked her legs around his, opening herself wider and taking him deeper as she met his every thrust with rolls of her hips. It wasn't romantic, not in the traditional sense. Their sounds were broken, their skin sweat-slicked. The sounds of need he made were more savage than they were heartfelt. Except it was real. It was real, and it mattered.

Because this wasn't a game.

This wasn't something manufactured to manipulate or embarrass her. They were both beyond control. It had nothing to do with showing anyone. With being legends for the sake of it.

They were just legends for each other. In this room, in this bed.

And as her orgasm crashed over her, making her cry out in ecstasy, she knew for certain that he might not think he was a hero, but he would always be one to her.

Always.

And then, on a low growl, his control snapped. His thrusts became hard, erratic, the intensity of it pushing her up the mattress so that her head met the headboard.

He gripped her hands, his fingers threaded through hers as he thrust within her, his eyes bright, a blue flame.

And she hadn't thought she would come again. She really would've said it wasn't possible, but when he thrust into her so hard their skin slapped together, and she felt a zip of pain through her body as her head made contact with the headboard and he went deep, something in her unraveled.

There was no anxiety. There was no fear. She was enough. This moment was enough. Together. The two of them.

And this orgasm was different. It was like shattering. Like coming apart and being made new. Because when she did, so did he, his body pulsing within her as he found his release. That raw, masculine energy infusing her with a matching feminine power.

She was destroyed. And yet remained.

And they lay there, together. She watched his chest

rise and fall, moved her fingertips over his bare skin. Across that sweat-slicked body, down to his scars. Back up again, so she could feel his raging heartbeat.

And somehow, this was maybe almost as wonderful as sex itself. Being naked beside him without shame.

Being able to look at him. His physical perfection and imperfection.

Everything that made him *him*.

He put his hand on her hip, and she wanted to purr. The security she felt with that basic, possessive touch. It was soothing and arousing all at once.

"You know if you don't go home, your sisters are going to send out a search party," he said, his voice rough.

As sweet nothings went for a post-sex moment, it did leave something to be desired. But...

"Snowy plover," she said.

"Termite," he countered.

"What?" she asked. "What did I do?"

"You misused the safe word. I'm being smart, not mean."

"Well, I don't want to be smart. I just want to lie here like this."

"*I* don't want to get skinned."

"Can I just stay for a while longer?" She felt a little bit like what he really wanted to do was separate from her so the intimacy wasn't so intense. But maybe not. Except, maybe.

The intensity was a little much for her. But she had decided she enjoyed it. Because it was him.

"But it wasn't just this once, was it?"

He shook his head. "I'm here for the month."

"So am I."

"Don't tell Lydia."

There was so much weight in those words. *Don't tell Lydia.* She knew that it wasn't just about the fact that they'd slept together, but about everything else he told her when they were up camping. Because she knew that was shameful for him. A secret. Something he hadn't figured out a way to come to terms with yet.

And she was sure, and understood, that he probably didn't want his family to worry about him, but there was more than that, and she knew it. Sensed it.

"Everything that's happened between us in the last couple of days is between us," she said. "You can trust me."

"I know I can," he said.

She kissed him, pressed her body against his, and it wasn't even subtle, and she didn't care. He wrapped his arms around her, and she found herself beneath him as the kiss intensified. She was ready for him again, would take him again.

"I can't," he said.

She felt him getting hard against her hip. "I somehow think you could."

"No. I mean *you* can't. That was your first time. We need to be reasonable. I don't want you to get sore. It's like any workout. Like rope climbing. You've got to build up some stamina."

That was frank. And betrayed his experience in ways that she didn't love.

"Have you slept with a lot of virgins?"

He looked a little bit sheepish. "Not since high school. And I wouldn't ever say that there were a lot of them. But that sort of thing didn't mean much back then. I mean, that was when a lot of people were losing it. It was just expected and part of it. This was different. I do want you to know that. It was different because it was you. And it wouldn't have mattered if you'd been with a hundred guys. It still would've been special. But you weren't. And I appreciate that. That it was me."

He reached out and touched her cheek. "I really do, Rory. I need you to know you're special."

Normally, she would doubt something like that, because her experience was that those kinds of proclamations were bullshit, and would only end up harming her. But she believed him.

There was a wealth of sadness in the silence between the words, though. A wealth of regret. They could never be simple. Because they weren't simple. Maybe he wanted to run away with her to Boston.

She had to stop herself from suggesting that. What a foolish thing to think. What a foolish thing to say.

Nothing about being with him scared her, but that thought did. It was a silly pie-in-the-sky sort of thought.

"I'll go home. So that you don't have to worry about Fia. She really would savage you."

"I know. She made that very clear."

She dressed slowly, and he watched. He watched closely. It aroused her, the way his eyes moved over her body.

It was sexy. So was he.

But she had to go.

She sighed and walked into the kitchen. He followed a minute later, still pulling his jeans on.

Then he took her hand in his, and her stomach hollowed out, her heart jumping up against her rib cage.

He walked her out like that, holding her hand, like he'd done up the mountain, and helped her into her car.

She didn't need help. But she did need him. Needed him to give her this last bit of attention. It felt good. She felt good.

And she cried a little bit on the drive back to Sullivan's Point; that was just a virgin's prerogative.

Fia wasn't downstairs when she got in, thank God. She went up to her room and took out her notebook. She stared down at the list. *Assist the legend.*

Get a kiss.

She had crossed off *makeover*, and she could cross off *climb the damn mountain* if she wanted to.

But what did you do when you weren't the same person who made the list to begin with?

It hardly felt like the Summer of Rory. It felt like something bigger. With more consequence. It was no longer about her leaving town with a certain sort of reputation. It was no longer about what anyone thought of her at all.

She was happy with herself. And that thought was truly the most jarring one she'd ever had.

She had liked putting that dress on, she had liked people thinking she looked pretty, but she didn't need it. She hadn't figured out exactly how to dress herself because she didn't care.

She liked to be comfortable, and she liked for things to be functional. She didn't need to attract attention. She liked to talk about books, and segue into whatever weird thing interested her. She liked having one lifelong best friend. She loved her sisters. Who understood her without the need for explanation or apology.

She didn't want to go out with Mike. She didn't want to impress all those old bullies who had been mean to her.

They didn't matter.

She was Rory Sullivan, and she was fine. And she'd had sex.

And... And... She pulled the paper out of the notebook and crumpled it up, sitting down on the bed hard as tears fell down her cheeks.

She didn't need it. She didn't care what anyone thought of her. All she cared about was that between now and when she left for Boston she got to spend as much time with Gideon as possible. He was healing her. And she really hoped—she did—that she was offering him some healing, too. If she could do that, then nothing else mattered at all.

CHAPTER TWENTY-ONE

THE LAST THING he expected was for his sister to show up when he was still standing shirtless in his kitchen, recovering from that evening with Rory.

He didn't even feel like he'd caught his breath.

"What are you doing here?" he asked.

"I knew you were…back." She frowned.

"I was getting changed after the hike," he said.

"Right. Did she finish?"

"Yeah," he said, trying not to think of Rory finishing, by tossing her head back on the pillow, arching her breasts up off the mattress and crying out his name. Because that wasn't what his sister meant.

It was the strangest thing, to have a good secret. All he'd had these last couple of years were shitty secrets.

Now he had Rory. Naked and soft and all his.

"She did great. She…" He kept trying to not think about the sex, but he was losing that battle. "She was brave."

Lydia smiled. "I *knew* she could do it. Everybody was just so mean to her in school. Can you imagine trying to do something like that with a whole bunch of people who are rooting for you to fail? I have always been her friend, but I understand why I wasn't quite enough. How could I be? When you have all those people, all those voices, saying all of that awful stuff to you, it just makes it not worth it."

"Well. She did great. And she didn't need me. She was an absolute champion."

"Thank you." Lydia looked down at her hands and made a study of her own thumbnail. "Will you please come over for dinner tomorrow?"

The realization she was afraid to ask hit him like a brick. That he was such a grumpy jerk so much of the time she expected him to turn her down.

"Yeah," he said, his voice rough. "I could do that."

"Would you mind if I invited Rory? I want to hear more about the hike."

"Oh. Yeah. I mean, you could," he said, feeling like the first time he and Rory saw each other after sex should maybe not be with his mother and sister, but...

"Great. I'll give her a call." She paused. "Thank you for doing that. For taking her. For taking care of her."

"Yeah," he said, feeling like a dick. "No problem."

She grinned. He felt worse. "Looking forward to seeing you."

"Yeah."

As soon she left, he realized that he didn't have Rory's number, which seemed ridiculous. But they'd done all their planning in person. He went over to the little binder that was in the drawer in the kitchen that had information on the rental, and inside was Rory's cell phone number. He opened up a text message and entered the number.

My sister is going to invite you to dinner. Just a heads-up.

He sent it off.

A second later, the phone rang.

"Do you want me to come?"

He stared at the back wall. "Yeah. I don't want you to be uncomfortable."

"I'm not uncomfortable."

"Good. I just... Given everything," he said.

"Do you not want me to go?" she asked again. "Because I can tell her... Oh, she's calling right now."

"You can go. Please go. If you can. I mean, don't rearrange anything on my account."

"I can handle myself. I'll see you later."

She got off the phone, and he went to find something clean to put on, then got into the shower.

He wasn't sure how he'd ended up here, but at least it wasn't a dark pit. There was that.

IT DIDN'T EVEN occur to him to go pick Rory up. He probably should have; it would've made sense. But he had some hesitation about whether or not they should show up together. Technically, she was there as Lydia's guest.

He had to ask himself why it mattered if anyone knew.

He couldn't have his mom and Lydia thinking it was something deeper than it was, or something more permanent. It was deep. Truth be told, it was as deep as it got.

He cared for Rory. He would rather die than hurt her.

But she was leaving, and he was starting a new life. He needed space and time; he knew he did.

There were too many ugly things inside him, and he didn't want to risk exposing Rory to any of them.

He had failed one person already. Profoundly. A person he had promised forever to.

It wasn't in the cards for him. Forever.

How could anyone promise forever? Life was way too unpredictable.

He would be an ass and an idiot to try again.

He would be cruel.

He just didn't see the point of announcing it. Maybe because it felt like opening a part of himself that he didn't want to. This was healing him.

That stunned him, that realization. That being with Rory had touched something deep inside him. He wasn't just doing this for her.

Maybe she felt like it was checking off a box. Maybe she felt like it was just moving toward that new life. That new sense of herself. But for him, it was more.

For him it was something.

It might as well have been his first time.

It was his first time as this man. And there was something incredibly hopeful about the fact that he could still feel. That he might even feel more during sex than he ever had before. Because he was different.

Because this new version of him didn't look forward to the moments of glory. He lived in the moment.

The old version of himself enjoyed pleasuring women, because he never wanted to experience glory alone, but he didn't think he had ever savored the journey in quite the same way that he had with Rory.

This new sense that nothing was guaranteed, that gave his life a precarious feeling, also made his time with Rory feel precious. Every moment. Every second.

He was so deep in his feelings he might as well be a pop song.

He put on a black T-shirt, a pair of jeans and then his dad's cowboy hat.

He got in his truck and headed out toward where his mother and sister lived.

His sister had a little house next door to his mother's, and the arrangement seemed to work fine for them.

When he got the ranch back, they would move there. There were enough outbuildings and other facilities for them to stay comfortably. At least, that was what he figured.

He hadn't talked to them about it. But…he didn't see why they wouldn't want that.

When he got there, Rory's car was already in the driveway.

His heart hit up against his breastbone. And he couldn't recall that ever happening.

He had loved Cassidy. She had turned him on. Made him happy. They had talked about the future. They had been united in things.

They had been shallow things.

He recalled an old story about a foolish man who built his house on sand. On temporary things.

But she never made his heart try to leap out of his chest. That was a whole new experience. He wasn't sure that he liked it.

He certainly had never asked for it.

His body could stop doing weird shit he hadn't given it permission to do anytime.

He walked up toward the front door and cleared his throat, then knocked.

His mom opened the door, and everything in him softened just a bit. He pulled her into his arms. "Hey, Mom."

She would always smell the same. Like his childhood.

Like a certain perfume he got her every Christmas—
because she asked for it every year—and Dove soap.

A hint of coffee and sunshine.

She was home.

When he'd woken up in the hospital, he had smelled
that smell. His mother.

He had never been more grateful for anything in all
his life. For a moment, he'd thought he was dead.

But it was just that she was with him.

His dad had smelled like Old Spice, coffee and to-
bacco. He would never smell that particular combina-
tion of things again, not the way that it sat on his skin.
And that was a grief he still didn't know how to manage.

So many things had changed in his world. The loss
of his father was the one he didn't think he could entirely ever accept. Too bad it was also the thing he could
do the least about.

There were ways he could rearrange his own life. He
couldn't bring someone back.

"I'm glad you came," she said. "You've been busy
the last week."

"Yeah," he said. "But happy to be here."

She reached up and touched the brim of his hat. "He
would be so proud of you. He was so proud of you."

What would his dad have thought about the pills? If
he'd known his boy had failed? As a husband, a care-
giver.

Dad had raised him to be all those things and more.
He never let hardship get to them. He'd had cancer. It'd
been painful and debilitating, and he hadn't lost himself.

"I hope so," he said.

"Rory and Lydia are just in the kitchen finishing up

dinner and chatting. Why don't you come sit with me in the living room?"

"Sure."

He walked into the living room with his mother and sat in the chair his father used to occupy.

"I should get rid of some of these things. They don't fit in this house."

A glow started at the center of his chest. Because for everything he'd done a bad job of in the last few years, he had this. This to offer his mother.

"Mom, I've been meaning to talk to you. I got the ranch, and you know I have a place for you there. I don't need the main house. I can stay in one of the smaller ones."

His mother didn't light up.

She frowned.

"Oh, no, I don't intend to move back to the ranch. I like being a little bit closer to town."

He felt like he'd been sucker punched. "Really?"

"Oh, yes," she said. "Your father loved that ranch. But it was never the life for me. It was only mine because he was there. And when he wasn't…"

"I thought you… I thought you wanted it back."

She smiled at him and he felt all of five years old.

"*You* wanted it back. And I'm very glad for you that you have it. But I'm doing well here. That isn't to say that Lydia might not want to move out there with you. But honestly, I didn't know that was something you wanted."

"I just thought we would…"

He thought they would go back to the way things were. Like it would fix something. He would buy that ranch and it would set to rights things that had been torn asunder, starting with the death of his father.

Like it would fix him.

And it wouldn't. He was just walking over the same ground, but with entirely different footsteps, and he was just kind of a fucking idiot.

"Sorry," he said. "I realize that I'm not thinking clearly about this. I guess I thought that everything would go back to being the way it was. But it can't." He looked around the space. This was a different house, but the furniture was the same. And the hole his father had left behind was the same as well. "He's not here. And he isn't going to be here even if I get everything set up at the house just the way it was. I'm sorry."

She reached out and put her hand over his. "There is a space that your father left behind, and nothing is ever going to fill it. But it's not entirely empty. Because the love that he had for all of us is still there. I don't mean to sound cliché, but he is with us. And everything we do. He's in you. I see him in your face and the way you hold yourself. You've grown so much. You've changed so much. You remind me more of him now than you ever have."

He was truly taken aback by that.

He didn't think it could possibly be true. His dad hadn't been the life of the party, that was true. He was kind of a taciturn old cowboy. A product of both his upbringing and his generation.

Not the quickest with a smile, but that made those smiles worth something.

"I'd like for that to be true," he said. "But I think I'm trying to fix something that maybe isn't fixable."

And he meant that to cover more things than his mother even knew.

"Sometimes you can't repair. Sometimes you have to get something new. I know your dad was opposed to that when it came to trucks and household appliances. But for this kind of thing, it is true. You're planning on doing something new with the ranch. That's a start. You can make a whole different life. That's what we have to do. I get to live where I want, in a nice little house that's easy for me to keep up. I would trade it all to have your dad back. I would. But I don't have that choice. So that means I will take what I do have. And that is this little house. My life is closer to town. My *choices*. The fact that I don't have to consult with another person to do what I want during the day. Not that your father controlled me, he didn't. But when you're in a relationship, you always have to consult that other person. You know how that is."

A partnership. Ideally. It was strange how all that had fallen apart. Had he and Cass really ever been a partnership?

And was he really the one to blame?

He shook that thought off. "Yeah. I do."

"Sorry. I know it's probably not a happy memory for you right now. Marriage. I am grateful for that. That mine always will be."

"Mine is a happy memory the way anything in my past is. There were good things. I just don't want it anymore."

And that, he realized, was very true. He didn't want it anymore, and he had seen it this whole time as a flaw. That his changing had shattered his world.

But he'd changed. So why be hard on himself?

Maybe because it was the only way he knew how to be.

Push, push, push. On to glory.

For whatever the hell it was.

For whatever it all meant.

Maybe this wasn't glory, sitting in his mom's living room, but it was meaningful. He would take that over glory now. Any day.

Because it wasn't just the glory days that were numbered, it was the every days.

The days of his father were gone.

He couldn't get them back. Any more than he could get back his high school football games.

Right now, he felt glory. Glory in the simple moment.

It reminded him of holding Rory. Just the joy in being present.

Lydia poked her head into the living room. "Dinner is ready."

He made his way into the dining room with his mother and saw that Rory was already seated.

Their eyes clashed, and he felt his heart give a jump again.

He felt like a high school boy with a crush.

And that was a hell of a thing. To be able to feel like that.

Maybe that was the good thing about not having as much control over himself.

There was something kind of effervescent and wonderful happening that he couldn't control.

It was better than the feeling of the darkness he couldn't control. So why not marinate in it? Why not enjoy it? Why not cling to it?

Dinner was a pasta bake that his mother had made

when he was a kid, that reminded him of his childhood and made him feel at home in a way that he hadn't thought possible in a house he hadn't grown up in.

Rory and Lydia talked about school days, and he found himself joining in and even laughing.

Rory's gaze would intermittently meet his, and they would share a smile.

And this felt like family. He hadn't realized how much he'd missed that. Feeling part of something. Not outside of it. But his memories were here. His foundation was here.

No, he couldn't go back.

He was going to have to build something new, but he did have his foundation. His mother was right.

His father wasn't here, but his father had loved him. Had loved all of them.

And that was one of the things he could build this new version of himself on.

He didn't have to throw out everything.

He had felt like he was an entirely different person for the last few years, but now he didn't feel like he was.

Just a different version of himself. A version of himself who thought a lot more about everything he did and why.

Maybe that was just the difference between being a person who had never made a mistake and being a person who had.

He'd made mistakes. He hurt somebody. Somebody he had promised to love and stay with.

If that didn't make you stop and reevaluate, how you'd gotten there, and how you can keep yourself from being there again, well, there was something wrong with you.

So he'd become a deeper thinker. And maybe that was what made him want more quiet.

Because you needed quiet for thoughts like that.

Maybe that was the thing.

It was all a little bit profound to be thinking about that over a casserole.

It did seem to pair even better with the apple crisp his mom served after.

He cleared the table and brought the dishes into the kitchen, and decided that since dinner had been served to him, cleanup was his responsibility.

"You don't need to do dishes," his mother said.

"Nonsense," he said. "You made the apple crisp, and Rory and Lydia made dinner. I ought to do something."

"I could pass out," said Lydia, fanning herself vigorously. "The golden boy doing chores."

He frowned.

Had he not done them before? He couldn't remember.

"Did I not help when I lived with you guys before?"

His mother laughed. "You did plenty in other ways. But no."

"No," Lydia said right at the same time.

He and Cassidy had employed a cleaner, so neither of them had done much in the way of household chores. She had been responsible for dinner, though she usually had dinners brought from a local premium grocery store.

He hadn't cared.

But it was just another way he hadn't fully engaged with that life. With the moment.

Maybe neither of them had. They hadn't cleaned their house or cooked their meals. Hadn't done their own yard work.

They'd been busy with other things.

Other things that surrounded their life, but so rarely life itself.

The whole memory of putting together that bookcase came back to him. Because normally, they would've paid for assembly, but for some reason he had been bound and determined to do it. Maybe because he felt so useless in every other way.

He hadn't been able to cope with the events anymore. He was being discharged, and he hadn't known who he was.

He had been drowning in his addiction, and that water was six feet high and rising, and he hadn't seen a way out.

He was trapped in it.

And he could see now that what he'd been doing was trying to go back and fix mistakes he'd made starting years earlier.

He was trying to be more present than he ever had been before, and he was trying to do that while he was already overwhelmed.

Hindsight on the situation never became less complicated.

Shit.

"Well," he said. "I think I ought to do the dishes now."

He went into the kitchen and started running water in the sink.

A second later, there was a hand on his shoulder.

He turned around and saw Rory. "I'll help."

She stood beside him, and as he washed the dishes, she took them and rinsed them. Dried them. And when they were through they both put them away. They didn't speak, but they didn't have to.

He liked that about Rory. She could still be a chatterbox, just like she had been in middle school. But she could also sit in the silence with him.

He put a cereal bowl up on one of the top shelves, just as Rory put a saucer in a neighboring cabinet and turned.

They were so close right then and he wanted to touch her.

But instead, they just stood and stared at each other. Until he heard the sound of a throat clearing behind him.

They both jumped.

Lydia was standing there, looking between them.

"Just doing some dishes?" she asked, a little too sweetly.

"Yes," he said.

"Yes," said Rory right at the same time.

"Great."

She disappeared again, and Rory did something completely unexpected. She covered her mouth and began to laugh.

"You think that's funny?" he asked.

"I do think it's funny."

"So much for being discreet."

"She's never going to think anything is happening. You're you."

"Yes, and you are you," he said, reaching out and taking a strand of her hair between his thumb and forefinger. "And I fail to see why anyone would think I wouldn't want you."

"Okay, your mother and sister are in the next room."

He forgot why that was a bad thing.

Oh, right. She was leaving.

"Right."

She was leaving. And he was him.

Which meant something different to her than it did to him, but he just couldn't…

He was still sorting himself out.

Trying to untangle all the bad decisions he'd made, trying to figure out where he'd gone wrong. How long ago?

"Finished," he said as he grabbed the last dish and put it in the cabinet.

"We should probably go play a game of cards."

"A little game of cards, not a euphemism."

"Not a euphemism."

They went back into the dining room, and his mother did have a deck of cards out and was getting ready to play Old Maid.

Of course, it wasn't gambling, because that was his mother. Just a family card game.

But they all joined in, and he felt content in a way he hadn't in a long time.

His mother and father had always liked to have a card game after a family meal, and he could remember being restless about that. Wanting to get on with the next thing. Wanting to get out of there so he could go hang out with his friends.

He didn't want that now.

He wouldn't trade in the slower-paced family game for much of anything.

Except for maybe another moment alone with Rory.

Lydia beat everybody and was obnoxious about it, which he appreciated about his little sister, and he offered to clean up the card game to applause from that same sister, who he now wanted to throttle a little bit. But in a good-natured way. A way that felt normal.

He was back at the game closet when he closed the door and Lydia was standing right there behind it.

"Be careful with my friend," she said.

"Everybody seems to be very concerned with that," he said.

He'd already been warned off by Fia, and that was before anything even happened.

"Because she's sweet. And I think a little bit naive."

"And you aren't?"

"Not as much as she is."

What struck him was how much his relationship with Rory—whatever it was—felt like a first time to him.

He didn't feel like he had any idea what he was doing, or like he could anticipate what would happen next, or control his feelings.

It was fucking weird.

But he could see why his sister would think he was the one that had to be warned. Like he was the one who had the experience. Like he was the one who might be experimenting or playing around.

"If you want to know what's going on, just ask. But, Rory is leaving. You know that."

Lydia frowned. "Well, maybe she wouldn't. Maybe she wouldn't if…"

He realized that his sister wasn't mad.

She was *hoping*.

"You want her to stay," he said.

"Of course I do. She's my best friend. If she leaves, then I'm not going to have anybody. I know that Rory felt like she was this big geek in middle school and high school, but I thought she was the greatest. And I never needed another friend. I don't want her to go."

"I can't make her stay," he said. "Rory has to do what's best for her. And I am not going to hold her back. I'm not even asking."

"She… She's in love with you, Gideon." That made him feel like he'd been stabbed through the chest. "You have to know that. She has been forever."

"Maybe she thought she was. With the version of me she knew back then, but I am not the same man, and the one I am now has only been around her for a week. Yeah, there's a spark there, but that's not love. Believe me. I know."

"Gideon…"

"I am not asking her to stay for me. Not for me. She has plans. She's going to make a new life for herself, and I'm proud of her."

"So am I. I just am going to be so lonely."

"I'm back. And I just talked to Mom. She's not interested in coming to live at the ranch again, but you know you're welcome to."

"Oh," she said.

"What?"

"It's great that you're back, Gideon. But you haven't let me come up to see you. If I hadn't stormed your house the other day I— Oh, *no*, I interrupted you and Rory didn't I? That's why you were *naked*."

He growled. "I was not naked. And finish what you were saying."

"It's just… Are you actually back?"

He looked toward the living room. Toward Rory. "Yes, I'm back. And it's something to think about. Moving to the ranch. You don't have to. But you can. There's something new for you to do, if you want. That's the point."

"I appreciate that. But you know, if you're going to sleep with my best friend, you could maybe try to make that work out for me." Her voice was dry.

"Who said I was sleeping with her?"

"Well, you didn't deny it."

"This is why I didn't tell you when I came back, by the way. You're nosy. And sometimes people need a little bit of privacy so they can figure things out."

"Sure," she said.

"Tell Rory you want her to stay," he said.

"You won't, why should I?"

"Oh, I don't think that you should try to get her to stay. I just think that you should tell her you want her to. Because I don't think she believes people care about her as much as they do. I think it would make her feel good."

"You think you know my best friend better than I do?" she asked.

"Some things about her," he said. "Yeah."

She squinted at him. "I guess I can't dispute that."

"No. Probably best not to."

"Gideon," she said, suddenly sounding very grave. "If you want her to stay, you should ask her to stay. You've been so unhappy... And I know there's more to it... We had so many years where we just didn't talk to each other. And I just want you to be happy. And if she makes you happy..."

"You can never count on another person to make you happy," he said. "It's not fair. Not to anybody. Because when things go wrong, and they can't do it anymore, everything falls apart. Trust me on that."

"I trust you," she said. "But I'm also not completely sure that you don't exist in a space where you're trying to self-destruct."

"If I was self-destructing, I would still be in Georgia."

"Okay."

She stepped away from him, and then they rejoined everybody in the living room.

"I should probably head out," said Rory.

"Me, too," he said.

They said their goodbyes and walked out the front door together.

"That wasn't very subtle," she said.

"Lydia knows, anyway."

"Oh."

"We were not very subtle. The whole time. It's fine," he said.

"She's not upset?"

"Not at all. She wants you to stay."

Rory looked devastated then. And he felt like a dick. Because that wasn't what he was trying to do. He didn't want to hurt her. And he didn't want to make her second-guess herself. He had just wanted her to know Lydia cared.

He'd misread that.

"And I can see that doesn't make you happy."

"I don't want her to be hurt. And I don't want to hurt anybody. My sisters are upset that I'm leaving, and Lydia is upset..."

"That isn't why I told you. I told you because I wanted you to know how much she cares about you. I feel like there's just so much shit you've taken on board from back when you were in middle school, and Lydia was never a pity friend. She cares about you. She always has. And that's all. I just wanted to make you feel good."

It was such a strange declaration, he realized.

Not quite what he wished he could say.

But given how badly this was going, it was the right move, if he was going to test out anything.

"Rory," he said, very intensely, very seriously. "I didn't mean to hurt you. And I'm not trying to tell you that you shouldn't go. You don't owe anyone anything. You don't owe anybody staying in one place for the rest of your life. But I wanted you to know that already, to a lot of people, you're a legend, Rory Sullivan."

Her eyes filled with tears. He was really making a mess of this.

"Thank you," she whispered. "I do appreciate that."

"I know we aren't the whole town. But, there's quite a few of us that think you're pretty amazing."

That was safe enough.

She wiped a tear away from her cheek.

"Well. I had a great time tonight. It was so good to be with your family. It was great. Even if it…it's a little sad. Your house is missing somebody. Your family is. It's like Sullivan's Point in that way. Even if it's a little bit different. My parents are gone, even though I can call them up anytime. The shape of it has changed. I'm about to change it again."

"Planes go both ways, Rory. I know your parents haven't made a lot of trips coming back to visit. That doesn't mean you can't."

"That's true. I'm not leaving under a cloud of smoke. I'm leaving on my own terms."

"And you can come back on your own terms, too."

She nodded. "Well… I guess I'll go…"

"Spend the night with me," he said.

He hadn't meant for it to come out so intense, so strained and tortured.

But he felt every bit of it.

"Okay," she said, her voice shaking.

"I want you."

Even feeling like it was complicated, like it was messy and might not be the best thing.

He wasn't a martyr, that was the thing.

That, at least, was consistent. He had never been a martyr.

He was willing to do uncomfortable things, but not so he could downplay his role in them. He wanted the glory.

He was hardly going around tying himself to wooden stakes.

And even though things were different now, he still didn't have the kind of restraint required to turn away when he really, really wanted something.

He knew how to go without unless he didn't want to.

That was a strange new revelation.

Because this version of himself had never really wanted anything.

Nothing beyond sobriety. Nothing beyond pulling himself back from the brink of death, simply because he knew that sinking into his own brand of oblivion was a piss-poor tribute to the people who had died.

And if he really wanted to do battle against the dark thoughts telling him he should have been the one who had been blown up instead, he needed to make a life worth living.

And that was the journey.

But beyond that, beyond survival, beyond building

something that from the outside looked functional, he hadn't wanted much of anything.

But now he wanted her.

He really fucking did.

"I'll meet you at your place."

HER HANDS WERE shaking as she texted Fia to let her know she was spending the night with Lydia.

Then she texted Lydia.

If my sister asks, tell her I'm going to spend the night with you.

OMG, what are we in middle school?

Maybe. Maybe a little. Except not.

I'm only going to ask you once. Are you lying to your sister because you are going to look at my brother naked?

Gross.

Are you?

I probably won't just look at him.

Have fun. Don't hurt him.

She stared at that.

I won't.

And that was it.

It felt momentous. And also not as weird as she had thought. For her friend to know.

And maybe she shouldn't find it intoxicating that her friend thought she had to warn Rory not to hurt Gideon.

No, she definitely shouldn't find that intoxicating. That was silly. It was madness.

But she took a little bit of pride in it. Even though she didn't believe it was possible. But now she had an airtight alibi because there was no point worrying Fia.

It was amazing how this had shifted. It was no longer about getting attention. She didn't want it.

She just wanted this to be about them.

About what passed between them. She didn't need it to be about anything else.

She didn't need it to be about her reputation, about the way the town saw her, about the way she left the place.

It simply didn't matter.

It just didn't.

She drove straight to his house and got out, walking with him up the front steps and inside.

Last night, she had never done this before. And that had given her a certain type of infusion of nerves.

The unknown.

This was different.

She had spent the evening with his family.

They had done mundane things like putting dishes in a cupboard, and it had felt transformative.

She looked at him, smiled, felt her heart beating like a wild thing, trying to escape.

Trying to get to him.

And when he kissed her, it was like a storm.

It wasn't tentative, and it wasn't careful. They already knew what she was doing here. They knew what they both wanted.

He lifted her up and set her on the counter, moving between her legs.

He cradled the back of her head and kissed her like he was starving.

He pushed her dress up her thighs, and she welcomed him in that space between.

Wrapped her legs around him, felt the hard ridge of his desire up against that cleft there.

This was wild, abandoned.

This had nothing to do with anything but passion. Wanting him. Needing him, and being wanted in return.

He moved his hands up her legs, grabbed hold of her underwear and pulled them down, effortlessly, easily, and then his hand was there, between her legs, stroking her and teasing her.

She was already so wet with her desire for him. Already so ready.

He was a glorious thing, the soldier in that moment.

Laser-focused and maybe a little bit dangerous, and she didn't mind.

Because she felt equal to him.

She didn't feel like she was the soft one, the weak one.

She didn't feel like a weirdo. Didn't feel like the sad girl mooning after a man she couldn't have. She felt strong enough, brave enough for him. The woman who had married him hadn't been strong enough for him. For the truth of him.

She hadn't stood with him. She hadn't helped him.

You are leaving.

That thought punctured a hole in that inflating sense of self, but she ignored it. And she kept on kissing him, rolled her hips in time with his touch.

Because he was glorious. Because she wanted him.

And that was more important than anything. Than what the future held, than who they were now, and who they would become.

This was what mattered.

He pulled the straps on her dress down, exposing her breasts, then lowered his head and sucked one nipple deep into his mouth.

With searching hands, she undid the buckle on his jeans.

He was still wearing his shirt, his cowboy hat.

She reached inside his pants and wrapped her hand around all that hard steel.

Then she exposed him, stroking the length of him, positioning him between her thighs.

She urged him into her, gasping when he filled her.

She had already been boneless and replete with the effects of one orgasm by the time he had been inside her last night. She was tender today, and it hurt a bit. But she didn't want him any less.

She wanted him so, so much.

If anything, this just proved how much. How much she was willing to pay for the chance to be possessed by him.

That desperation almost frightened her.

Because she knew what it was like to want things she couldn't have.

To want things that could be taken away from her.

She was far too familiar with it. With that freefall sensation that happened when the rug was pulled out from beneath you.

Those things had formed her. They had made her.

But she had climbed the mountain; she hadn't fallen off. And she would climb this mountain, too.

Because she wanted to.

Because she wanted to acclimate. That was enough. They had decided that. That just wanting to was enough.

So she clung to his shoulders, and she met him thrust for thrust, kissed him with wild abandon as he moved in and out of her, the sweet slide of his hardness inside her softness making her feral.

Turning her into her own brand of soldier.

A warrior.

His equal.

She wasn't Rory from middle school any more than he was Gideon from high school.

They were both changed. They were both different. More now than they had ever been. But somehow they had come to this moment together. And it was perfect. Glorious and brilliant, a shimmering testament to their strength and their need.

He was everything.

And so was she.

He planted his hands on the cabinet above her head, leaned in and kissed her mouth savagely as he continued to thrust, then he gripped her hips and pulled her against him even as he slammed home.

She could feel him beginning to unravel. With one strong arm around her waist, he lifted her up off the counter, and she clung to him, locking her ankles behind his back.

He was still buried deep inside her, and he carried her into his bedroom, laying her down on the mattress, thrusting harder, deeper, as he guided her legs up over his shoulders so he could drive himself in until she wasn't sure where he began and she ended.

Until they might as well have been one body.

Until they might as well have been one soul.

The savagery of her need was shocking. But she didn't want it to stop.

Didn't want this to end.

She felt, in that moment, that this might be the truest example of who she could've been if she hadn't been an object of ridicule. If her father hadn't left. If her mother hadn't left. If she had never been bullied at that frat party.

Would she have been this Rory all along? Brave and full of abandon, absolutely fearless when it came to the pursuit of her own pleasure. When it came to claiming what she wanted.

Maybe. But she couldn't regret it, couldn't spend time worrying about it, because right now she was that version of herself. Right now, it was like she was suddenly walking a whole different path. One she might've been on if only things had been different.

But she could taste it now. Test it now.

With his heat and strength above her, and their cries of pleasure mixing, their need and desire tangling together.

How she wanted him.

And she had him, and still, somehow it didn't feel like enough. He was so deep inside her she could barely breathe, and it still didn't feel like enough.

She turned her head and bit his neck, and he growled, pinning her hands down to the mattress as their climaxes reached a blazing finish at the same time. As he roared his satisfaction while she cried out her own.

"Dammit," he cursed, kissing her shoulder. "That was... That was crazy."

"I'm not complaining," she said.

"It wasn't too rough for you?"

She sniffed. "I'm capable of letting you know if something is too much." She smiled. "I hear safe words are a thing."

"Thanks for not shouting *snowy plover* in the middle of that," he said, lying on his back and throwing his arm over his eyes.

"I told Fia I was spending the night with Lydia."

He shifted his arm and looked at her with one eye. "Really?"

"I made sure Lydia knew what I was doing."

"Wow. My sister is willing to lie for you?"

"On the off chance that Fia texts her, yes." She rolled over onto her side and put her hand on his chest. "Fia means well, but she's very protective. And she gets very weird when any of us is with somebody. I don't know if that's because of her experiences, her heartbreak or what. But it's not something that I want to deal with right now. Because we only have a few weeks. Three weeks. I don't need to spend any of that time getting warned about my own feelings by my sister."

"Fair enough."

"I'm not ashamed of it."

"I didn't think you were."

A smile touched her face. "Of course you didn't. Everybody brags about sleeping with you, don't they?"

He frowned. "Yeah. I guess so."

"If I was going to worry about anybody being embarrassed in this...relationship, it would be you."

"I'm not embarrassed. I am sorry that anybody ever

made you feel like they would be. They were assholes.
You're beautiful. But that's not even the most interesting thing about you. I just like you."

Absurdly, that made her grin. Silly and wide.

"Well, thank you."

"It's just true. You are strong. And just…so damned
accepting. And you don't try to give me advice, but you
also don't clam up and stop talking to me. I've never met
anybody like that. And it's funny, because I've known
you all this time, but I didn't have the same baggage that
I do then, so I didn't appreciate it. I'm discovering a lot
of things about myself. Things that are different now
that I've experienced what it's like to make mistakes.
To not be able to cover when things are hard. I thought
that I could take a pill and just magically sort myself
out. Because I had never in my life had something that
I couldn't just overcome, and it was my pride that led
me down the darkest part of that path. I was an idiot. I
was. I didn't respect what I had.

"And I sure as hell didn't have empathy for anyone
else who wasn't me."

"I don't think that makes you a bad person. I think
that makes you human. We are all limited in our understanding."

"I think some people know it a little more. Sometimes I wonder if I'm just different now because I have
to think about what I'm doing. Because I do have to put
limits on myself. Because I have to walk around knowing I'm not invincible and I could destroy my own life
with ease. I don't know."

"You seemed bothered by the idea that you didn't
help with the house back then."

"I am. Because I don't remember that. I was self-absorbed. I don't…" He turned over onto his side. "I don't want to be the person that I was. I don't think I liked him. At least I don't now."

"I always did. You were never rude. You were never unkind."

"I wasn't kind, either, was I?"

"You were to me," she said. "And in the grand scheme of my life, you meant something. You always have. So don't write off everything that you were. Just like you can't write off everything that you are. Yes, you might've been the man who hit rock bottom, struggled with addiction, but you are the same man who climbed out."

"That's because I knew there was a path out. And some people don't. I knew people were waiting for me on the other side. I'm not stronger than anybody else. And I don't ever want to fall into the trap of thinking that I am again. That's how you fuck your life up."

"Did it ever occur to you that maybe after all these changes…you've changed for the better?"

"Not until recently. But now I'm starting to wonder. I was celebrated for the man I was then. But I'm not sure the man I am now would want to have a drink with him. With that person who believed he was as great as everybody said he was. Who was just…kind of full of himself. I don't feel like Cassidy and I built a life together. We built a really beautiful facade. We had a beautiful house that somebody else maintained. Wonderful dinners that somebody else cooked. We got to go to parties in formal wear, and everybody looked at us and thought we were to be envied. And we both thought that, too. Because we had everything. But our love wasn't based on loving the deepest parts of each other. And I am not immune to that. I don't know the deepest parts of her. I don't think she does, either. *I* didn't. She's never had a reason to think twice about who she is and what she wants. I can't blame her for that. That's just…a side effect of having had things very easy. The first struggle she ever had was her husband falling apart. I'm not mad at her. I'm not."

"It's okay if you are hurt, though. That she didn't love you as much as you thought."

He shook his head. "I don't think I loved her as much as I thought. Because I didn't know what to do with her when we weren't bonded together by the stuff we did. It's hard to explain. I thought we were in love because we liked to do the same things, because I thought she was beautiful. She thought she was in love because I was that model man she had always wanted to be with. That soldier. That man who would give her the lifestyle her parents had had, that she wanted to replicate. We liked the shallowest things about each other, and when those things were stripped away, we didn't like what we found. She didn't like me injured. She didn't like me weak. And I didn't like her dissatisfied. We couldn't face the ugliness in each other."

"What do you think the ugliest thing in you is?" she asked, for some reason compelled to hear the answer. She looked into his eyes and felt tenderness rise up inside her.

"That I don't know how to struggle. I don't know how to be uncomfortable. So I just tried to medicate it away. Because once I had to sit still, I had to acknowledge I had joined the military as nothing more than a little boy playing war. Men died around me. When I have to sit still, when I have to contend with what I am,

I don't know that I like any part of it. What was I ever worth? What did I ever do for anyone?"

"You fought for your country, don't let hardship and injury and disillusionment take that away from you."

"But I didn't do it to protect people. I did it for the glory."

"And you changed along the way. You realized new things. You changed. That matters. And it's important. That proves you are a man of substance. You didn't stay in one place. Everybody starts somewhere. And then things happen. Things happen to you, and they break you down a little bit, but it's what you do afterward— that's what matters. And I don't know what it's like to struggle, not the way you have, but I know what it's like to be hurt. I know what it's like to feel that you aren't enough. Like you're just a disappointment. I really do know what that's like. And sometimes, even though we've been through different things, the feelings are the same."

"Tell me about that book you're reading again?"

"Well. It is about a woman who doesn't know she's a witch. But it turns out that she's the magic all along."

He leaned in and he kissed her on the lips. "I have to say, that sounds an awful lot like someone else I know."

And when she fell asleep, he was holding her.

CHAPTER TWENTY-TWO

IT WAS A hell of a thing to wake up in a woman's arms. To wake up in Rory's arms. He had taken her a couple times during the night, and she had taken him, joyously.

Enthusiastically.

He wondered what the hell he had done to deserve this.

To deserve this reprieve from the intensity of the bullshit he'd been enduring these last few years.

But he was sure as hell grateful. Sure as hell grateful that he had been given this even for just a little while.

He got up and put on his jeans. Then he went into the kitchen and opened up his fridge.

He decided to make her breakfast because it almost felt like the least he could do. Of course, it wasn't like he was paying her back for the sex, but it did seem courteous to make a woman bacon and eggs after she'd had sex with you three times.

He almost wanted to sing. And that didn't remind him of himself in any life.

But he fired up the pan, got out the eggs and bacon, and started humming to himself.

Rory appeared a few moments later, standing in the doorway wearing nothing more than his white T-shirt. It barely came to the top of her thighs, and if she moved just so, he would be able to see all that glorious treasure between her legs.

He'd always been a man of substantial appetites, but he had never paused to appreciate the details. The beauty of Rory, the way her red hair spilled over her shoulders, the way her freckles dusted her nose. That little bend in her knee, as she rubbed her foot against the side of her ankle, a nervous little gesture that struck him as being ridiculously adorable.

He was all about the details right now. With her.

Maybe he was different.

Or maybe she was.

Maybe he would never know for sure.

It was a funny thing. He'd spent years feeling like he had it all figured out. After all, somebody who was as successful as he had been surely knew something the rest of the world didn't. He'd had a beautiful wife, a promising career.

He hadn't known shit.

He hadn't known what loss was. He hadn't known what struggle was.

He hadn't known the kind of darkness a person could endure without actually dying.

He hadn't known the strange numbness that ensued after a marriage broke apart.

And how bizarrely disorienting it was to realize that maybe you hadn't loved your wife the way you'd always thought you had.

Yeah, he still carried some guilt.

Over time, it had all unraveled.

But he had to wonder if some of the problem was he simply didn't like failing.

He wondered if it was more than the loss of her.

Than the feeling of letting her down.

He suspected that what he had loved was his image. Himself.

And it had taken having himself dismantled to see that. To understand it.

"Good morning," he said.

"Good morning," she replied.

"Breakfast?"

"Well, that sounds lovely."

"I'm going to go out to the property today. Do you want to come with me?"

She flushed. "I'd love to."

"Good. Let's do that. I want you to see the ranch. You know, the rest of it, not just the boot-camp part."

"I won't recognize it when I'm not sweating!"

He didn't know why he felt so compelled to share it with her. This thing that was going to be his permanent home. She wasn't staying. But it still felt right. She got dressed, and so did he, and he was regretful they were leaving the bubble, but he supposed he couldn't be annoyed about that since he was the one who suggested they go out.

They made the drive over in silence, and it wasn't a bad silence. Not awkward or unhappy.

He had sat in so many silences all on his own.

They felt isolating. They had been the evidence of the fact that he had cut his mother and his sister out of his life, and that Cassidy had cut him out of hers.

They had been the deepest evidence that he had done something wrong. That his life had gone off the rails somewhere back there, and he was never going to be able to figure out how to get it back together.

At the same time, he had needed the silence sometimes. The headaches were less frequent, the fatigue and the forgetfulness a little bit less severe. He still didn't crave a crowd. Still didn't crave noise, but it wasn't as bad as it had been.

Now the silence didn't feel like isolation. Or like a punishment. Not with Rory. It was like being understood. Like these pieces of himself could be met just as they were, not resisted or changed.

And he thought he ought to say that. But he didn't want to.

Because he was still examining these new places inside himself, and he didn't know what the hell he thought of them. He just couldn't say.

So he kept that to himself because he had betrayed so much of himself last night. In his hunger, his desperation.

Maybe he could just find freedom in that. Because they had a time limit on this. And that was like boundaries.

Boundaries that would keep them safe. That would keep them whole.

Instead, he turned on the radio, and she leaned her head against his shoulder, and he gave thanks for the bench seat in his truck that allowed him to sit touching her while they drove.

They pulled up to the place, and he saw that the owner wasn't in residence.

"We can just wander around the outside. I want to show you what I've got planned apart from making people do rope climbs."

She nodded and got out of the truck. He took her hand; it was amazing how easily he had gotten used to that.

It was strange what a simple, innocent thing it was, and yet how deep and intense it felt.

It did feel like so much more than just locking hands.

It was like they were getting each other through.

He wasn't leading her, and she wasn't leading him. They were walking together, holding each other up.

He knew it was easy for her to see herself as damaged because other people had treated her that way. She wasn't, though. That was the thing.

She had this whole beautiful fresh life ahead of her.

She could find herself a nice man who lived in the city, who could stand all that noise.

Someone who would treat her exactly like she deserved, for more than three weeks.

Someone who hadn't already broken his vows. Someone who wasn't broken in all the ways he was.

And he didn't deserve a woman as pure and perfect as her. She was brave. In ways he could never be.

He had already transferred more poison to her than he should have. He'd needed that. It had been cathartic. To tell her his story.

There were dark things in that. The survivor's guilt. The things he didn't like saying out loud, and he never wanted to burden her with all of that.

It was better to imagine her away from him. Away from here. From all the baggage and the bullshit.

To imagine her happy. But right now, he wanted to walk with her.

They went down a narrow path, through towering pine trees and into a field.

"I want this place to have a little tiny house village. Put a big firepit in the middle. We'll be able to stage excursions here."

"It's funny," she said. "You're building a community, whether you recognize it or not. Maybe it isn't the parades, but it's bringing people together with a shared objective. Not totally unlike the military, I guess."

"Well, except without violence."

"Yes," she conceded.

"I just am looking forward to being out in nature."

"You think that's the only reason you want to do this? I think you still want to connect with people. It's okay if you don't recognize that. It's okay if you can't. But I think you do."

"It doesn't matter what I want or don't, there are limits. There's a reason we have a safe word."

"I don't think there's anything wrong with you. I just think you're different. Different to how you work. It's not fair to try and shove you into a box based on who you were thirteen years ago before you saw so much, and experienced so much. We need to stop acting like you're broken. You aren't. You're just different. Changed by what you went through."

"But that has to be some kind of broken," he said, the statement welling up from deep inside him. "Because doesn't it? How could it not be? It's like everybody changes a little bit in their lives. But maybe just this much." He held out his hands, his thumb and forefinger spaced apart just enough for him to hold a playing card between them. "You're not supposed to change completely."

"Who says? We get one life, yes, but we can stop and decide to live it differently anytime we want to."

"I didn't decide, though. We're different. You deciding to go away to Boston—and I think that's great, Rory, I do—but it isn't the same as getting blown to hell and seeing…seeing things you can't get out of your head." Fuck. He hadn't meant to go there.

"I know," she said. "But what should somebody do when they see those things? Should they stay the same?"

"If there are other people in your life, then I think you should. For them."

"There is nowhere in wedding vows that says you won't get sick. That you won't get poor. You're supposed to stay together through that. You're not the one who broke your vows."

"I changed. She wasn't obligated to."

"I think if you love somebody enough, you should. Because I don't understand how nearly losing your husband doesn't change you. I'm sorry. I can't wrap my brain around that. That she came out the other side of that experience entirely the same. Do you think that your mother is the same? I know that Lydia isn't. When she found out you were injured… Gideon, her world was rocked. She was devastated. She called me sobbing. And all she wanted was to get to your side. I was changed by my father leaving. He didn't die, he decided to leave. I have been changed by all these little traumas in my life, and she wasn't changed by her husband getting blown up. I'm sorry. I don't think that you're the wrong one. I think changing when you've experienced intense trauma just shows that you're not a sociopath."

"Cassidy isn't a sociopath."

"I don't have any loyalty to her. All I know is that she hurt you."

He growled into the back of his throat. "Yes. I guess. But not like you think. Not like you mean."

"What are you saying?"

"The disturbing thing was finding out that I wasn't

all that in love with her. Once I didn't want the whole thing, I just didn't care anymore. I don't know if that was the drugs or not. I just know I was angry with myself. For being a disappointment. For failing. But that mattered a hell of a lot more than losing her."

"You didn't love her."

"Maybe that's the problem. Maybe I can't love her. Maybe I can't love anybody. What I loved was the image. That's fucking scary."

"You're different now. It doesn't matter."

"It does matter. Because I can't unknow it. And I shouldn't. I need to remember. I need to remember. Who I was. Who I am. At the end of all things. Who I *fucking* am."

"You're a man who left part of his heart in Afghanistan. Because not all your men came home. That's who you are."

She walked ahead of him, and he was left speechless.

"How do you know that?"

She turned to face him. "Because I know you. Because I know this isn't about just physical pain. As awful as I know it was. And as real as I know all the injuries that you sustained were. They were your men. Like you said. Why wouldn't that change you?"

He stopped there and looked up at the sky. This familiar sky that he'd been a boy under, a golden hero under.

And he wanted answers now, but as ever, it was silent. It had been ever since that bomb had gone off.

He lost his connection to everything that day.

"Eight men lost their lives that day." He very slowly said all their names. Their ages. "And I didn't get to call their families. Because I was laid up in the hospital. It was my responsibility. Because they were my responsibility. All I thought about was glory. Glory on the other side. Fuck that. I watched twenty-year-old boys… They were there one minute. They were gone the next. Just gone. It's such a merciless way to go. You can't even say a proper goodbye. Their bodies don't come back, because there's nothing there. Fuck."

He watched her. Watched her pallor change.

He was supposed to protect her from this. His father-in-law had told him that. It was his job. Protect the civilians from the horrors of war. And listen to him now. He had thought he wasn't going to burden her with this, and here he was burdening the hell out of her. Great job. Great fucking job.

But she didn't turn away from him. Instead, she took a step toward him and wrapped her arms around his shoulders, conforming herself to him. And she held on to him tight.

"I think we need to change the idea of what a legend is," she said softly. "It's not always the guy who has it all together. Sometimes it's the guy that bears every loss, every burden. Every responsibility. With the deepest, clearest pain. The guy who *wanted* to make the call. No matter how much it hurt. Sometimes that's it."

Her words were a balm for a wound he hadn't imagined he carried.

"I shouldn't have said all that to you."

"Why not? You saw it."

"Rory, you were a virgin until two days ago. You've lived here all your life. You've never had to see anything horrible. You've never… Shit, honey. I've taken all this stuff from you."

She frowned. "You haven't taken anything from me.

You're giving me something. You're treating me like I'm strong enough to bear this. You're treating me like an equal. How is that hurting me? I asked. Because I want to know. Because I want to be part of your life."

He could see the moment she heard what she'd said. She looked down. "I mean, we'll keep in touch after I leave."

"Yeah. We will," he said.

He didn't think they would.

Because there was no way she would be able to keep one foot here and one foot in Boston to quite that degree. He sure as hell wasn't going to be able to do it. This thing between them had become all-consuming in a matter of a week. How the hell was it going to work for them to stay in touch? Like they were friends. He supposed that was the game. That they were friends.

"When will you actually get to move in?"

"Right about the time you leave."

"Right."

She looked away, and he felt something tear in his chest. "You want to come see the obstacle course?"

"Yeah. I think I might want to try to climb the rope again."

"Have you been doing push-ups?"

"Is sex exercise?"

He laughed.

She wrinkled her nose and looked at him. "It's a valid question."

"Sure."

She trundled over to the rope, and jumped, reaching up, and there was something different about her movements, something lighter and freer.

She made it farther this time. And then she looked down at him. "I don't think I'm making it to the top yet."

"You did amazing."

"And it's okay that I didn't go all the way. And I can get myself down."

He smiled, but there was something that made him a little bit sad about that.

She didn't need him to catch her.

But he already knew that.

He was a mess. And it was a documented fact. She was coming into her own while he had basically exited his own, wandering off in the twilight years.

He was sitting in a strange spot.

He couldn't say that he wanted to go back to where he'd come from, but he didn't think it was something to aspire to, either.

He was in his retirement, essentially.

And Rory was just beginning everything.

There were only a few years between them, but a wealth of experience. A wealth of life.

It was… It was just so different.

She climbed down and ran toward him, wrapping her arms around his neck.

She kissed him, on the cheek. Like he was the one who had accomplished something amazing when it was her.

"Look at you," he said. "Fearless."

"Not quite."

She put her hands on either side of his face. "But I'm getting there. You inspire me. Your bravery. You make me look at myself and wonder what the hell I'm doing. Why I'm holding on to all these things."

"I told you, it's not a trauma-dick-measuring contest."

"Maybe not. But there is a big difference between fatal and nonfatal fear. To see what you've been through, to see you standing there, makes me want to do something more. To be stronger. To just find new strength inside myself."

"Whatever works."

"It's more than that. I…" She looked away from him, and his breath caught. "You're amazing. That's all."

"Come back to my place?"

"Yes."

Because they wouldn't stay friends. And this wouldn't continue on past her leaving.

It couldn't.

But he would keep being with her while she was here. She was the one he wanted to share all this with.

She was some kind of miraculous, and he hadn't thought he would have any kind of miracle again in his life, at any stage. He was walking off into the sunset. The glory days were long since passed.

Her own were just beginning.

But that didn't mean he couldn't enjoy this last little bit. Like that sliver of light just before the sun disappeared behind the mountain.

She was that light.

"You going to lie and say that you're having a sleepover with my sister again?"

She looked at him thoughtfully. "No."

"Even if your sister asks?"

"I'll tell her. Unless you have a problem with that. But since Lydia already knows…"

"I don't have a problem with it."

"Okay, then. Neither of us has a problem."

But he did. A big one that went all the way down to his soul.

And that was unfortunate.

But there was no point ruminating on it, not now. His decision was made. And if there was one thing he had learned through all of this trauma and recovery, it was that when he made a decision, he had to stick to it. It was the only way forward.

But right now, there was a little sliver of sunshine left, and he would take it.

CHAPTER TWENTY-THREE

IT HAD BEEN two weeks of spending every night in his bed.

Fia hadn't asked, but she was fairly certain Fia knew.

Maybe because Quinn had had a talk with her, or maybe something else.

It wasn't like it was a huge mystery, she supposed.

The bigger mystery was why Fia wasn't questioning her.

But that could be because Rory was leaving.

She looked at all her clothes that she had laid out on the bed.

Her phone lit up.

I'm here.

It was from Lydia.

Rory smiled and went downstairs. Fia was by the front door, but she was busily stirring the pot on the stove.

"I think Lydia is lingering on the porch," she said.

"I know."

"What are you doing?"

A rare question from Fia, who had been very hands-off.

"Choosing which clothes to bring to Boston."

The sadness in Fia's smile betrayed the fact that it

probably was the reason she was leaving her alone about Gideon. The move.

She opened the front door, and Lydia came in.

"Hi."

"Hi. I am here to choose your defector wardrobe."

She hadn't talked to Lydia about what Gideon had said to her. In fact, she hadn't talked to Lydia about the situation with Gideon at all.

But she supposed tonight was as good a time as any.

Lydia came up to Rory's bedroom.

Most of Rory's precious things had been packed away.

"I can only bring one suitcase of clothes. I can't be crazy."

"Well," said Lydia. "I think Boston is very cold in the winter, maybe colder than it is here. And I wonder if your winter clothes are going to be sufficient or if you should just get new ones."

"That feels like a very well-thought-out directive."

"I'm trying to be helpful. And supportive. Because I am happy for you."

"Yeah," she said. "I... Gideon said that you wanted me to stay."

Lydia sighed. "Of course I do, Rory. You're my best friend. Not having you here is going to be really lonely. I can't leave. I've got my mom. And I know that Gideon is back, but that's an even bigger reason I can't go." She looked up at her. "I thought he might be a reason for you to not go."

She remembered that day at the ranch. When he had told her about the men he'd lost.

When he had shared that pain with her, and she had felt something shift within her. Rearrange.

A core of steel, a sense of resolve.

It had been shifting inside her ever since, and she didn't quite know what it meant.

She knew that she cared about him. That she even might...love him.

Not like the poems she wrote when she was a girl, about the blue-eyed boy who seemed so perfect. No. She loved the man. This intense, broken, put-back-together, beautiful man.

She had from the moment she saw him in the woods.

But she wasn't quite sure what she was supposed to be learning from all this.

Because she still felt like he was holding a piece of himself back, and she had to go to Boston, otherwise she was a quitter.

She felt something shift inside her yet again. Like turning away from something. A renewal of something.

"Well, I think that depends on if he would want me to."

"Well." She shook her head. "It's like that?"

"Like what?"

"I mean, that you would stay for him if *he* asked."

She sighed. "Please don't take that in a hurtful way. We've been friends for a long time, and I... I care about you."

"But you're in love with my brother."

She nodded. And she couldn't say everything that maybe needed to be said about Gideon. About what he'd been through. Because it was his story to tell.

"He seems so different," Lydia said softly.

"He is. But I love this version of him even more."

"But you aren't staying."

"I said that I was going to do this. I've been a quitter for so long. I just can't be a quitter anymore."

Right there, all that shifting inside her crumpled. Fell. It was like an extreme shift in her soul.

Which thing was she actually quitting?

Was it quitting to recognize something new was happening in your life, and maybe you needed to be there for that?

She remembered the most important thing that she got from him talking about his marriage.

He had changed. But Cassidy hadn't wanted to change for him.

And here she was, finding all this new bravery inside her soul, changing because of her interaction with him, but not recognizing what it all meant.

She had hugged him, folded herself around him when he had told her about the dead men. About how responsible he felt. How much he grieved it.

And that had been the evidence of what needed to happen inside her.

He had changed. And he was changing her. So that they could fit around each other.

Was it quitting to understand that? Was it quitting if she redirected when a new path presented itself? She had been convinced that it would be.

That she had to go to Boston no matter what.

Because she had set herself on the path. But this wasn't choosing not to climb a rope in gym, or being afraid to go down a narrow path.

She wasn't reacting to anything. Not fear, not to what anybody might think of her.

That was actually the greatest tragedy. When people kept on paths they weren't meant for.

Knowing when to quit was a skill.

Being in control of it was even more important.

It wasn't fear guiding her now.

It was her heart.

It was love. And nothing could be more diametrically opposed to the anxiety she had struggled with for so many years.

She wasn't making this decision from that place.

"I can't leave," she whispered.

Lydia's eyes went wide. "What?"

"I've been sitting with this, with this feeling, for the last week. I felt like he didn't want me here. He doesn't want me to not go to Boston, he doesn't want to have another life. I think he's shot that part of himself down.

"But I also think that he might need somebody to make that bold decision for him.

"No, I can't make him be with me. But as long as I'm going off to Boston, he gets to tell himself that he's being some kind of hero by not giving us a chance. And I think he needs to feel like a hero. And believe me, he is one. He is so profoundly wonderful. He is so brave. And he is so…everything. And he has rebuilt this part of me that was so weak. Built me up." She had to smile, because it was like weight lifting for her self-esteem, being with him.

And maybe that wouldn't make sense to Lydia. But it did to her.

"I'm strong enough now. To do this. To step back, actually make my own choices. Instead of just quitting because it's hard, or trying to prove myself because other people made me feel bad. I do not care what anyone thinks. And I'm not running from anything. So… I'm staying."

"Are you sure, Rory?" Lydia asked. "Because it was such a big deal that you got that job, and you were very excited."

"I know. I was. I am. It's not nothing. Giving it up isn't nothing. But I wanted to leave here because I was ashamed. Of how little I had done.

"And I'm not anymore. I'm good at my job, and I'm good at it here. We started the farm store here. We have accomplished a lot. I have. I just couldn't see it because nobody was throwing me a parade. And he's right, I can't live my life toward that. It's a stupid thing. A foolish thing. I'm staying."

Lydia reached out and hugged her. "I'm really glad. And I'm really, really glad that you're there for him. That he has you. That is so amazing. And I am... I'm overwhelmed, actually. Because I didn't feel like I could reach him. And I think you did. You are extraordinary, Rory. I think you were maybe always exactly the right person to love him."

It was bigger than destiny. Rory knew that.

Because there were so many paths that he could've taken. Dark roads he could've gone down that would've led to oblivion.

Just like she could choose to walk away now. But she wasn't going to.

She had felt all her life like she didn't match up to other people.

And he was feeling that as well.

And they had both shifted just enough to meet each other's needs.

It was better, honestly, than finding someone who fit her perfectly just as she was.

She found somebody who had changed her in all the

right ways. Whose story gave her the kind of perspective she never had before.

Who listened and accepted her, and never tried to make her hurt feel less, and who somehow accomplished all that at the same time.

Because he was Gideon.

There was part of her that did feel like maybe they were meant to be. Like her heart being set on him from middle school to now was something sort of predestined.

There was a magic to that.

But there was also magic in knowing that they had to claim this. That they had to make choices now. To have that life. To have a new life for both of them.

Yes, she could go off and have one alone.

But it would never be as wonderful as the one she could have here.

With love.

With Gideon.

"I have to tell Fia."

"Oh," Lydia said.

Rory flung the door open. "I'm not going to Boston."

Fia appeared at the bottom of the stairs. "What?"

"I'm not going to Boston. I don't want to go anymore. I want to stay here."

"Rory," said Fia. "If this is because I've been sad…"

"It's not. It's not for you. Or you," she said to Lydia. "And it's not for Gideon, either. I swear to you. It's for me. Because it's what I want."

She went down the stairs, and headed out the front door. "Where are you going?" Fia asked.

"I'm going to go see Gideon. I think I'm going to tell him that I love him."

And then she got into her car, and drove to his house.

CHAPTER TWENTY-FOUR

HE WAS SITTING there in one of the kitchen chairs when headlights appeared in the driveway.

He stood up and went to the door, his body tense.

He knew who it was. It could only be Rory, but he had expected her to be spending the evening with his sister. She'd said she was packing for Boston. Weeding out her clothes, and things like that.

The countdown was on.

For him to start his new life, for her to start hers.

For them to be realistic.

She flung the door open, without knocking. And then she was in his arms before he could ask what she was doing here.

She kissed him, and he kissed her back.

Whatever he'd just been thinking, the dark thoughts about it all ending, they evaporated in the heat of the moment. Her mouth was confident, she was confident.

In the last couple of weeks, Rory had transformed into a demanding and bold lover.

He'd never experienced anything like it.

She gave what she got, and she was never performing.

And that in and of itself was the most attractive thing he could even think of.

And when she kissed him, right now, she went for broke.

It was deep and delicious and wonderful. It was just the two of them. And never for show.

He'd been in a relationship where half of it had always been for show.

Where half of what they got out of it was what other people might feel when they saw them together. Envy. Because they were successful and attractive and desirable.

And he knew that his wife had gotten a whole lot out of that. But Rory kissed him with her eyes closed tight, and Rory kissed him in secret.

And he had never been anyone's secret. He had been someone they trumpeted to the world.

Until he had just one flaw. A big one, but still.

It had taught him a little something about when he mattered and why.

But Rory made it feel different.

Rory kissed him just to kiss him.

And that was a hell of a thing.

He stripped her shirt off her, admired her glorious curves.

He had loved watching her grow in confidence in her body as well.

Her curves were slender but perfect. Her breasts high and firm.

Her nipples were pert and pink and tight, begging for his touch. Begging for his tongue. He lowered his head and sucked one tightened bud into his mouth.

She was leaving. And he was starting over, and it just felt bleak. The sun going behind the mountain.

He accepted that it had to be that way. He did.

And hell, he didn't want to take anything to dull the pain. In fact, he wanted to live in it. Wallow in it. Because at least he had felt something.

If there was one damned broken thing he could give thanks for in the middle of all this, it was that she made him feel something.

But she was leaving.

And he was glad for her.

But it might kill him.

He stripped the rest of her clothes off her, all the way bare, and lifted her up, setting her down on the table and laying her down like the feast that she was.

She blushed, all over her body, and he relished it. Welcomed it.

There was something so beautiful about that.

That she could do all these things, be this bold and also still blush.

He got down on his knees and put her legs over his shoulders, pulling her toward the edge of the table, holding her prisoner as he began to lick that tender place between her legs.

Just like she liked.

He knew exactly how to do it. Knew the way that she cried out inside, how she signaled the rise of her desire.

He knew all that.

It was beautiful.

And so was she.

There was nothing more incredible than watching her come. Knowing it was about to happen. Tasting the evidence of her desire.

There was nothing better. And when he felt lonely in the middle of the night, he would comfort himself with this memory. The memory of what Rory Sullivan tasted like on his tongue.

Because it was truly glorious.

And so was she.

And this was the beginning of their goodbyes.

He knew it.

So he feasted on her with all the desire inside of him. Because if he could make her understand one thing, it would be this.

How much he wanted her.

How much he would let things be different if they could be.

If they had lived a different life.

Right then, he let himself imagine it. If he'd never left. If he'd stayed there, and so had she. If they had found each other ten years ago.

If they had just fallen in love then.

Married each other. Instead of him going into the military.

But you wouldn't have. You wouldn't have seen her. You never would've slowed down long enough to do it.

He growled, pushing two fingers inside her, and she came apart.

Beautifully. Under his tongue.

And he couldn't wait anymore. He stood up and undid his jeans and freed himself, thrusting inside her, feeling the silken heat of her close around him.

What a shitty, horrible thing, to realize that he could never have been good enough for her before, either.

He would never have seen her.

He would've been looking at flashier things.

More obvious things.

He wanted glory. He cared what other people thought.

He never would've just taken her.

Because he was a fool.

He was a fool.

And now he was broken. And what was he to do with that? What the hell could he do with that?

It was just desperately sad, and all he could do was have her. Over and over again. Until neither of them could see straight, until neither of them could breathe.

Until maybe, just maybe, he could forget the grim reality of it all.

That he had to be broken to find her.

That he never would've been able to have this if not.

And that either way, keeping her was impossible.

She clung to him, her fingernails digging into his shoulders.

"Gideon," she whispered. "I love you."

He growled, his climax overtaking him completely. He couldn't see straight. Couldn't think straight. She loved him.

He lowered his head and pressed his face into her neck, and he felt moisture rising up in his eyes.

She loved him.

She wasn't supposed to love him. She was the sun, and she was supposed to go off and rise somewhere else. That stupid girl.

She was supposed to go away.

She was supposed to leave him to be broken, because that's what he was.

An addict, a junkie, a man who had abandoned his promises.

It's what he was.

He knew that.

"Rory."

He said her name. He said her name instead of telling her no.

He came hard, pouring himself into her, instead of saying no.

Instead of telling her it was impossible.

Dammit.

Dammit, dammit.

He kept his face pressed tightly into her neck.

He just let her hold him.

Because no one had held him in a long time.

Except for her.

And there were a thousand thoughts and feelings rolling through him, and he couldn't readily identify what any of them were. What he was supposed to do with any of them.

He was afraid. Afraid of this feeling that was so intense, that felt like the heat of battle more than it did anything else, that reminded him of being a different man. In a different time. He was afraid of that, because it was like dreaming again, not like walking into the sunset. Not like letting glory go.

It was a fucking parade *inside his soul*, and he was terrified of it.

And all the ways that he would fail her.

Because he could not stand to watch the light go out of Rory's eyes.

He had survived Cassidy.

But he had loved things about Cassidy, and never her. Not really. Not entirely.

He knew that now, because he knew what it felt like when it was different.

Oh, he had loved her. He had loved her as much as he could at the time.

But he couldn't love anything more than he loved himself. Not then.

Not more than he loved his own self-image.

But Rory...

Rory was all-consuming.

And if he fucked up with her he was never going to be able to survive that. He had been brought to the brink once already. He would never be able to do it again and come back.

He would die. He would quite literally die.

He was realistic enough about himself to know that. This time it would end in the gutter.

But if he let her walk away, if he let her go live her life, if he didn't disappoint her, if he didn't make her fall out of love with him, he could live with that. And he needed to be in a reality he could live with. Because he had been so close to one that he couldn't.

She had told him once there was a difference between fear that could be fatal and fear that wasn't.

This was fatal. He damn well knew it.

But he couldn't let go of her.

So he picked her up and took her to bed instead.

He laid her down there beneath the covers, and held her tight, and didn't see how destroyed he was.

He kissed her temple, and they lay like that for a long time.

"I want to stay," she whispered.

He felt like he'd been stabbed straight to the center of the chest.

"No," he said. "No, honey. You're not staying."

"Gideon, I love you. I don't want to leave."

"Rory," he said, the word tearing at him. "This isn't a rope climb, sweetie. This is your life. You decided that you were going to go do this, and you need to go do it. You need to do it for you."

"Gideon," she said. "I am doing this for me. I want to be with you. I want to give this a try."

"Please tell me that you didn't quit the job."

"I didn't. I came straight here after talking to your sister and realizing what I had to do. I came straight here because it was important. I couldn't have Lydia and Fia knowing and not you."

"Rory," he said. "You can't do this to yourself. Not for me. I am a shitty partner. And I have proven that. I don't have anything to offer you. I don't. I am a fucking mess. Or did you not get that from anything that I've told you recently?"

"But I love you. I liked you before. But we didn't… It wasn't the same. That was just you. That was the Gideon you showed the world. It's like your shell. It was never you, Gideon. Maybe this is you."

"Great. That's what I always wanted to know. That I was always a fucking asshole who actually hates everybody. Great. I am just thrilled to have come to that conclusion."

"No. You're somebody who thinks very deeply about the people around him. You're someone who helped me do a rope climb, just because you cared about me meeting my goals. You bought your family ranch so that you could try to give your mother some of her life back, so that you could try to get something of your life back. You climbed out of your addiction. You fixed yourself when your wife wouldn't stand by you. And you refuse to blame her, even though she deserves some of the blame. Because she didn't give you a chance, Gideon. She couldn't handle you when you weren't perfect, and her marriage vows didn't mean anything. And that isn't a failure on your part."

"Rory, you don't understand. I am never going to be able to give you that life. You wanted to go experience things. You wanted to go eat different food. I am not going to ever be able to be the guy who gives you the life you deserve. The life you worked for. That you climbed a rope for."

"Maybe I was climbing the rope for you. For this life. Maybe this was supposed to be the destination all along and I didn't realize it yet."

"Rory," he said. "Go to Boston. Because I can't have you here."

He watched her dissolve, and he hated that. But it was better than breaking her over time. It was. Whether she understood that or not. It was better than letting it get too far, and disappointing her.

This was bearable.

Even as it stabbed him straight through the chest, it was bearable.

"Gideon…"

"Go," he said.

And he thought with some irony that it was strange he was the one throwing her out when he'd been the one thrown out before.

And that made him have a metallic taste in his mouth.

"I think you should go. I think you should go and you should pack. Because you need to go to Boston."

"Does it matter what I think?"

"Right now you're blinded by the sex. But the reality of what it means to be married to me, it would break you. I know it would."

She huffed. Not a laugh. Not a sob. Somewhere in the god-awful in-between. "I don't recall proposing to you."

"You know where that was headed."

"You are so full of yourself," she said, and then suddenly she was shouting. "You're still trying to be a legend, instead of a man. Wake up, Gideon! The only person that needs you to be perfect is *you*."

"Rory—"

"No! Don't interrupt me. Don't you dare. You're the one that still can't let go of this idea that you need to be the hero. You've done enough for me. I don't need you to tell me what I need, too. You helped me climb the mountain. You helped me climb up the rope. I'm grateful for that. But you don't need to tell me what I want. What's good for me. You don't get to do that." She took a breath. "This isn't just the Summer of Rory Sullivan, this is *my life*. And I make the decisions. I'm in charge of what I want, not some guy who poured beer on me in college, not some kids who bullied me in middle school. Don't treat me like I'm fragile after all that. Don't build me up and then try to tell me what I can and can't handle."

She got up and went into the kitchen, and he could hear her dressing. He got up off the bed and went to stand in the doorway.

"Do you have something to say?" she asked.

He was frozen.

He hated that.

And all the rage that welled up inside him was only directed at himself. He couldn't blame her. He couldn't blame anyone but his own damn self.

Fuck.

"I want everything, Gideon."

"I can't give you everything."

She let out a primal scream and picked up an apple in the bowl on the counter and threw it. It didn't hit him, not even close.

"I deserve everything! I'm not beige. I'm not insignificant. And my feelings are not stupid. They aren't. I'm allowed to feel them and I…" Tears ran down her cheeks. "I have checked off every item on my list because of you. Mountain climbing and makeovers and kissing and now this damned tantrum. And I hate you for this. I really do."

She turned on her heel and she walked out the front door, slamming it behind her.

He put his hands over his face. He tried to breathe.

She would thank him. She would go to Boston. Because she had to. Because if he made her into a quitter, she wouldn't want them anymore. Because she would realize at some point she had passed up something good for something broken.

But this felt like a bomb blast and he ought to know.

And the only thing that shocked him was there wasn't literal shrapnel lodged in his chest right now.

So he lay there, bleeding out. Like he was lying on the ground in Afghanistan.

But he knew there was no medic to fix this.

Because nothing ever could. Nothing at all.

CHAPTER TWENTY-FIVE

RORY DIDN'T WANT to go to Boston. She wasn't going to stay there. But she had her plane ticket to get there, and she had some money saved up, so she had felt like she really should go. At least see it. At least to get moving for a while, rather than sinking into depression. Because that's what the last few days had been. Nothing but crying. She had really gotten her heart broken.

It was strange, though. Because it wasn't over a breach of trust.

It wasn't like her dad leaving, it wasn't like getting bullied.

It wasn't because she'd quit.

She'd checked off all the items on her list, after all.

It was *life*.

She had watched him. She had watched him come up against the edge of his strength.

And not be able to push past.

She was asking him to get over all his trauma very quickly.

And even though she thought he could, she really did, she knew he wasn't doing this to hurt her. He thought he was doing it to help her.

And he was probably protecting himself.

When she had talked to Fia and Quinn, Fia had been in a rage.

"I told him not to hurt you."

"Yes. You did. But in fairness, I think he has convinced himself that this is better."

"Well, he's an idiot."

"Yeah. But it comes from somewhere…good."

Fia grumbled, but didn't argue. She supposed that was because she looked so sad, and even Fia, who had a propensity toward being a hard-ass, couldn't be mean to her when she was that devastated. If she had to be pitiable to get softness from her older sister, she supposed that would do.

For her part, she was grappling with this very adult heartbreak.

And trying to figure out what it meant for her.

It was her third walk through Boston Common today. And she would be wandering from there to the north end to get some pizza. She'd had the cash-only Italian food last night, and it had been amazing, but she had a feeling her appetite was going to be compromised for a while.

Which she felt wasn't fair.

She went into the bustling pizzeria after waiting in line for a while, and looked at all the eclectic photos lining the wall.

There was a celebratory atmosphere, and she tried to absorb it.

One thing she thought was so amazing about Boston was the way it felt familiar, even though she had never been there before.

There were so many iconic places she'd seen in movies a hundred times. This pizzeria was like that. Ingrained in her as a sense that this was what a pizzeria should look like. And so it felt as if she had walked into

this place numerous times before. Like she was a regular, and just maybe everybody might know her name.

Even though she was a stranger. Just passing through.

She hadn't thought a city could feel like this, but
this one did.

But not even that fully soothed her. Not when everything was so precarious inside her. The pizza was
delicious, though.

She could have been starting her new life here. Instead, she'd fallen in love.

Not just with Gideon, but with the possibility of what
she could do in Pyrite Falls.

With her own list of accomplishments.

She'd needed to escape when she had felt inferior to
the people around her.

She didn't feel that way anymore.

Something in her had changed. And she knew that
was because of Gideon.

She knew that it was.

And she could be thankful for it, even though it hurt.

She pulled her phone out and called Fia. "I had pizza.
I thought of you."

"Liar."

"I did."

"Are you wandering around all sad?"

She looked up the street, at the red brick buildings
and the bustling crowds lined up in front of restaurants.
There was an especially big line in front of a bakery
that served Italian pastries, and Rory decided to get in
it while she talked on the phone.

"I am not wandering around sad."

The women in front of her turned around and looked

at her as she said that. And judging by their quick appraisal of her, they knew Rory was a liar.

But she would never see them again.

That was the interesting thing about wandering around the city. She might feel like she *could* know them, but she didn't. Her pain was anonymous. She wasn't even the only woman wandering the streets looking sad. There was a woman just across the street screaming into her phone with no regard for anyone or anything else but her own rage. These people were all strangers. She was the main character. Why bother to rein her anger in at all?

It was very different than Pyrite Falls in that way. Where she would always run into people she knew.

And that just didn't feel like as big of a disaster as it once had.

"Well that's good," said Fia.

"I'm going to order pastries. So I'll get one and think of you."

"I appreciate that. Are you going to be sad that you didn't move there?"

"No," she said easily. "This place is beautiful. But it's not home."

Though she realized something interesting. She could be at home here. If she wanted to be. Just like she could now be home in Pyrite Falls.

Because she was at home in her own skin.

That was what had happened to her over these past few weeks.

She had found that she could be brave. She could climb a rope and a mountain, and she could declare her love for a man who couldn't declare it back.

She was beautiful, when it mattered.

She felt that now, too.

She didn't need to prove anything. She simply didn't.

And that was its own kind of triumph.

What a terrible thing to know that she could never have achieved this growth without Gideon. Without walking through this particular valley of the shadow of death.

Without this dark night of the soul.

She couldn't have found this wholeness without being broken.

And it really sucked.

"Well, I'm glad you're staying. You know we have a lot of work at Sullivan's Point. And the new era is just beginning. We are finally pulling our weight. We aren't beholden to the Kings."

"No. That gives us less of an occasion to have town hall meetings, I suppose. And less reason for you and Landry to fight."

"I'm sure we will think of reasons," said Fia. She sounded just a little bit distracted.

"Fia," she said. "I've been very consumed by my own feelings of awkwardness and inadequacy for the last... My whole life. And you have done so much for me and Quinn and Alaina. And sometimes I wonder if we've missed some things with you."

"You've seen everything I wanted you to."

That was what she was afraid of.

"Fia. I love you to pieces. You would tell me if there was something? If there was something you needed to tell me."

There was a slight break before Fia responded. "I would. I might not have before. I believe that you're strong enough now, Rory. Because I've seen your growth. And it's pretty amazing."

Well, the fact that her sister saw it, that made her feel better. That made her feel like maybe it was a real change. A lasting change.

"Well, in the meantime I will enjoy my Boston sabbatical for the next couple of weeks."

"Good. Do that. Enjoy it. Don't let a man stress you out."

"I'll do my best."

She got off the phone just as she went into the bakery, and she ordered herself a cannoli, and went back to her room and ate it.

It wasn't being in love. But it was an adventure. And suddenly that on its own was kind of amazing.

She could have these adventures sometimes. Could take time off to travel.

She could be whoever she wanted to be.

And she'd been able to do that all along.

But it had taken Gideon to show her.

She took a deep breath and looked out the window at the city below.

Another thing she learned from Gideon was that healing didn't happen overnight.

But that you could heal. From pretty much anything that didn't kill you.

And she had just discovered all this great new stuff about herself, so she wasn't going to die.

She laughed into the silence of her hotel room.

As triumphant declarations went, that was sort of the bottom of the barrel.

But sometimes the bottom of the barrel was all you had, and the trick was to just keep scraping.

Because Rory Sullivan wasn't a quitter.

Not anymore.

CHAPTER TWENTY-SIX

HE HAD BEEN WRONG. This was the worst thing he could imagine.

He was supposed to be starting things up at the ranch, and he couldn't concentrate. He was just a miserable dick.

And he felt...isolated. Rory had connected him. To his sister, his mother. Because Rory had been the one person he was vulnerable with. Who he was honest with.

Rory had been the one person who had known the truth.

All of it.

And he wondered...he wondered if he had to change that.

He didn't know what to do.

Because he was miserable.

And he'd been miserable before, but this was different.

This was brokenness.

He cleared his throat.

And he went inside. He unzipped his bag, and he took out his Purple Heart, which he generally never looked at.

What was the point?

Why hadn't he died in Afghanistan?

So that you could live.

And it was like that wall he put up inside of himself had been broken down.

So that he could live.

Not as a symbol, not as a legend, not as anything damned near close to perfect. Just a living, breathing man.

He was fucked up and broken, and wanted to do better.

What was the point of going off into the sunset? It was selfish.

It wasn't living.

It was dying before his time.

He found himself driving to his mother's house.

Lydia was over there for dinner, and she gave him the side-eye when he came in.

"Rory's in Boston," she said.

"I know," he grunted. "I told her to go."

"*I* know," she said. "She told me."

"Well, I'm glad she went. But… I need to talk to you. I need to tell you something."

"Me?" Lydia asked.

"Both of you." He looked at his mother, and he could see the worry in her eyes. He hated that he'd put it there. He took a sharp breath. "Remember, Mom, when you told me that Dad would be proud of me?"

"Yes," she said. "He was. He was so proud of you."

"I want to believe that. He would be proud of me, but it would only be because he didn't know everything about what happened after my injury."

And he told him everything. All the things he had decided he needed to keep bottled up, to protect them from.

"I couldn't call you," he said, when his mother had

asked through her tears why he hadn't asked for help when he was homeless.

"I was too ashamed. I didn't want you to see me like that. I couldn't stand to see the disappointment in your face. It's a thing that scares me more than anything. That if I'm not perfect, if I'm not a legend, who's going to…" He took a sharp breath. "Why would anyone *love me*? Why would anyone be proud of me? That's what I've been this whole time. It's what I've had to be. And the minute I wasn't… Cassidy was done with me. I blamed myself, and I carry some blame. Trust me. I wasn't a great husband to her those last few months. But the truth is she didn't love me. Not the darker parts of me. Not the deepest parts. I was living two lives even before my injury. One as a deployed soldier who was beginning to question what we were doing, and who had reservations about a lot of things, and one who came back and relished in the military life. In our status. But I couldn't share any of that with her."

He breathed in deep. "So when I couldn't do that anymore, she was done. And that confirmed what I think I always feared. If I wasn't chasing glory, if I didn't find it, who would stand by me? Rory always felt like there was nothing special about her. And she had to find that strength inside herself. And that's what draws me to her. She is just herself. And I've never known quite how to be that. I just know how to be a thing. A symbol. I don't want that anymore. I can't want it."

"Gideon," said his mother, wrapping her arms around him. "We would never stop loving you. We were proud of you. But you were born naked, and not good at anything but screaming your head off and eating. You hadn't done a damn thing for me and you were the apple of my eye, and still are. You both are. I'm sorry if that was never clear to you. I'm sorry if us being proud got mixed up somehow. But I don't need you to be a military hero."

His mother's scent enveloped him. That same scent that had been there waiting for him when he woke up after his injury.

And of course, she loved him.

"I just couldn't stand the thought of letting you down."

"We're all going to let each other down. Because we're human. You were disappointed that I didn't want to move back to the ranch. I don't know that you understand it, but you love me."

"Well, yeah."

"I don't need you to be perfect, Gideon," Lydia said. "In fact, it's really damned annoying. I don't like you perfect. Because that just makes me feel inadequate."

"Well, I think you can safely say that you're maybe doing a little better than your addict brother."

"Don't say that. You're a hero. Because you're here. And that's it. You will always be a hero to me. Not in spite of the fact that you have weaknesses, but because you do. You're not an invincible robot. Don't you see that only makes everything you've ever done that much more brave? Don't let Cassidy's failures speak for the rest of us." Lydia swallowed. "And don't let her speak for Rory."

He realized, though, that it wasn't really Cassidy. That was a convenient excuse. He just didn't want to risk loving like this.

But he knew he had to be brave again.

He thought that his days of that were over. That now

that he wasn't in the military he didn't have to suck it up quite so hard.

But he did.

"I might need to move to Boston," he said. "And I bought the ranch. I was going to make that our thing. But I think I need to go to Rory."

"What?" Lydia looked confused.

"If Rory is in Boston, then that's where I'm going. I'm in love with her. And I can't live without her." He took a sharp breath. "Boston would be too loud, and it would be a step closer to my personal hell, but I'm in hell without her. So."

"Rory didn't move to Boston. She's just visiting. She already had a one-way plane ticket, so she thought she would buy a return one and spend a little time there. Eat some food."

"Lydia," he said. "Do you know where she's staying?"

"Yes."

"Can I have her contact details?"

"Of course. What are you doing?"

"I think I have to do a grand gesture. I think…it has to be nothing short of a parade."

"Well. This is perfect. Let's get you a plane ticket."

"Yes. Let's get me a plane ticket."

RORY WAS ON her nightly circuit, wandering the north end, looking for delicious food. She had found some and was carrying her pastry bags back to her hotel room when she stopped. The sun was setting, a glorious pink backlit by the bridge in the distance.

And there he was.

Like that day in the woods. All in black. As if needing him had made him appear.

Like magic.

Like love.

She knew it was him. There was no mistaking him.

Gideon Payne.

The legend of Pyrite Falls.

"Rory," he said.

He sounded broken and hopeful, and it was the hope that got her.

It was the hope that just about did her in.

"Gideon," she breathed. "What are you doing here?"

"I came for you. To visit, to move here, whatever you need. I would give everything up to have you. I need you to know that."

"Why?"

"Because I love you. Because I love you, and I can't be afraid of that anymore. And I was. I feel like I have nothing to give you. And by that I mean I feel like I don't have what I used to. The ways that I used to be sure that I was good enough. All my life I have needed a parade. But I don't need one for me. Not anymore. I just need you."

Rory's heart jumped in her chest. "Gideon…"

"But, I did think that maybe you deserved a parade. Because you're the legend, Rory. And legends should have parades."

She turned just as a group of men in uniform came around the corner, holding a banner in front of them.

It said *I love you, Rory Sullivan.*

"What is this?"

"I called in a favor. It turns out that I still have some connections that I can make use of."

They marched and saluted her, and then went back around the block and around another time.

And Rory was effectively speechless. "This is… It's too much."

"No. It's just enough. Just enough for you. For me. For us. Rory, I love you. I have lived two lives now. This life is filled with glory and the pursuit of it. This need to prove myself, because I had been doing it from the beginning, and I didn't know another way. But even though I've had the thought for a long time that I didn't want to go back, it occurred to me that if I could choose to live one of these lives twice, it would not be that one. It would be this one. With you. You make the silence sweet. You make me feel like my moods aren't something broken in me. You are strong when I need you to be, and you also asked me for help. And that… I need that. I do need it. I want to be needed. I need it. You tell me about books so that I don't have to read them."

She laughed. "It wouldn't hurt for you to read a book."

"No. It probably wouldn't. And see, you're going to change that for me, too. Rory, you are everything."

"It's so funny," she said. "Now that I have a parade… it turns out I just want you."

He scooped her into his arms and kissed her.

"I just want you, too. You make me feel like I'm not broken."

"You aren't," she said. "You're you. This version of you is just fine to me. More than that. This version of you is the one that I love. I don't need you to be unscarred or unscathed. I don't need you to be perfect. I like you like this. Because you're the man that was strong enough to climb up from rock bottom. And we don't have enough stories about that. Because people think it's romantic to write a character into a corner and leave them there. To let them die. But the bravery is in getting back up. The bravery is in healing yourself. The bravery is in defining yourself not by the bad things, but by choosing to embrace love again, and *that* is glory."

"Hell yeah," he said. "Rory Sullivan, you are my glory. I thought you were a sunset. The last sliver of my sunshine disappearing behind a hill before I went on to nothing. But you're my sunrise. You're the reason I'm here. I have asked myself why. I've asked myself why so many times. And now I know the answer. It was to live. And it was to love you."

"I realized something, too, that I was going to have to go through this to be fixed. To be as strong as I needed to be. And it hurt, but… I needed you. And even the way that it ended, and has started again, I needed all that. To get to who I needed to be."

"I realized something similar. I needed to have that block removed. I needed the Jenga tower to fall. Because it's what made me a man who could love someone more than I love myself. It's what made me the man who could be with you. And I would walk that road a thousand times if it brought me here. It brought me to you."

She closed her eyes and folded herself into his arms. And then they went upstairs to her hotel room, and they told each other how in love they were with their hands, with their lips. And with words.

So many words.

"I love you. We can go back home now."

"Let's stay here for a while. Let's make Boston ours. And then after that, we will go home."

WHEN GIDEON PAYNE returned home this time, he didn't need a parade. And he didn't need to hide in the dark-

he walked down the main street of town
...ry Sullivan's hand.

...nd he knew beyond a shadow of a doubt that they would all think she was a legend.

But he already knew that.

And best of all, so did she.

Rory Sullivan was his. And that was all the glory he would ever need.

* * * * *